Praise for

'Heartfelt, poignant, properly g...
To...

'An eye-opening, fun ...
read . . . truly spectacular'
Rebecca Ryan

'Funny, joyous and wise, this is a story which reminds us it's OK not to have the answers, to be working things out, and to be living life on our own terms'
Simon James Green

'The right balance of laughs and compassion'
The Times

'The most insightful book about love I've read in a long time . . . I LOVED IT'
Kate Weston

'Funny, charming and unique'
Lauren Forsythe

'Compelling'
Daily Mail

'Refreshingly candid, whip-smart and painfully funny. A perfect exploration of what it's like to navigate the never-ending challenges of love, dating and adulthood'
Hannah Tovey

'A powerful female friendship at the heart of the story makes this book a strong and fascinating read'
My Weekly

'A joyful, chaotic exploration of love and monogamy . . . Laughs out loud guaranteed'
Lizzie Huxley-Jones

Chloe Seager is Director of Children's and YA at Madeleine Milburn Agency. Chloe lives in London and in her spare time she likes listening to noughties emo music, watching reality TV and shouting at Spurs games.

You can find her on:
𝕏 @chloeseager
◉ @chloenseager

P.S. you're the worst

chloe seager

ONE PLACE. MANY STORIES

HQ
An imprint of HarperCollins*Publishers* Ltd
1 London Bridge Street
London SE1 9GF

www.harpercollins.co.uk

HarperCollins*Publishers*
Macken House, 39/40 Mayor Street Upper
Dublin 1, D01 C9W8, Ireland

This edition 2025

1
First published in Great Britain by HQ,
an imprint of HarperCollins*Publishers* Ltd 2025

Copyright © Chloe Seager 2025

Chloe Seager asserts the moral right to be identified as the author of this work.
A catalogue record for this book is available from the British Library.

ISBN: 9780008598167

Set in Sabon LT Std by HarperCollins*Publishers* India

This novel is entirely a work of fiction. The names, characters and incidents portrayed in it are the work of the author's imagination. Any resemblance to actual persons, living or dead, events or localities is entirely coincidental.

All rights reserved. No part of this publication may be reproduced, stored in a retrieval system, or transmitted, in any form or by any means, electronic, mechanical, photocopying, recording or otherwise, without the prior permission of the publishers.

Without limiting the exclusive rights of any author, contributor or the publisher of this publication, any unauthorised use of this publication to train generative artificial intelligence (AI) technologies is expressly prohibited. HarperCollins also exercise their rights under Article 4(3) of the Digital Single Market Directive 2019/790 and expressly reserve this publication from the text and data mining exception.

Printed and bound in the UK using 100%
Renewable Electricity at CPI Group (UK) Ltd

For more information visit: www.harpercollins.co.uk/green

*For anyone who's ever felt
The Tower's cruel wrath*

Dear Becky,

With 30 looming ominously over the horizon, it's time for some home truths:

1) After nearly a decade of saying your job is 'temporary', it's probably time to accept you really do have a career in recruitment.
2) You can no longer pretend living at home 'to save for your own place' is working. It's been a year and you've managed £2k, so only another £142.5k to go for the average London flat deposit.
3) For a long time now, you have questioned whether you actually like any of your friends anymore, and whether they like you.
4) Your dad will never call. Get over it.
5) Your ex-boyfriend has moved on. GET OVER IT.
6) You'll never find another decent relationship.
7) You'll never get married.
8) You'll never have babies.
9) You'll never have a shiny career that other people are jealous of.
10) You'll never have ANYTHING that other people are jealous of.

11) You'll never be on Strictly Come Dancing.

Happy 29th birthday! It's time to grow up.

Best wishes from,
Yourself

Chapter One

Twenty-nine. I count to twenty-nine on my fingers. That is A LOT of fingers. Have I really lived through *twenty-nine years*? How can that BE?! I still have pink-tipped hair, for God's sake. I still sometimes buy WKD and listen to Britney Spears. No one who still listens to Britney Spears can be twenty-nine . . .

Except, that's exactly how old people who listen to Britney are. Because 'the youth' don't know who she is . . . do they? I start googling 'do the youth know who Britney Spears is?' and then stop in my tracks. Anyone googling facts about 'the youth' is indisputably no longer 'the youth'.

I just don't know when it happened. I swear to God, I blinked and ten years passed. Ten years ago I was still nineteen. Just a naive simpleton waiting expectantly for her cocktail parties, exciting career – I was always nebulous as to what exactly it would be, but I knew it would be *exciting* – and sophisticated dates. I've never been to a cocktail party, my boss still sends me to buy her sandwiches from Pret and the last date I had asked me if I'd rather have a beard or feathers for pubic hair. (I opted for the feathers.)

I groan, remembering him taking off my underwear and 'checking for feathers'. And I still slept with him. Sometimes it's like I'm actively *trying* to lower my self-esteem.

'Becky!' Mum calls. 'The car's waiting!'

Oh God. Is it time already? I look at myself in the mirror. I have one eye made up perfectly and the other is still naked. I look ridiculous, but there's nothing I can do now. Mum gave me three warnings twenty, fifteen and ten minutes before the taxi was supposed to get here. If I keep her waiting now there will be an *atmosphere* for the rest of the evening. At least I'm wearing clothes.

'Becky!' Mum calls again, sharper this time. 'Did you hear me?'

'Coming!' I yell, grabbing my handbag and racing downstairs. I'll have to finish my make-up in the loos when we get there. *It's fine*, I tell myself. We'll have ages, because Mum is chronically early for everything. The party doesn't even start until eight.

When I get downstairs Mum looks at my face and sighs deeply. 'Honestly, Becky . . .'

I consider telling her this is just how young people do their make-up now. Make her feel really *old* as revenge for making me feel so useless. But then I'd have to walk around like this all evening and that would probably be cutting off my nose to spite my face.

'I'll do it later,' I mumble.

She's stopped listening and is midway through setting the alarm. It beeps ominously.

'Five seconds!' she urges, ushering me out the door. As if I don't know. The sound of those little beeps have filled me with pure, unadulterated dread every day for the last twenty-nine years. What would happen if we *didn't* get out of the door before the beeps stopped? We'd anger the home security gods and they'd punish us by weakening our door reinforcement hardware?

I suspect – and have suspected for some time now – that moving back in here was the wrong call. I'd suffered through so many years spending two-thirds of my pay cheque to live in mouldy hovels with housemates who eat weird amounts of mushrooms or try to get you to go for group runs that, when Mum offered, it seemed like a sensible alternative. I thought if I wasn't paying rent I'd be able to save a decent amount and work towards getting my own place one day. But in between the cost of living skyrocketing, trying to keep up with my wealthier friends' lifestyles because I'm too embarrassed to say 'sorry, I can't afford that' and the ever-rising price of London flats, that day still feels *very* far away, and living with Mum has turned out to be worse than the group runs. At least then, I had some modicum of self-respect and didn't get out of breath walking up stairs.

On the ride to the restaurant Mum is deathly quiet. The driver asks us where we're off to and a look of confusion crosses his face when she answers 'birthday party' in the reverent tone one might use if they were going to a funeral. We hit some traffic and she starts looking at her watch, muttering about 'not setting off on time'.

'What?! Do you mean that *ten seconds* it took me to come downstairs?' I demand.

'I don't know why you can't just be waiting at the door,' she mithers.

I don't know why you keep organising events when they make you so anxious, I think. It's definitely not for my benefit. I'd much rather have stayed in and watched *Heathers* for the tenth time – you can never watch *Heathers* too many times – and eaten my body weight in lasagne. But I don't say anything.

At least the taxi driver gives me a sympathetic look in the rear-view mirror. I cling to our secret mutual understanding like a sad crumb of comfort.

We pull up outside Antonio's. My stomach clenches and I suddenly feel a bit sick. It's like I've been keeping the reality of the situation at bay until I see the glint of balloons from inside the window. This is real. It is happening. A *birthday party*. Organised by my *mother*. What was I thinking? Why didn't I say no? Why am I so weak?! WHAT IF NOBODY COMES?! And how old do I have to get before I stop worrying about no one showing up to my birthday party?

Probably when I'm ninety and all my friends are dead. Then I'll know for *sure* that no one's coming. I might be a bit lonely but my God, I'll be relaxed.

It's very . . . sparkly . . . inside the restaurant. And balloony. I can barely move. Why did Mum order so many balloons? Oh God, was it to make the room seem less empty in case no one turns up?! *No. Don't be paranoid, Becky.*

'I ordered extra balloons to make the room seem less empty,' Mum says.

Oh good. It's always comforting to know your most neurotic thoughts might be entirely accurate. I head to the bathroom to finish my make-up.

When I get into the loos and reach inside my bag, my heart sinks. No. No no no.

Noooooooooo.

I tip the contents out and scrabble around. Lip gloss. Tampon. Condom (optimistic but you never know). Fiver. Tissues. Pen. Emergency Maoams. *No eye make-up*.

How can that be?!

I think back to my bedroom. UGH. I'd just finished off my right eye when Mum called me downstairs. In my desperation not to piss her off I must have left it on the sidetable. I stare at myself in the mirror and move my head from side to side. Could I pull this off? Act like I was going for some sort of alternative *Clockwork Orange* look?

No. I'm nowhere near cool enough for that. I sigh and prepare myself for battle.

'Mum,' I venture, stepping out of the bathroom. My soul feels heavy. She is going to *kill* me. 'I need to run back home.'

Mum's fiddling with the giant '2' and '9' balloons. Her neck snaps towards me.

'What for?' The storm brews in her voice.

'I left my make-up at home.' I point to my naked eye.

She sighs deeply. 'Honestly, Becky.'

There's a silence. I let her disapproval hang in the air for a moment and try to look repentant, so she can feel like she's punished me sufficiently before letting me go.

'*Why* didn't you just finish your make-up before we left the house?' she continues.

'I'm sorry,' I murmur. Maybe if she hadn't rushed me to get here several hours early.

'Can't you ask Angie or Damilola to bring something?'

'Well, Dami says she'll be here at seven thirty, but you know that means at seven she'll try-leaving-work-but-just-answer-a-few-more-emails and then it will be nine. And Angie's coming from Clapham.'

'For God's sakes. Why is she in *Clapham*?' Mum accuses, as if this is all Angie's fault.

'A meeting. I don't know.' I shrug.

'Well, you can't go now.' She goes back to fiddling with the balloons. 'There's too much to do. You'll just have to put up with it.'

'But . . .' I start. 'I look like I've escaped from an asylum!'

Mum smirks.

'What is there to do, exactly?!' I know I should keep my cool. I know I'm going to regret this in a matter of moments. But it's too late. I'm already flailing my arms around wildly and raising my voice. 'All the balloons are blown up. The booze is bought. Someone else is making the food. Why are we even here?!'

Mum doesn't answer and keeps her eyes fixed on the balloons. A waiter peers through the window in the door to the kitchen, about to bring a tray through. He clearly thinks twice after seeing us arguing and his head disappears.

'I'm sorry that my throwing you a party is such an *inconvenience* for you, Becky,' Mum says coolly.

There it is. Hello, Regret, my old friend. I've been expecting you. Regret shakes his head at me and wags his finger. I shouldn't have said anything. The truth is, this *is* an inconvenience. I never wanted a party but instead of just telling Mum no, like a grown-up, I went along with it to avoid a fight, but have been grumpy and unhelpful and made everything as difficult as humanly possible every step of the way.

I'm about to respond when there's a tap at the door. A dark mop of ruffled hair emerges, followed by grinning brown eyes.

'*Knock knock.*' Max's voice reverberates around the room and my heart leaps into my throat. Why is he here?! Suddenly my limbs feel very meaty. My arms are no longer arms but big, fleshy noodles I have no idea what to do with.

'Max!' My mum beams. Her whole manner softens now that we're in company. 'Becky said you weren't coming until later.'

'Yeah, the shoot finished early. It's looking good in here, Ms A.' Max changes the subject as he pulls away and looks around the room. His gaze finally lands on me and a bemused expression crosses his face. *Shit*. My hand flies up to cover my left eye.

'Thank you, Max. You don't think it's too much glitter?' Mum carries on.

'No such thing.' Max shakes his head solemnly.

'You're looking tanned,' Mum says. It sounds like an accusation. 'Have you been away?'

'Not since the summer.'

Mum makes no reply, hiding a glittery balloon behind a plain one. She often stops listening partway through conversations.

'Your shoot must have finished *very* early.' I change the subject back, now that Mum is distracted by balloon placement.

Max shrugs. 'Well . . . yeah . . . okay. I took some quick snaps and pegged it out of there. Said something about losing the light.' He laughs awkwardly. 'I thought you might need help setting up.'

'Did you get everything you need?!' I panic. This was a big deal for him. He's been talking about it for months. I can't believe he left an important job to help set up my stupid birthday party. But also . . . *I can't believe he left an important job to help set up my stupid birthday party.*

'Ngegh.' Max makes a non-committal noise and shrugs again. 'It'll be fiiiiine.'

Mum leaves to go and inspect the caterers. Max moves closer and leans over me. I can smell his aftershave and my body turns even more noodley. I tilt my head up, keeping my eye covered. 'Everything all right, Becky?' He grins.

'Yeah, um, got something in my eye,' I say.

'Huh, let's take a look, shall we?' he says, peeling back my fingers. He brings my hand down to my side and we look each other in the face. We both burst out laughing.

'It's a good look,' he teases.

'I left my make-up at home.' I don't need to explain to Max why I can't go back and get it. He knows my mother.

'I'll go to the shop.' He smiles, still holding my hand. 'What do you need?'

'Mascara, liquid eyeliner, some sort of grey eyeshadow.'

He looks at me like I just spoke Spanish. Eventually I write it down for him and he heads out. He'll probably get it all wrong anyway but oh well. *Max is here. Running around helping me because he cares about me.*

The quiet, unhinged part of my brain whispers: these are definitely the vibes of a boyfriend, right? Not just a friend? Friends don't show up early at parties to hang out with people's mothers, do they? UGH. *Shut up, brain.* Yes, they do. Because you are just friends. You have been just friends for a long time. Because YOU BROKE UP WITH HIM, remember?

Max returns with the right make-up and I sort my face out. Mum feeds Max about a million different entrées and he humours her with an in-depth discussion about the tones, flavours and textures of each one. Mum's boyfriend, Gavin, arrives and starts scoffing them until she slaps his hand away and he laughs. Gavin cracks open the champagne. For a beautiful moment I stop worrying about whether people will turn up. I stop worrying about living at home, my lukewarm feelings towards my job and having zero interest in every date I go on. I stop torturing myself with the fading, hazy dream of what my life should have been, versus the reality of nearly thirty years on the planet with nothing to show for it.

Then Dami arrives with The Folder.

Dear Damilola,

I truly think you're a nice person and a good friend, and I'm sad that we've grown apart over the last few years (I know you've noticed it too). I've been thinking a lot about why that is, and I can't help but trace it back to when you started at KD.

With the late nights, the last-minute cancelling of plans, and – when you do turn up – the eye constantly on the inbox, it became hard to reach you.

And once wedding planning began, I didn't stand a chance. Any spare moment you get from work feels like it's focused on flowers, chairs, flooring. Do you really care about any of this? Because the Dami I knew was non-materialistic and it seems more like Phil's big, splashy wedding than yours.

I just want the old Dami back. I don't know who you are anymore and I miss you.

Love,
Becky

P.S. I had a dream that The Folder got roasted in Angie's new wood-burning stove and I woke up really, really happy.

Chapter Two

The Folder was once just a folder. An innocent sliver of a thing, meant to contain 'a few ideas' for Dami's wedding. Then a few weeks after Dami got engaged (six months ago but it feels like I've been talking about cake forks for at least six years), Angie took joint ownership of The Folder in the name of being 'helpful', but I'm pretty sure it's partly so she can make unsubtle hints at her commitment-phobic boyfriend, Jacob. Across the months it grew and grew to the size of a poodle, and then a small child. Now The Folder might as well be a fourth person in our friendship group. I'm thinking about buying it a little hat.

Dami taps on the window, carrying it underneath her arm. Old Dami never would have brought it to my birthday party . . . But apparently, New Dami, who has been taken over by work and by Phil, would. At least she hasn't started dressing like Phil yet (an unsettling amount of V necks, badly fitting jeans and pointy shoes). She looks the same as ever: understated, classy, her black hair drawn in a smooth, high bun.

'Hi, Dami.' I smile as she enters, eyes on The Folder. Sometimes I feel like it's watching me. 'You're on time!'

'Of course!' She looks confused, as if she's not constantly running late because she will never leave work at five thirty. She runs forward for a hug and squeezes me into her chest.

The Folder gets pressed in between us and sticks into my rib cage. 'Happy birthday! Have you had a nice day?'

Despite having become increasingly absorbed in her inbox, and now her wedding, Dami is genuinely lovely. She, Angie and I have been friends since we were at school. I sometimes feel like we don't have anything in common anymore and she nods at things I say with a faraway glaze in her eyes, like I'm an alien creature who she's intrigued by but in no way understands, but she is lovely.

She follows my gaze to The Folder. 'Sandra just wanted to see a few bits,' she says.

Oh, so Mum asked her to bring it. Of course. I can feel Max shaking beside me, trying not to laugh. I've spoken about it so much it's like a legend to him. He didn't believe me when I told him how big it was.

'I've chosen the white dress now, but I still need some help with the gele.' They're having a hybrid British ceremony with traditional Nigerian elements baked in, so there are a few outfit changes across the night.

Dami goes to put her things in the cloakroom and Max grabs me by the shoulders. 'BECKY,' he hisses. 'Holy fuck. That thing is GINORMOUS. I think it grows by eating human souls. It's going to devour us all.'

I snort, instantly comforted. Max and I always see things in the same way. I never meet anyone else that makes me laugh as much as he does. I silently wish that I had had this foresight at twenty-four, before ending things and making the biggest mistake of my entire life.

As if to remind me, Dami returns from the cloakroom and says, 'So, Max! How are you? How's Fran?'

Fran is Max's . . . ugh . . . I can't even say it in my head. Girlfriend. They've been together about five minutes. Before I can hear his answer, I pretend to go and help Mum with something. It's not like I'm not aware of Fran's existence, but that doesn't mean I want to hear about her. Kind of like Trump being president; you know he is, but that doesn't mean you want to scroll through his Twitter feed.

I would have invited her, if Max had been planning to come on time. But as he said he was just going to put in a late appearance and has showed up last minute, it's a bit late for that, thankfully. I don't think I could have withstood the pain of watching them together at my own birthday party.

I note with relief that quite a few people have started arriving. Not because I actually enjoy parties – I'd much rather live vicariously through *Booksmart* or . . . *Animal House* – but at least it *looks* like I have friends. For all anyone else knows I'm just another normal, functioning member of society. There are some neighbours and a few family friends . . . mine and Max's old pals from the bar . . . Phil, Dami's fiancé . . . and at about eight Angie arrives with her slimy boyfriend, Jacob.

'Happy birthday, poochie!' she trills. Blonde hair cascades perfectly past her pale shoulders. Her silk blouse is tucked tightly into her short, black leather skirt, showing off her tiny waist. Even after a day at work, her hair and make-up are the kind of perfect I could never achieve after hours getting ready. Angie is always immaculate and, being a personal trainer, spends most of her time in the gym.

'Hi, Angie.' I let myself be enveloped in her warm hug. Angie can be one of the most loving, fun and attentive people you will ever meet, if she likes you.

'Oh. Hi, Max.' She shoots him a false smile.

Not so much if she doesn't like you.

'Angie.' Max nods.

'Max finished early,' I explain.

'Yay.' Angie delivers flatly, clapping her hands together. Max opens his mouth to ask her a question, but she's already heading for the booze. He shrugs at me and I smirk.

Angie, unlike Dami, would never be described as 'lovely'. She's fiercely protective if you're her friend, but mildly scary if you get on the wrong side of her. Basically, she doesn't bother to hide her feelings and she's never liked Max very much. Probably because they're both quite outspoken and have conflicting points of view on almost everything. Angie isn't a fan of being disagreed with.

She notices Dami and Mum with The Folder and rushes to sit down with them, instantly entranced by whatever dress or floral arrangement they're looking at. Even though I'm annoyed they're doing this on my birthday, for a moment I feel a rush of warmth looking at the three women I love most in the world sitting around a table together, and I long to be included.

I send Max off to chat with our old friends from Scintilla – the cocktail bar we worked at in our early twenties – and go to join them.

'I find wood panelling very oppressive,' Mum is saying as I sit down.

'Hmm, yes, I see your point . . .' Dami says politely, looking down at her venue options, all of which feature wood panelling. 'What do you think, Ang?'

She doesn't ask me.

'I think they're all classy, but I especially like this one.' Angie points to a semi-gothic stately home with a moat. Dami smiles.

'Very *Saltburn*,' I try.

No one says anything.

'I meant the building, not like, we'll be drinking each other's cummy bathwater,' I add.

Mum rolls her eyes.

'Did you decide on the family colours yet?' Angie interjects.

'Phil's keen on lime green.' Angie wrinkles her nose and Dami adds, 'Don't worry. My entire family are already talking him out of it.'

'What about the cake?'

'Oh, let's have a look.' Mum flips to the cake section. 'Gosh, this one's unusual.' Mum points.

'It's cheese,' Dami answers.

'*Cheese?*' Mum repeats.

'I love cheese . . .' I try to interject, but Mum cuts me off.

'Still, I suppose you can do whatever you like these days. Cheese instead of cake is probably just the tip of the iceberg. I'm a bit out of the loop.' She glances at me.

'My mum's not a fan of the cheese stack either. It's gone.'

'Gosh, your mum must be having *so* much fun helping you plan this.' Mum sighs deeply.

'She's very involved,' Dami agrees tactfully.

'Well, thank you for allowing me to throw in my two pennies. It's unlikely I'll ever be helping to plan a wedding.'

I wait for Angie and Dami to deny it, but Angie just presses her lips together, and Dami looks at me like you would a homeless puppy. Okay. And I'm out. Any warmth I was feeling evaporates and I want to be as far away from all three of them as possible.

If you'd asked me ten years ago where I'd be romantically, at twenty-nine, I'd have said 'engaged' or at least 'in a stable relationship'. I'm painfully aware of how far away from that I am and I don't need them to make me feel any worse about it.

It's not like I haven't tried to meet someone. I have tried *hard*. But if the date's not truly horrendous (feather guy) then it's lacking in chemistry (woman who was clearly so bored by me she started playing Royal Match on her phone waiting for her Uber). Most of the time it feels like there's so much choice that everyone's constantly looking for something better (woman who organised another date *during our date*) or like they're trying so hard to counteract the disposability of the dating scene, they're willing to commit to just about anyone (man who asked me to adopt a shared dog on date number three).

'Right, got to make the rounds.' I stand up and make my way over to Max. None of them follow me.

Half an hour later, they are *still* crowded around The Folder. So much for 'a few dresses and then it's away'.

Thank God Max is here. We sit in a corner, mocking them from afar.

'On my *birthday*,' I rage. I'm on cocktail number six by now. And it's only nine thirty. 'What is the definition of a *birthday*, Max?'

'The anniversary of the day on which a person was born, typically treated as an occasion for celebration and the giving of gifts,' Max answers dutifully.

'And does a birthday, by your understanding, have

anything to do with *weddings*?' I drain cocktail number six and reach for number seven.

'By very definition, no!' Max slams his fist on the table.

'Answer me this. Can you order a HAPPY WEDDAY card, or a HAPPY BIRTHING card from Moonpig?'

'Maybe . . . if someone got married on their birthday?'

'But who would DO that?'

'Only a psychopath,' Max reassures me. He puts his arm around me. 'It's out of order, Becks. They're wankers. Fuck 'em.'

Yeah, fuck them. Max is here. Max is the only person that I need. If everyone else on planet Earth died except Max, I'd probably be pleased because then he'd *have* to get back together with me.

Oh God. I'm drunk. And as Angie once said, 'Drunk Becky is just the opening act for Desperate Becky.'

I'm about to say something else to Max when his phone rings. 'Sorry, I have to take this,' he apologises, standing up. I grab his arm.

'What?! No. You can't abandon me.'

'Becks, it's your party.' Max grins. 'You know everyone in the room.'

But you're the only one I want to talk to, I think, as he leaves.

I can't *believe* everyone is still poring over The Folder. I unsubtly stare at them. Mum and Gavin are nodding intently at everything Phil is saying. Phil, as usual, has his arm around Dami in that way that looks like he's got her in a chokehold. You can barely see her little head peeking out from his big, stifling, muscular arms. Angie's sitting gracefully, perfect posture, occasionally laughing, playing with her hair and brushing Jacob's leg. Jacob is perched on the edge of the seat, looking around the room, obviously waiting until he can go home. I dislike Jacob but, if he has one upside, it's that he's about as interested in The Folder as I am.

I think about going back over there. Then I remember the 'I'll never plan a wedding' comment and no one jumping to my defence, and stay where I am.

'Your parents are so cute!' A sing-song voice interrupts my self-indulgent marinating. Sara, one of mine and Max's friends from Scintilla, is pointing towards Mum and Gavin. Sara was a crazy drama student who was always leaving you stranded at the bar to rush off for last-minute auditions and, when she was there, was mostly role-playing with kitchen appliances. She once made me try to vent my 'pent-up frustrations towards my mother' to a spoon.

Max and I don't see that group often, but it's always nice to catch up now and then and get tickets to Sara's bizarre performances. In the last one we saw, she played the shoe of a Nazi. I'm not certain I fully understood the play but I'm pretty sure it was something along the lines of 'Nazis are bad.'

'That's my mum's boyfriend,' I correct her. 'Not my dad.'

'Oh, sorry!' Sara puts her hand to her mouth. 'Well, they're cute, anyway. Oh, I almost forgot. Birthday present!'

She rummages in her bag and I'm expecting her to bring out some flowers or a bottle of gin to add to the pile, but she produces a dark blue, shimmering gift card covered in stars. It reads 'Spellbound' in lettering that I recognise.

'Oh, is that . . . ?' I join the dots. Spellbound is a magic shop – magic shop? witchy lair? occult cave? what does one call this sort of establishment? – on the next street over from the bar we used to work in.

'Yes! Right by Scintilla!' She claps. 'I've been going to Sue for readings for years.'

Max and I always laugh at how Sara never has money for food, but always has enough for psychics. I've sometimes secretly wondered if there's anything in it – on some level, I've always liked the idea of there being some sort of wise, omnipotent magic that has all the answers, plus Sara was told she would meet someone who'd cause trouble in her life *right* before she met Toxic Tina – but Max would disown me if I admitted that out loud.

'She's been so helpful for me with . . . well, everything, to be honest. I finally dumped Toxic Tina after a particularly cathartic reading. And found the courage to keep auditioning for things when I was having a massive crisis of confidence. Then I got the goose!'

Sara is currently playing the goose in a children's production of *Charlotte's Web*.

'So this is for . . . ' I falter.

'A tarot reading!' She beams. 'I mean, you can use it for anything. They do all sorts in there. But I'd really recommend tarot. It's especially great when you're feeling a bit . . .' She doesn't finish her sentence and bites her lip. I'm guessing she was about to say 'lost'. Wow. Even Sara thinks I need to get my act together. I'd be offended, but she has a kind heart and is genuinely trying to be nice.

'Fun!' I say. 'Thank you so much!'

'And enlightening and informative,' she replies seriously.

'Of course.' I nod, tucking the gift card away in my bag,

alongside the gift card for a massage from Ang and Dami and the BFI membership from Max. I'm surprised and touched – Sara is incredibly sweet to get me a gift – and I'm secretly a little excited, too. I would have felt foolish booking something like that for myself – I can already hear Max's laughter pealing in my head when I tell him about this – but as Sara got it for me, I sort of *have* to go, right?

'God, can you believe we're all nearly thirty?!' Sara goes on. 'There's Seth with his tooouuur.' She gestures to Seth, beside her, who is too wrapped up talking to his date to notice. 'And Max with his flaaaaat. When did we all get so fucking old?! Oh, did you know Andi Summers had a BABY?'

Sara's eyes widen. She clearly thinks this is juicy gossip, even though I can't remember who Andi Summers is. All I hear is 'Max and his flat'. What about it? He's had his flat for ages.

'Max?' I repeat. 'I mean, *yes*, the man has a mortgage, but he still has his Pokémon card collection, so . . .'

'I mean Fran moving in!' Sara delivers the words casually, taking a sip of her drink, like I must already know.

It takes a second for my brain to catch up. Thankfully, Seth leans over to ask Sara the name of Andi Summers's 'foxy baby daddy' and she's too distracted to notice the sheer soul-devouring horror that's swallowing me whole.

Fran . . . moving in? With Max?
Since when?!
It's like someone turns down the volume button of my life. Every conversation around me fades into silence as I process this life-altering information. I retreat inside my own imagination, picturing Fran and Max cuddling on the

sofa together. Pouring wine after a long day's work. Making dinner together. Taking baths together. Having sex in the bed they sleep in together. Spending the rest of their lives together.

I abruptly leave the table and dash for the bathroom. Every single sausage stick I ate this evening is threatening to come back up. I make it to a stall and lock myself inside, trying to take long, deep breaths, but they're ragged. Now that I'm alone, behind a closed door, the tears I've been holding back start to burn. They spill down my cheeks.

Can this be right? How does Sara even know? Why would she know and not me? They haven't even been together very long. How long *has* it been? Not long enough to move in together, surely? That's a huge, stupendous, cataclysmic life-changing decision that requires *significant rumination?!* Max is usually a thoughtful person. This is so unlike him. Maybe this is all a big misunderstanding. That thought doesn't stop me feeling nauseous.

I lean over and vomit into the toilet.

Dear Max,

Hi. I love you. I love you so much that if you told me the end was coming and the only way to survive was to follow you to the desert and let you lead me into the new world, I would drop everything IMMEDIATELY and tattoo a giant 'M' on my forehead, no questions asked.

    That is all. Just thought you should know.

OK bye,
Becky

Chapter Three

Locked in my cubicle, I do something that on some level I *know* is pointless and emotionally reckless, but I do it anyway. I search Fran's name in my WhatsApp to check when she and Max first started dating, to find evidence that their decision to move in is ridiculous. What, how long can it have been? Eight months tops?!

I scroll back through the mentions of her name in my thread with Max – there aren't many, I don't ask about her often – and with a horrible, lurching sensation, I see the date. The first time I heard her name was two years ago.

Two years. No. It can't be. Did they really meet *two years ago*? How can it have been *two whole years*?!

On paper, I have to recognise that does sound like a perfectly reasonable amount of time to know someone before agreeing to cohabit. That's nearly as long as Max and I were together. This shocking discovery is almost worse than finding out they're moving in. I stand up abruptly, knocking my knees against the wall. I don't want to be here. I need to go home. I stumble out of the loo, the taste of sick fresh in my mouth.

I try to maintain composure as I walk past the line of people waiting for the toilet I've been hogging, but my ankle wobbles and I totter on my heels. I am but a sad, weak-ankled clown, and they my nightmarish audience of shame. How am

I going to do this? You can't leave your *own party* without everybody noticing, thus drawing attention to yourself and inviting unwanted questions.

It's not like Dami and Angie don't *know* I'm in love with Max – everybody does, except Max – it's just one of those things we don't talk about. We used to, before Phil was on the scene and before Angie moved in with Jacob. But now they're in real relationships, with an actual wedding on the horizon, nobody wants to hear about how I'm still pining after the boyfriend I broke up with five years ago.

I move stealthily past my table of friends, where it looks like The Folder actually has been put away. For once I'm disappointed. It would have been a good distraction.

I can hear them talking about Dami's ridiculous workload.

'Yeah, wow,' Dami is saying, 'it's never-ending. And we've just got a new intern, so it's that thing where asking her to do something takes longer than just doing it myself—'

'Babe,' Phil cuts across her. 'You just gotta throw her in the deep end. Trial by fire.'

'But there are so many things that—'

'How is she ever gonna learn?' he interjects again.

My blood boils. I don't entirely disagree with what he's saying; Dami is nearly incapable of delegating. Partly because she's so polite she ends up offering to do everything for everyone else. But must Phil always interrupt her? Must he always boss her around? Must he always *project*?! The sound of his voice makes my ear-drums bleed.

At least when Phil's talking it's easier for me to get past them unnoticed.

I scan the room, checking for Max. I don't know what

I'd say if he asked what was wrong. I'm relieved to see he's engaged in one of his heated arguments with Angie. Thank God. That will keep him preoccupied.

'Yeah, not everyone's going to *get* it . . .' he's saying.

'What is there to get?!' she shrieks.

'Look, it's okay, Angie. Art can be challenging . . .'

'Max, there is nothing *challenging* about an eight-foot photo of an anus.'

I slip past them into the coat room, where I bump into someone blocking the rack. It's Angie's boyfriend, Jacob. Talking to Sara's friend Something-Or-Other whose name I can never remember. They look at me like I'm intruding. It feels like I've just walked into a bedroom, not a public area for hanging outerwear garments.

'Errr . . . sorry,' I say, pointing behind Something-Or-Other's head. 'Can I just . . . ?'

'Oh, sure.' She steps out of the way.

I rummage for my coat in silence. I feel the pressure mounting. They want me to find it and leave so they can get back to their unsavoury-but-just-about-socially-acceptable flirtation.

Eventually I find my coat and hurry past them, mumbling a goodbye. I'm too drunk and sad to think too deeply about Angie's boyfriend being holed up in a space the size of a broom cupboard with someone else. Tonight, I've only got space for my own mess.

I escape without anyone seeing my red-rimmed panda eyes and find my Uber, where I manage to keep the tears at bay. There's something too bleak about crying in the backseat of an Uber and either having to explain your life story to the driver or have them awkwardly pretend not to hear you. I text Mum saying, *sorry, felt ill and had to go home.*

When I get home I run to my bedroom and throw myself onto the bed. I let my mind return to events I've gone over more times in my head than Dami's gone over her future wedding: my break-up with Max.

Max and I met on my first shift at Scintilla. It's small, dark, underground and prides itself on making fine cocktails, so God knows how I – or, for that matter, Sara – got a job there. It was my first job out of uni. He'd been working there a couple of months and was instantly amused by my inability to do even the most basic of tasks, like successfully cutting lemons. He helped me practise the recipes outside of hours and, when people sent my inadequate cocktails back, would redo them for me. I'd probably have been fired without him.

Within a week we were having sex. Within a month we were exclusive. We spent the vast majority of our time drinking and spending money we didn't have on takeaways in the middle of the night, getting to know each other's favourite films. Max has a very specific taste in cinema – David Lynch, Jordan Peele, Tarantino – and marvelled at my love of all movies; the good, the bad, the downright terrible.

For a couple of years after university, our lifestyle felt exciting and tinted with a kind of destitute glamour. We were officially 'struggling in the city', bartending alongside out-of-work actors, models and writers – serving people with vastly more disposable income than ourselves – and enjoying feeling young and hard done by. But two years later, the post-uni bubble was popping. I knew I wanted to be 'successful', but still had no idea what I actually wanted to do with my life, and everyone else seemed to have plans. After a lot of internships, Dami had landed her first PR job. Angie was getting into personal training and was already plotting how to go about one day setting up her own business combining fitness and wellness. And then Max got his first gig as a photographer.

A small travel website wanted someone to go around Europe on the cheap, photographing 'off the beaten track' destinations. It was perfect for Max, who wanted to see the world. I desperately wanted to go, but I had no money saved on a bar worker's salary and paying extortionate rent.

We avoided the subject until just before he left but, in the cold light of day, the realisation hit me that I didn't know when I would see Max again. Six months? A year?

He was leaving. I was staying. In my mind that equalled a break-up.

I can still see his hurt face as I delivered the news. Him looking like he's about to cry but saying, 'Yeah, that makes sense. Obviously. Don't worry about it, dude.'

Don't worry about it, dude.

And you know what? I didn't. He went off and I didn't think about him much at all. He was doing his thing and I had my own thing to find. In my head it was just inevitable that we'd go our separate ways. I would see his pictures, doing fun things in different countries, and feel okay about it. The right decision had been made. I accepted a job at We Work, You Win and at that point, even though I knew it wasn't what I wanted to do, I was just enjoying the novelty of being employed somewhere that gave me paid annual leave and health insurance. I was getting drunk with Angie and Dami, using dating apps and meeting all kinds of people. I'd figured out I was bi and was exploring the novelty of dating women. I was relishing the feeling of being 'a grown-up'.

It was only a couple of years later, when Max came back, that I started seeing it differently. He asked if I wanted to go for a drink and as soon as I saw him it was like nothing had changed. I was right back there; all the in-jokes, the attraction, the feelings.

At first I thought that was inevitable. If you see any ex there's going to be *something* that's still there, right? Especially if you broke up because of circumstances rather than things being wrong with the relationship.

Except, as time went on, I realised it wasn't a case of 'something' still being there. I thought about him when I woke up. I looked forward to his messages more than anything else. He popped into my mind when I was on a date. I wanted to tell him every tiny thing that happened during my day. A few months after he moved back I realised I was still in love with him.

There have been so many times since he moved back to London that I wanted to tell him I made a mistake. But by age twenty-six he'd friend-zoned me and I wasn't sure there was a way back. I was terrified of him rejecting me, so I didn't say anything. We were both dating other people on and off and there was never a good time. I tried to be happy to be back in his life, even as a mate, and I figured – once we had built up trust between us again – I would work up the courage to tell him how I felt one day.

Except, I never did.

He met Fran.

And now here we are.

I try watching *Grey Gardens* to cheer myself up but even big Edie and little Edie can't help. I spend the rest of the night crying and clutching my old, mangy teddy bear. When Mum comes back later that evening, I think she might walk past my door and go straight to bed in a textbook display of passive aggression, but she stops outside.

'Hello? Becky?' Her voice is muffled but I can tell she's worried. For a moment I'm as happy to hear her as a five-year-old who's fallen on the playground. The door opens and even her entering without knocking doesn't bother me like it normally would. 'What happened?'

'Mum,' I sob. I don't know what else to say. Mum and I don't share much personal information with each other. I'm sure she suspects that I'm still in love with Max, although I've never voiced it to her. It's on the tip of my tongue to say something. Maybe this gap between us can be breached. Maybe if I told her more we'd be closer. I have the overwhelming urge for her to tell me it's going to be okay.

'Mum . . . I . . .'

Then she spots the bucket I've put beside my bed – just in case – and sighs.

'Honestly, Becky. How much have you had to drink?'

'Only seven cocktails,' I say.

'Only?!' She raises her eyebrows.

'It's my birthday.' My voice sounds small and defensive. 'It's not that many.'

Mum sighs again. 'Oh, Becky. *When* are you going to grow up?'

She disappears off back to her own room, probably too repulsed that she created such a hideous monster-child to look at me. Probably wondering where it all went wrong and if she should have told me Santa Claus wasn't real sooner.

I cry some more and eventually fall asleep.

Dear Mum,

First of all, thank you for letting me move back in with you. I don't want this letter to sound ungrateful. But let's face it, we both know this isn't working.

I can't live like this anymore.

I can't be home by a curfew. I can't worry every time I leave a mug on the coffee table instead of putting it in the dishwasher. I can't feel like I've murdered someone if I forget to eat leftovers. I can't sleep in a bedroom that hasn't been redecorated since I was twelve.

I'm aware how much money you've saved me this year and that you wanted to help me out. It was a good plan in theory, but I've felt infantilised and miserable, and I've barely saved up enough to make a dent in a deposit anyway.

I still want to buy my own flat one day, but not like this.

I know this will be a disappointment to you. I know I'm a disappointment. I love you. I'm sorry.

All my love,
Becky

Chapter Four

When are you going to grow up? My mother's words resound in my head the next day as I lie in bed, staring at the ceiling, remembering with a sinking feeling that I have a date today. *Why did I agree to a date the day after my birthday party? I've not been on a date in months, this is surely the worst moment I could have chosen. Why did I agree to said birthday party at all?* I guess that brings us back to question number one. Only children are told what to do. I'm just a big, grotesque child that's allowed to drive and have raging hangovers.

Not that I can drive.

I have a bunch of messages from Max, Dami and Angie, all asking what happened to me last night. I haven't replied yet. Another one from Dami pops up.

Babe, we're a bit worried. You ok? x

Bless Dami. She is sweet. I stare at the words. Am I okay?

Honestly, I can't remember the last time I was okay. I think it was the week before Max left. I was in his house-share and we were packing all his stuff up, painting over Blu Tack marks, wrangling with the insane jungle of a garden and drinking beers with zero thought for the future.

Before I can reply she says:

Come meet me and Ang tomorrow? 6pm at The Grapevine? x

I agree, then hear the front door slam downstairs. My stomach lurches. Oh God. What time is it? I look at the clock. It's midday. *Shit*. Mum must be coming back from her water aerobics class. She hates when I'm still in bed after nine. I jump up and scrabble on the floor for some clothes, but all I can find is more pyjamas. The sound of Mum's footsteps on the stairs tells me it's too late anyway.

She enters my room without knocking. This time it does annoy me.

'Honestly, Becky.' She shakes her head. I stand up.

'Sorry, Mum,' I mumble.

'The weekend's nearly over. You've slept it away,' she says.

I don't point out the fact that I'm still in bed because of a party that she made me have. It will only start another argument and it won't change her mind. Even after a late night, she's always somehow up and dressed at seven, probably having done all her chores and devoured a novel the size of *War and Peace*. Mum was a lawyer – she used to work incredibly hard for ridiculously long hours – and her frenetic efficiency lasted into retirement. This means my dysfunction is even more distasteful to her than it would be to a regular human.

I do try to please her. I really do. I set an alarm for 9 a.m. I must have shut it off in my sleep.

'What are your plans today?' she asks.

'God . . .' I reply, accidentally putting a sock on my hand. My brain's not switched on yet. 'I have a date.'

Why do I keep doing this to myself? I suppose in the vain hope that I *might* meet somebody. That this next person, in all the eight billion people on the planet, might be *my* person. One day it's got to happen, right?

'You sound thrilled,' Mum remarks. 'What's their name?'

My mind blanks. I frown.

'What do they do?'

I purse my lips.

'Honestly, Becky.' Mum turns and leaves the room again.

At least my miserable dating life distracted her from the fact I left her party to eat Doritos in bed and cry. Silver linings.

I don't have long to get ready before meeting my date whose name, it turns out, is Vera. Did I really agree to go on a date with someone called Vera? In the *afternoon*? I don't generally organise dates before 7 p.m. because why would you meet new people at a time when it's socially unacceptable to consume alcohol?

I check back through my thread with Vera. She's very pretty – plus. Likes hiking – minus. She wanted to show me Primrose Hill before it got dark, hence why we're meeting during the day. She seemed determined that I couldn't possibly live in London without seeing it and I must have gone along with it, even though drinking in the dark is much more my scene than strolling in the sun. I glance through my uninterested responses. She must be hard up if she's keen to meet after that. I consider cancelling – it won't be any different from any of the dud dates I've had over the past few years – but it's a bit late now.

I throw on something half acceptable and reluctantly make my way to the tube station. The journey passes in a blur of caffeine, painkillers, and hangxiety. Apart from worrying about how tragic it is to leave your own birthday early, I'm going over and over every conversation I had last night, analysing whether I said something stupid, *before* I left in a blur of tears. (Did I ask enough questions about other people's lives? Was it obvious that I couldn't remember the name of Gail's second child? Or, *shit*, is it her third child? Did I offend Sara when I called her dress maroon and she thought it was burgundy?) So I'm nice and relaxed when I show up for my date.

When I see Vera I note, happily, that she is one of those people who is more attractive than her pictures. Her tanned, freckly skin has a kind of natural, golden glow and her smile has an energy that a camera can't capture. Her honey-coloured hair flows past her shoulders in natural waves that make it look like she just stepped off a sail boat. I actually . . . fancy her?

My heart sinks. What's the catch? There must be something wrong with her. I'm sure, shortly, I'll discover that she irons her knickers or takes baths with her brother.

'Becky!' She throws her arms out and pulls me into a hug. 'It's great to meet you.' She beams like she's genuinely pleased to see me.

Okay. No one is *that* happy to see someone they don't know. Definitely a sociopath.

'Nice to meet you too,' I reply, already plotting my escape. Could I say I need to return home for something? I need a wee?

'I need a wee,' I say.

Vera bursts out laughing. 'All right, there's your bush.' She points to a shrub.

'Err . . .'

'Not an outdoorsy girl, I gather?' she jokes. 'Come onnn, you'll be fine. Holding it in is good for you. Maybe. Helps exercise bladder control, anyway, so when you're eighty and in a care home and everyone around you is pissing themselves you'll look back and think, *Thank God for that nice lady who took me on that very long walk and taught me to strengthen my bladder muscles.*' She takes my arm and, reluctantly, I am dragged alongside her.

It doesn't take long to realise she's *chatty*. I'm normally irritated by excessively talkative people, and write her off immediately, but somehow as we walk she worms her way back into my affections. She's not talking in a boring, blathers-at-you way, she just seems to have a lot of opinions. And it's not like she's only interested in spouting about herself. She also asks questions about what I think like she sincerely cares and properly listens to my answers. And her favourite film is *Cocoon*, which is a weird, weird choice but intrigues me.

This will go wrong *any* moment now. Even if I like her, she won't like me. The older I get, the more I realise the odds of two people both actually liking each other on a date only get slimmer and slimmer.

'So Becky, where do you live?' she asks as we walk through a patch of trees. It's a grey, gloomy day, and there aren't too many people around. For London, anyway.

'North West, and you?' I ask quickly, even though she

already told me. I'm trying to dodge the inevitable 'who do you live with' question, but she doesn't buy it.

'What's your set-up?' Ah, there it is.

I pretend I don't know what she's asking, to buy myself a few more moments where she thinks I'm functional. Or at least, that I *could* be functional.

'Flatmates? Cat?' she presses.

'My mum,' I admit, my cheeks flushing. 'I'm saving for a flat. Well, trying to,' I garble.

Well, that's done it. She might as well order her Uber and play Royal Match while she waits.

'That's cool,' she says, without so much as a blink. I feel myself relax, which makes me deeply uncomfortable, so I immediately unrelax.

'What about your dad?' she asks.

Oh God.

'Uhhhh . . . I . . . He . . .' I start.

'Don't go there. Don't worry, it's cool.' She grins.

She's so . . . open and uninhibited? And unfazed by my awkwardness? She's like, actually a nice person, without being nauseatingly boring?

We keep walking, and talking, and eventually stop at a bench. I glance at my phone and am surprised to realise a few hours have passed without me noticing. She sits down and gestures for me to join her. It occurs to me that, miraculously, during the course of the date she still hasn't said or done anything to physically repulse me. How can this be? I cast my eyes over her ears. Ears are weird, right? They're bound to disgust me. But no. Her ears are solid. Nice, well-formed lobes.

We don't say anything for a moment and just admire the London skyline. I feel her watching me from the corner of my eye. I look back and she doesn't glance away for a moment too long. Is this . . . *sexual tension*?

'Do you iron your knickers?' I ask.

She bursts out laughing.

'Erm, no, but I can if it's your kink?'

I laugh. I can't be sure, but I *think* this might be a 'good date'.

Except, with a familiar, heart-sinking feeling, I realise it can't be. Because I've thought about whether Max and Fran have had sex today at least twice. And now I'm wondering what they'll be making for dinner this evening. Perhaps they'll get a takeaway?

Vera leans towards me. The heady scent of her perfume sends a pleasant, calming shiver down my body, like I've just had an aromatherapy massage. I notice her tanned collarbone, speckled with little moles, and think about how I want to kiss it. About how I want to push her sleeve off her shoulder and start kissing my way down. I realise I've been staring at her neck and look up. She's smiling at me and leans in closer. I vault away like a lemming.

'Shit! Time!' I squeak. 'I've got to go.'

'Oh, that's cool, no worries.' She stands up and pulls me into another warm, deep hug. She's so soft and the feel of her boobs against mine make me want to throw my top off. I stand very still, trying to make myself as unhuggable as a big, steel rake. After stumbling out my goodbyes I effectively bolt back across the hill.

I didn't have to go, obviously. I decide to walk home and then regret it. Walking has this way of forcing you to focus on your own thoughts. Why didn't I get the tube, where I could concentrate on how annoying the person cutting in front of me on the escalator was instead? Part of the whole appeal of living in London is having no headspace for your own thoughts, because you can't hear them above the noise of everyone else's.

I'm not entirely sure why I feel so awful. The date was *good*. Miles better than most of the ones I go on . . . So why did it make me feel worse than the bad ones?

I ponder this all evening and can't come up with any answers.

The next day, I'm looking forward to seeing Angie and Damilola. As I approach The Grapevine – a wine bar near Angie's we've frequented since she moved into her current place – I see them sitting on stools in the window, laughing with drinks in hand. I feel an instant swell of solace and relief. They look like home.

I sit down beside them, pleased to simply be in their company. For once I don't care if we talk about the embossing on wedding invites or napkins or *even* napkin-holders. I just want to sit quietly and listen to their comforting chatter. But both their eyes are firmly on me.

'Becky? Why did you leave so suddenly the other night?' Dami rubs my shoulder.

'I felt sick,' I say. It would be a lot more convincing if my lip wasn't quivering.

She and Angie share a look.

'Are you sure? Do you want . . .'

'It's nothing,' I insist. 'I just had a bit too much to drink. I'm fine,' I say when they keep looking at me.

I'm too ashamed to tell them I'm upset about Max moving in with Fran. My friends are as tired of me as my mum is. As tired of me as I am.

Angie shakes her head with weariness, confirming that I'm right.

'Okay, well, if you're sure,' Dami says gently. 'How was your date?'

'Uh, it was . . .' My reflex reaction, by now, has become to dismiss their questions. Say 'meh' and move on, like I normally do when the conversation gets turned on me, so that no one gets bored of hearing the same old thing over and over.

But something compels me to say more this time. I stopped talking to them about how much I hate my job, or living at home, or not being able to get over Max, because those things got old a long time ago. But this date has brought up a lot of new feelings. Maybe it might *actually* be nice to examine them with my pals, like we used to.

'It was . . . fun?' I answer with apprehension.

Dami's eyebrows shoot up her forehead. Angie practically spits out her drink.

'Excuse me?! Who are you? What have you done with Becky?' Angie jokes.

'Ooh, that's exciting! What was she like? What was her name again?' Dami gushes breathlessly.

Naturally, they stopped bothering to learn the names of anyone I date years ago.

'Vera. She was nice. Cute. Smart. Warm. Sexy. Cheerful without being stomach-turning. Made me laugh. She *hikes*, but, I don't know . . . I didn't mind that she hikes.'

Dami claps her hands together. She looks so pleased that I feel bad about dashing her hopes a second later.

'But . . . I don't know. I don't know if I'll see her again,' I add.

Neither of them says anything. I continue.

'I mean, we could potentially have some not-entirely-terrible sex. I bet she wouldn't ask me whether I'd rather have a beard or feathers for pubic hair, at least. But, I don't know . . . She just wasn't . . . You know?'

I don't say it, but we all know what I mean.

She wasn't Max.

I wait for them to chip in with their analysis. Why am I still not interested after a good date? Should I give up on apps altogether? What should I do now? But I've lost them.

'Sure,' Angie says, looking defeated.

Dami's phone lights up and I see her click an email icon. This conversation is not even worth ignoring her inbox for on a Sunday.

They were briefly interested in my life and now they're back to being tired of it. I squash my hopes that we might reconnect.

It's a blow. Often their advice on this front is more annoying than useful; Angie's been with Jacob since university, so she's never even used a dating app, and Dami met Phil through a friend at work. They don't get what it's like out there. But . . . it stings that they've given up even *trying* to advise me. I remember this is why I don't share with them anymore and vow not to make that mistake again.

There's a moment of silence while Dami answers the email – she never can read an email and not reply immediately – and Angie studies her nails, then Dami changes the subject.

'Ang . . . should we be celebrating your news?'

I look between them. News?

Here it comes. I brace myself to hear that Angie's getting married now, too. They've been living together for a few years and she's been angling towards it for a while. Angie usually gets what she wants, eventually. Despite feeling hurt by her, my gut clenches with protective unease at the thought of her marrying Jacob.

'Yeah, I'm finally setting up my own business,' she says.

'Oh. Congratulations.' My stomach muscles relax.

Dami notices my relief and a moment of understanding passes between us. Dami would never say it out loud – she's too classy for that – but we have a tacit agreement about our mutual dislike of Angie's boyfriend. I've seen her watching Jacob hitting on other women, like I have.

'Ang, that's seriously great,' I go on.

She smiles. 'Thanks. Yeah. I'm really pleased. I should have done it ages ago. What's the point in working for a gym that's taking fifty fucking per cent when the clients are there for me? I have enough clients now to go it alone; ones who are interested in more than just fitness. They're willing to pay for the whole wellness package, you know? And I've got the nutritionist qualification. I've got funds for the space.'

'Yeah, it makes perfect sense,' I say. She's wanted to open her own wellness centre for years. She's one of those people who's naturally a boss, not an employee.

We toast to Angie and the tension between us is forgotten. I am genuinely thrilled for her, but as I listen to her talk about her plans for her new website and where she's looking to rent a studio, I can't help but feel lonelier than ever. Just one more thing to add to the list of people living their lives, when I seem to have a total inability to live my own.

Angie is starting her own business.
Dami is getting married.
Becky is not doing anything.

I think about how odd it is that my two best friends since school are sitting right across from me and yet I've never felt so distant from them. The table might as well be a vast ocean between us. They're little, tiny specks on the other side of it and I'm trying to wave and jump and get them to see me but they're just squinting, going, 'Do we know that person?'

I knew talking to them was a terrible idea. Why did I even try? They don't understand. Of course they don't understand. We're not in the same place. We haven't been in the same place for a long, long time.

Dear Angela,

Do you remember how grossed out you were by the alien in The Thing when I made you watch it? How you said if it touched you, you would shower until you had no skin left?

Well, that's how I feel about Jacob.

Your boyfriend's a creep. The kind of man whose mere glance makes me want to wax off my eyebrows so he would never look at me and find me attractive. I say this because I love you and you need to hear it.

There's no good way to sign off here,

Becky

Chapter Five

On Monday morning I'm hiding under my hangover cap, shielding my eyes from the sun and my face from my colleagues. Quite frankly, I could do without looking too closely at Ted and his overly moistened lips when I'm already feeling delicate. The sad truth is that my hangovers last for several days now.

For some reason – probably the tarot gift from Sara planting a seed of desperation for a sign from the universe – this morning I find myself downloading an astrology app called Co-Star that I've heard Dami and Angie talking about. After filling in details about when I was born and getting all my various signs, my horoscope says:

Forward motion requires lifting one's legs.

Is that supposed to be helpful?! What does that even mean, Co-Star?!

I delete the app immediately. If Max ever found it on my phone, I'd never hear the end of it.

I look back at my computer. What am I supposed to be doing again? It doesn't help that, despite having showered several times this weekend, I feel like I somehow still smell of sick.

When I first joined – which feels like a million years ago, although apparently it's only five – I was *good* at this. I had energy for finding people roles they'd be brilliant in and helping companies grow. I used to *care*. I never loved the job itself, exactly, but I was invested in having a job and being good at something. But the years went on, and the cyclical nature of the work began to feel like a relentless hamster wheel. Nothing is ever enough? You find someone a role one day and then it's on to the next? Just more, more, more, all the time?! The thanklessness of it began to wear me down. No one is that grateful when you find someone a position they excel in, but when it all goes wrong, it's somehow all my fault? Somehow, somewhere along the way, I lost my motivation. And then, if you're not enjoying your own job, the irony of finding other people jobs *they* love feels like the universe is laughing in your face.

Everyone I originally worked with began leaving for greener pastures, which made it even more depressing. Eventually, I looked around me and I was the only OG left, apart from Ted. All the new people coming in had the boundless enthusiasm I once had, and lost, and that made me feel even worse.

Around last year, I gave up entirely. I developed a highly sophisticated method of trolling through LinkedIn going on people's 'vibes'. You can actually tell a lot from someone's profile picture. Say, for instance, someone was looking for someone to take over a senior role in their 'consumer packaged goods' department. Fuck knows what 'consumer packaged goods' means, exactly. I mean, loo roll is a packaged good but so are jam tarts. Where would anyone begin targeting people? So I would just stare into their eyes for a very long time and ask myself, would *this* person want to work in consumer packaged goods? If the answer was probably not, they look like they do larping on weekends, move on. If I leant towards, possibly, their smile doesn't quite reach their eyes and it seems like their souls are ninety per cent dead anyway, etc, etc, then I'd put them in the 'maybe' pile.

It's as good a method as any. Probably?

My boss Margaret clearly disagreed because six months ago, she moved me into marketing and my job became even more nebulous. Fuck knows what it is that I'm doing these days. I suppose I should be grateful she didn't just fire me. Despite everything, she does appear to have a soft spot for me. I think it's because she remembers the effort I put in when I first started. Sometimes she brings up something great I did about a billion years ago with a confused look, as if she's searching for evidence of That Becky and Now Becky being the same person. She's always trying to encourage me by giving me 'important tasks' to make me feel needed and reignite my enthusiasm, and can't seem to accept that while That Becky had hopes and dreams – vague as they were – Now Becky just wants to sit at her desk comparing all thirteen *Halloween* movies.

I cast my eyes over the notes on the new 'urgent' task that she's given me. I'm supposed to be 'developing content for the website that illustrates vibrant, busy office life'.

Can I just take a picture of Leanne from Accounts smiling vacantly as she rearranges the communal pen pot for the four hundredth time and go home?

My phone buzzes.

Recovered yet?

Against my will my heart flutters and I feel like I might vomit again. It's Max. I type a reply.

Why is everything so loud? And bright? Ted's lips are glinting in the sun

Bahah. Just stay under the cap

He knows me so well.

Anyway, respect for peaking pre-10pm at your own party, but I had something to tell you! Drink tonight?

I'm dreading hearing the words come out of his mouth, and having to plaster on a fake smile and pretend my heart isn't withering into a little shrivelled raisin. But I already know that I'm going to go.

Sure :)

Even though he wants to meet up with me *to tell me he's moving in with another woman*, I still want to go, just so I get to see him. How sad is that? How does one make their unrequited love profound and philosophical, like Gatsby, rather than just pathetic? Maybe if I wrote a poem?

'TO DO: write poem,' says a voice from behind my shoulder.

UGH. It's Ted. I cover up my notepad.

'Hi Ted?' I question, without turning in my chair. I remember to click off Amazon Prime, where I'm watching *The Godfather Part III*. I finished parts one and two last week.

Giving films their due attention can be quite challenging when you're being constantly interrupted by colleagues.

'I didn't know you were into poetry!' Ted continues, ignoring the hint of 'what do you want please go away' in my voice. 'I've always rather liked haikus.'

'I'm not,' I say.

'Oh, I see, okay.' I finally turn to look at him, because clearly we're having a conversation now. He presses his finger over his mouth as if agreeing to keep my secret. 'Sure.'

He licks his lips. Why is he always licking his lips? Ted is only five years older than me, but he has the mannerisms of an eighty-year-old grandma. Unfortunately, as he's the only person apart from Margaret who's been here long enough to remember I used to be invested and friendly, I can't shake him.

'You okay, Ted?' I say.

'Tea run.' He points at his mug.

'I'm good, thanks.' I point at my flask of coffee.

'Oh, of course. How was it?' he asks, referring to my birthday party.

Our conversation is cut mercifully short by Margaret. She strides across the room and stands abruptly before us, a vision in camel. She starts talking urgently about something, but as usual, I am too distracted by her outfit to pay attention. After five years of working for her it never ceases to amaze me that she dresses, every single day, head to toe in pure camel. Where does she shop?

'. . . so if you could follow up, Becky, and report back,' she finishes.

Shit. I wasn't listening.

'Will do.' I nod firmly. Over the years I've learnt Margaret responds to assertive body language as much as tasks actually getting done. Maybe that's partly why she still holds out hope for me as an employee. If you have no idea what you're doing, but type furiously and stare at your computer, looking determined and alert, then you'll fly under the radar. Poor Ted. He works really hard but he doesn't have a purposeful walk, so Margaret's always bitching about his 'lollygagging'.

'All right then, thank you, Becky.' Margaret returns my nod, eyeing my cap with disapproval. She's usually as confused by my state of dress as I am by hers. 'Ted, stop standing around yammering.' She strides back to her office as Ted springs towards his desk like a chastened frog.

'All right, back to work we go.' Ted grins sheepishly. 'See you at four.'

'Four?'

'The announcement!'

'Oh, yeah.' I cannot muster the same enthusiasm as Ted, but at least whatever this 'announcement' is will break up the day somewhat.

At one point during the afternoon, I think I might feel an echo of the gratification I used to feel, when a lovely woman named Cassidy takes the time to email me to say how much she's enjoying her new position and thank me, as she only found the recruitment company through one of my marketing campaigns. I am happy for her, and it's sweet of her to update me, but then it just reminds me how uninspired I am by my own career.

Annoyingly, people keep clustering behind my desk all day, so I get to the end of *The Godfather* trilogy but I can't start *Goodfellas*. For a little while I try to distract myself by looking around and imagining having sex with various co-workers. But it's not that interesting because there isn't a *single* person in this office I would wank over.

Most of the time, I avoid thinking too hard about working here. But today my mind keeps sliding back to being twenty-four, ready to leave Scintilla, full of hope about finding a fulfilling purpose. I applied for all sorts of things that sounded fun and interesting. But I found job-hunting a bit like dating apps; there's an oppressive amount of choice in candidates, which means it's competitive, cut-throat and no one will give you a chance. I didn't have a clear idea of what I wanted to do and, in this job market, it feels like if you haven't known what you wanted to do since birth and been working your whole life towards it, you don't stand a chance.

I interviewed for a publishing assistant role for about 2p an hour. I read a decent amount and I thought I could be good in editorial. They gave the position to a girl who'd written three novels, ran a book blog and spent weekends reading to blind kids. I applied to work at an environmental charity – again, for about 2p an hour. I care about the planet and I'd like to make a difference. They gave it to a guy who saved some kind of nearly extinct bug and had a side business cobbling vegan shoes.

I took this job because I needed money for rent and was so happy to be given *any* kind of work, always with the intention of leaving. But then having this job made interviews even harder, because people kept asking 'so why did you start working in recruitment?' and I didn't have a good enough answer. Eventually, I gave myself a break, always with the intention of getting back on it and finding something. But when I returned to job-hunting with renewed energy, the amount of time I'd been at WWYW became even harder to explain away. Eventually I gave up entirely.

And now here I am.

Margaret finally calls us to stop what we're doing for the 'big announcement'. Everyone gathers together in the kitchen. Margaret's holding a bottle of bubbly and has bought a big box of cupcakes from the fancy bakery down the road. Ted licks his lips.

'Everybody, if I could have your attention. Thank you.' She looks around the room with her square grin. Margaret's expressions of pleasure always look like she's baring her teeth rather than smiling. 'It brings me great excitement to come together today to celebrate a very special employee. Someone who you all know very well. Someone who's been at the company a long time, who knows it inside out, and whose years of dedication haven't gone unnoticed.'

She makes eye contact with me. My heart jumps into my throat. Oh no. God, no.

Is she talking about me?

'Recently we've been stepping up her duties and she's been carrying them like a load-bearing wall. So, we've decided she's surpassed the role of recruitment marketing executive and will now be . . . recruitment marketing manager!'

Oh my God. Is this why she's been giving me extra shit to do? She was priming me for a promotion . . . ? I peek out from under my cap. My head starts swimming. I *cannot* get a promotion. I've spent years actively avoiding increased responsibilities for this very reason. Everybody knows a promotion means you have to stay at least another year. And then you get another promotion and have to stay *another* year, and on and on it goes until you're too old to do anything else. Once you get a promotion THERE IS NO ESCAPE.

'Without further ado . . .'

My lungs aren't working. I feel like I might collapse.

'If you could all raise your glasses . . .'

Everyone around me holds their champagne aloft. I try to take a deep breath.

'To Jessica!'

'To Jessica!' The rest of the team breaks into cheers.

'Hear hear!'

'Woooooop!'

'Go, Jess!'

It takes my brain a second to catch up. Errrrr. That's not my name.

Jessica is getting a promotion? Jessica has 'been at the company a long time'? Jessica 'knows it inside out'? Jessica 'hasn't gone unnoticed'? *Jessica?!* JESSICA?!

Jessica is only twenty-four. The exact age I was when I started. Jessica has been at this company *two years*. I have been here *five*.

FIVE.

Jessica makes her way through the crowd and stands next to Margaret. She flicks her long, dark hair and smiles and starts babbling about how happy she is and how her time at We Work, You Win has been the most rewarding experience of her life.

OH PULL THE OTHER ONE, JESS.

I stand until the end of the speech, but as soon as everyone starts talking amongst themselves, I make a break for the bathroom.

Ah, the familiar, comforting second-floor loos. The well-worn grey linoleum floors. The dingy mirrors and harsh, unflattering lights. I run my hand over a sink. How many collective minutes have I wasted in here, dawdling to avoid going back to my desk? I dive into a stall and lock the door behind me. As soon as I'm alone tears start rolling down my cheeks.

This is the second time in three days I've ended up crying in a toilet.

Why am I upset? What's wrong with me?! Five minutes ago I was dreading getting promoted . . . I don't *want* to be promoted. But . . . watching them promote someone else above me, when I've been here so long, somehow feels equally devastating.

I sit for a few minutes, wondering how long I can stay in here before anyone notices I'm gone. My phone buzzes. For a moment I hope it's a well-timed message from Max, or Angie or Dami, but it's an email from Ted.

> Saw you run off. To cheer you up . . . T x
>
> Climbing a ladder
> Is more than reaching the top
> There's beauty in the climb

I continue sobbing.

Dear Margaret,

I gave you the best years of my life and you shall have no more. I realise you are just a cog in this soul-guzzling corporate machine, but I refuse to let you keep sucking me dry. May Jessica's fresh, tasty youth soon sour in your mouth, as mine has.

I QUIT.

Goodbye, Becky

P.S. I've worked out all the times you forgot to pay me back for your Pret sandwich and it added up to £55.45. Bank transfer will be fine, thanks.

P.P.S. everything else withstanding, your outfits really are quite glorious.

Chapter Six

I spend the rest of the afternoon fantasising about walking into Margaret's office and resigning on the spot. There are several scenarios that play out in my head. In the first, I'm incredibly dignified. I walk through the door, looking her straight in the eye, and she just *knows* from the look on my face what I'm about to say.

'Becky . . .' she starts.

'Stop.' I put a hand out to stop her. 'Don't bother. Nothing you say will change my mind, I'm afraid.'

'But . . . Becky . . . I only promoted Jessica because you're *too* important. I simply wanted to keep you by my side . . . But I see now that it was wrong of me. *Of course* you deserve a promotion. Look, I'll create a senior management role . . .'

'Hush, Margaret,' I say. 'It's too late. You're embarrassing yourself.'

In the next, she gets down on her knees and begs me to stay, but I remain unmoved. In one, she demotes Jessica in front of everyone and makes her recite 'I never held a candle to Becky' while washing up my mug, but it's still not enough to persuade me. Then it takes a different turn. I scream at her, yelling that I'm the only person who knows exactly how she likes her tea. I rip her favourite camel jacket from the coat rack and fling it out the window onto the street below and then I run next door and tell everyone about the time she left her Slack open and I saw her call Mary from HR 'a brainless potato'. In another, I pour milk all over her head.

At five, just before I'm about to leave, Margaret calls me into her office. I'm so deep in daydreaming that actually walking towards her glass walls and immaculate desk feels surreal. *The time is now. Am I really going to do this?* I open her door. The camel coat glints at me from a corner. *It would be so easy to grab it . . .*

'Becky.' Margaret's typing something on her computer and doesn't look up. She's very obviously avoiding eye contact. 'The file you asked for is on my desk.'

Is that it?! Is that all she has to say? I've been here five years and she promoted Jessica above me, and she's really not going to acknowledge it? I open my mouth. *Words . . . forming . . .*

But nothing comes out. I linger for a few seconds, staring at Margaret, but her eyes never leave her screen. I take the file and go.

When I exit the building, Max is waiting for me on the street. At the sight of him it's like a plug is pulled inside me and all the stress starts draining away. So Margaret wants Jessica. Who cares?

We head to Scintilla, as usual. We partly still go there because they always have seats, but mostly for the nostalgia. Hanging out in there always feels like going back in time, so it's worth paying for the outrageously priced cocktails.

'I thought we'd established that hair of the dog doesn't

work for you, Becky.' Max laughs, as I order two dark and stormies. I grin.

No matter what time it is in Scintilla it's always dark and there are always candles lit. We settle in our corner, on a dark green velvet banquette. There's a stain on one of the seats from where I spilt a tray of cocktails all over a table of unsuspecting customers. Max and I still laugh about it.

'So Becks, best birthday gift?' he opens as we sit down. 'Mine, obviously?'

I smile. His BFI membership gift card was definitely my most thoughtful present.

'I don't know.' I move my hands like scales. 'BFI membership . . . Tarot reading with Spellbound Sue . . .'

Max snorts. 'Oh my God! Sara didn't!'

'She did.'

'*Please* don't join the armies of otherwise seemingly intelligent millennial women who believe in horoscopes. I don't think we could remain friends if you started spouting about the romantic compatibility of Sun and Water signs.'

'Sun signs are just star signs. Water, Fire, Earth, Air are the . . . You know what, never mind.' I can see Max giving me a look.

Definitely not mentioning that I downloaded Co-Star earlier. Or that, since Sara gave me the voucher, I've been increasingly curious about a tarot reading. I mean . . . it couldn't make me feel any *worse*, could it?

'Becks.' Max clears his throat. 'I have news.'

I've been playing innocent up until now, but suddenly I know I can't hear him say the words. 'Actually, I know,' I admit hurriedly. 'Sara told me.'

Max looks up from his beer. 'Oh. Fuck.' He leans back against the upholstery, looking me dead in the eye. 'Sara ran into Fran at Point 22. I wanted to tell you first.'

'What? Sara's *not* the first person you tell all your important life events to?' I joke, but it still hurts. The news itself and the fact I heard it last.

'No, Sara's not.' He smiles, keeping on holding eye contact, and I know he means *you are*. Max finds it hard to articulate how much he cares about people, but he always says it nonverbally.

'Congratulations,' I say. I *think* I manage to sound sincere. When I wasn't imagining throwing Margaret's possessions out of a window today, I was practising for this moment. 'That's . . . wow. I never thought I'd see the day.'

'What? What are you saying?!' Max puts his hand across his heart like I've shot him.

'I don't know. Living with a *girl*. It's very grown-up.' I force a smile.

'*We* practically lived together.' Max shrugs and takes a sip of his beer.

I look away. 'I guess . . .' I try to sound as if I'm recalling faded memories, even though I think about those times every day. Sleeping in Max's T-shirt. Borrowing his pants and socks when I ran out and eventually abducting his entire wardrobe. Keeping orange Body Shop face cream in his grimy bathroom cabinet that Max's housemate once ate when he was high. Max buying Coco Shreddies because he knew I liked them even though he's morally opposed to Nestlé.

I briefly wonder if he thinks about those times, too. He does bring them up a lot . . . I quickly squash the rising hope in my chest. *Be quiet, Desperate Becky*. He mentions stuff from the past because we're mates. If he still thought about me like that it would be too awkward to mention. Like how you can sing along to your friends when a dramatic love song is playing, but not look people you actually fancy in the eye.

'Was it okay with work, by the way?' I change the subject, not wanting to dwell on his future flatmate any longer than necessary. 'Did you get in trouble for leaving?'

'Oh, it was fiiiiiine,' Max says, and then *he* changes the subject. He's trying to cover, but obviously it wasn't fine. This is why it doesn't really matter that Max is bad at expressing his feelings; his actions speak louder. My heart warms as I realise he got into shit at work for me and he doesn't want me to feel bad about it.

We spend the rest of the evening plotting my revenge on Margaret, ranking Sara's plays in order of weirdness and debating whether Ted likes a pinkie in the bum. I say not but Max thinks he's got that glint in his eye. Somehow it gets to nine o'clock. I see the time and panic. *Shit*. If I don't get home soon there will be hell to pay at home. Mum goes to bed at ten and she can't sleep unless I'm back.

Max sees me looking at my phone in horror. 'Gotta go?' He smiles.

I grimace. This is why I love hanging out with Max. I never have to feel ashamed of any of the crap things about my life. He just takes me as I am.

We hug goodbye. As I'm holding him I smell his aftershave and it's like a million memories hit me at once. I see myself sitting across from him on his blue bedspread, his Polaroids strewn all over the floor. I feel logical and free, and life is full of possibilities. I'm rationally explaining that we obviously need to break up. Surprise crosses his face. He tries to cover it, but I've blindsided him and he's in pain. I want to scream at Past Becky.

Present Becky pulls away. The same eyes from all those years ago stare back at me.

'Max . . .' I begin. There's so much to say that's on the tip of my tongue.

'Becks . . .' he mimics. Silence hangs in the air as he waits for me to speak.

'See you soon.' I chicken out. What was I planning on saying anyway? *Don't move in with Fran? Abandon your solid two-year (two-year??) relationship and get back together with me instead, a girl who coldly broke your heart a lifetime ago?* It's exactly what I want to say, and something I would never say unless under the influence of sodium thiopental.

We break apart and head in opposite directions. On the way home, I stew about how everything around me is racing forward and I, Becky, have stayed entirely still since my early twenties. In fact, I've actually gone backwards since then. I'm a minus adult.

I try to adjust to my new reality. There was a part of me that genuinely thought Max and I would end up together. A tiny, ridiculous, unjustified part of me, but a persistent part. I feel like an idiot.

In a weak moment, I get out my phone to message Angie and Dami. Since I've been out with Max there are sixty unreads in our thread. I open them up and start scrolling through the pictures of Dami's new wine rack, Angie's new workout routine, and close it again. Angie and Damilola have lives. Real *lives*. What am I supposed to say? Guys, Max is moving in with his girlfriend who he's been with for two years and somehow I'm shocked by this . . . give me sympathy?!

Deep in rumination, I notice that my feet are taking me on a slight detour, and when my brain catches up to my body I realise that I'm not headed to the tube station. A few minutes later, I find myself approaching *Spellbound*.

The doorframe is painted black and the words 'your future awaits' are written across it in gold, swirly letters. There's a chalkboard on the street that says, 'Crystals, energy healing, light work, tarot readings, spiritual guidance'.

Whenever we've walked past this place before, Max has scoffed and bemoaned who on Earth would spend money on something like this, and I've agreed with him. But I find I've stopped outside and am staring through the window. *Spiritual guidance*. That does sound nice, doesn't it? I mean . . . I've got the gift card, right? It would be rude not to. What did Sara say about it . . . ? 'Enlightening and informative.'

Okay, so Sara also once said that playing a dead body in *Holby City* was 'cathartic', but she's got her life together more than I have, so who am I to judge?

A large blonde woman with a nose piercing and a lot of eyeliner sits inside. She's at the counter, sewing beads onto some sort of purple blanket with the intensity of a surgeon at an operating table. She looks up and sees me standing there. Her eyes light up and she scuttles towards me like a spider, and from that moment I'm prey caught in her web. It's like when charity workers come to your house. If you don't say 'sorryIhavenomoneybye' and slam the door in their faces before they start talking, you're trapped. It only takes five minutes before you're donating money you don't have to deaf children and then being eaten alive with guilt when you cancel the direct debit ten days later.

She approaches the door with a glint in her eyes. 'Can I help you, dear?'

'Errr,' I say, dubiously staring up at the witchy markings painted on the window. She probably sacrifices small animals to Satan.

'I'm about to close.' She nods at the sign. 'But you look like a soul in need of some direction, if I ever did see one. I'm Sue.'

Part of me knows this somewhat terrifying woman – Sue – is just trying to make a quick buck before she goes home, and I'm already cutting it fine to get back, but something about her use of the word 'direction' feels like a little warm candle I want to stick my cold hands around. Suddenly I want to put my head on her matronly bosom and have her stroke my hair and tell me everything is going to be okay.

I look at my phone. If it's quick, I might still make it home on time. 'How long will it take?'

'Fifteen minutes,' she assures me.

I look at my phone again. The wafting smell of aromatherapy oils feels irresistibly inviting. 'Yes please,' I answer in a small voice. 'I have a gift voucher.' I pull it out of my bag and hand it to her.

She looks less interested now she realises she won't be making extra money from this appointment, but she stands to one side and gestures with a sweeping hand for me to enter.

'Oof.' She shivers as I walk inside, drawing her shawl around her more tightly. 'Your energy is *supremely* negative, my dear . . .' Her eyes drift above my head. 'And your aura is really rather dingy. Can I interest you in a healing cleanse?'

'Errr, just the reading for today, thanks,' I say.

I follow her to the back of the room, where a table is set up with a deck of cards and a long, tapering candle that she lights with a match. She dims the overhead lamp.

'You should seriously think about it,' she says, sliding a price list across the blue star-covered tablecloth.

'Noted,' I reply.

She picks up a remote control, presses a button and the sound of trickling water fills the room. Tranquil piano notes begin to play over it. Sue closes her eyes. I feel weird staring at her when she has her eyes shut, so I do too. We sit in silence for a moment with the soft, calming music playing. Eventually, she speaks, and I open my eyes with a start.

'Hold these,' she says, pressing a deck of beautifully illustrated gold-embossed cards into my hands.

'What do I do?' I ask.

'Whatever you need to do in order to connect,' she answers. 'The cards need to absorb your energy.'

I hold them in the same way I held my cousin Glen's newborn baby Ethel. Awkwardly and at a distance from my chest.

She shakes her head – probably still thinking about my dingy aura – but doesn't correct me. Eventually, she takes the cards back. She begins to shuffle them, holding them out towards me.

'Stop me when you *feel* it,' she commands. I get a little thrill; I can't believe I'm doing this.

'Stop.' I put a hand up after a beat.

'Did you *feel* it?' She inspects me accusingly.

'No,' I admit.

'We go again.' She continues shuffling. Eventually I 'feel' something – although I can't be sure whether it's magic or the social anxiety of sitting in total silence with a stranger – and ask her to stop again.

This time she lays a card out on the table. On it, two children are playing in a flower-filled garden, in front of a sweet little house, by a row of gold cups. 'Let us begin with your past position. Ah, the Six of Cups.' She grimaces, looking me up and down.

'What?' I ask. 'What does it mean?'

'The element of water,' she barks. 'The suit of emotions. A nostalgic card of childhood harmony, old friends, and memories.'

'Oh. Isn't that . . . good?'

'Look closer. See this child, holding the cup? It's overgrown. She's wearing a fairytale costume that no longer fits, living in the *past*. This card, in this position, suggests to me that you have been stuck. That to move forward, you need to reconcile your past memories with the reality of the present, in order to create the future.'

She's peering at me and I try to avoid eye contact. I feel like I've been put under a microscope. It's so . . . accurate. I wasn't actually expecting this to *work*. I don't know what I was expecting when I stepped in here. But that card does feel eerily resonant. A tingle runs down my spine.

'Tell me, have you been burying your head in the sand? Allowing time to move around you, while you yourself remain frozen? Clinging to things long gone?'

I shiver, and nod. It's like she's encompassed everything I'm feeling in one card. I'm fully afraid now. Maybe Sara was right about this. Maybe there *is* such a thing as witchcraft. She lays a second card on the table and looks aghast. Thunder crashes into a building; smoke rises into the sky and bricks break away, revealing large, gaping holes. People leap from the burning structure and hurtle towards the ground.

That can't be good.

'What? What is it?!'

'*The Tower*,' she whispers. 'Your present position. Major Arcana. The Minor Arcana suits – Cups, Wands, Swords and Pentacles – are nothing to the Major Arcana. These are the most impactful life lessons that resonate throughout your entire consciousness, transforming your whole being and marking the soul's journey to enlightenment.'

When I look confused, she adds, 'The big shit.'

'Right,' I say. 'Well, what does The Tower mean?'

'It means, if you've been shutting yourself away in an ivory tower, you're coming back down to Earth with a *bump*.' I swear she sounds gleeful. 'The Tower is a necessary fall from grace, the burning to the ground of what we thought we knew, the destruction of everything we've built.'

'Right, so, nothing too intense then,' I joke feebly, trying to lighten the mood. I feel like I've been punched in the gut.

'I would guess, from this card, that currently *everything* is coming crashing down around you. Probably as a direct result of remaining here, for too long.' She points at the Six of Cups.

I gulp, as fear strikes into my heart. Everything *is* coming crashing down around me. This is genuinely spooky.

'Does this sound familiar?' she asks.

I nod.

'It's not so bad,' she adds in a gentler tone. Probably remembering the potential one-star Google review coming her way. 'In order that our horizons can expand, it is sometimes necessary, first, to tear down the walls holding us in. This card tells us that in order to rebuild, the total obliteration of our current circumstances is necessary. Sometimes, this includes illusory prisons of our own making. But destruction is the first step on the path to reconstruction.'

'Uh huh,' I say, not in the least bit comforted. I can't stop staring at the haunting expressions of the people on the card, as they jump from the burning building.

She must sense this, because she quickly moves on to the next card. 'And your future,' she says brightly, laying down a card with a picture of a skull that says 'DEATH' on it in big, black letters.

'Death?!' I shriek, jumping up from the table. '*Death?!*'

'Please, sit down . . .'

'Are you telling me I'm going to *die?!*' I wail.

'Please, do remain calm . . .'

'*Calm?!*' I yell, plagued with images of myself lying in a casket. Of my own tombstone. *Here Lies Becky: She Always Made Curfew*. 'I can't *die* . . . I haven't *lived*!' I shout dramatically. 'I still live at my mother's house. I've never had a job I enjoy. I don't have a meaningful romantic relationship. My mates are leaving me behind. I'm forever stuck in the role of "chaotic bi friend" in the movie of my own life.'

Sue is frustratingly silent. She listens to my rant pensively. I so badly want her to tell me I'm not going to die, but she doesn't.

'Tell me,' she says slowly. 'If you knew you were going to die, what would you do differently?'

'Are you saying I *am* going to die?!' I whisper quietly, sitting back down in the chair opposite her.

Once again, she says nothing. Oh my God.

Oh my God.

'If you were dying, what would you do?' she asks again.

'I would . . . I would do *something*. Anything,' I answer.

She nods. 'Then . . . yes. I'm afraid so.'

Dear Dad,

I'm contacting you to tell you not to contact me.

Sorry that you missed out on the TRUE SPLENDOUR that is knowing me but, I just wanted you to know, I will no longer be here waiting for you to reach out like some sort of sad, abandoned lemon.

I mean this in deadly seriousness: please **never** try to get in touch with me (even on your **deathbed**/if you happen to pass me on the street **do not say hello**), because I'm drawing a line.

The line is drawn.

From,
A Stranger
(Becky)

Chapter Seven

That hag is so lucky she was paid *before* the reading. As if she got £25 to tell me I'm going to *die*. I was swept up in the experience but, hurrying back towards the tube, my sanity has returned. *If she's going to con me*, I tell myself, *she could at least tell me what I want to hear.*

I get a text from Mum:

It's quarter to ten . . .

Sorry, will be a bit late tonight, coming!

She doesn't reply. I start legging it home as fast as I can.

'It's not real,' I whisper to myself. 'It's not *real*.'

I'm crossing the road towards Tottenham Court Road station, when I hear screeching brakes and a loud horn. A car comes to an abrupt halt to my right.

I stand, dumbfounded. The driver gestures 'what the fuck?' at me.

He rolls down the window and yells, 'Lady! Get out of the road!'

I collect myself and run to the other side of the street. I could have sworn I *looked*. The pedestrian light was green, wasn't it? How did the car appear so quickly?!

I'm filled with sheer horror, but shake it off immediately. I wasn't paying attention, that's all. I was too focused on pissing off Mum. Even in light of the news that I'm about to *die*, I still fear my mother's wrath for breaking curfew more than potentially getting hit by a car.

There must have been delays, because it's busy on the platform. Five minutes until the next train, so it's touch and go whether I'll squeeze onto it. I'm debating whether to let Mum know, when the man next to me turns around too forcefully, knocking me flying with his huge backpack. I stumble towards the edge of the platform and teeter. There's a moment where everyone on the platform does a collective intake of breath, before I trip and fall onto the tracks.

There's gasping. Someone screams.

'Oh my God!' a man calls. 'Someone help that girl!'

I'm on the floor. My hand is grazed from where I stuck it out to break my fall and it throbs. A rat scuttles off in surprise as I sit up and a tangle of arms extend towards me from above. I stand up, noting how I'm basically unscathed but how filthy my jeans are, and then think this probably isn't the time to worry about my clothes. My mind is blank; I've gone completely outer-body. Somehow, I manage to reach for an arm and watch myself get pulled back onto the platform, with four minutes still to spare before the next train.

'Are you okay?' people around me keep asking.

'Oh, yes, fine, thank you,' I repeat multiple times, in a daze. But I'm not fine. I'm literally in *Final Destination*.

Sue was right.

I stand for four minutes, rubbing down my disgusting trousers. A woman passes me a wet wipe and I clean up my hands. The only benefit to my near-death experience is that, when the next train arrives, everyone stands aside to let me on.

One of the people on the platform explains what happened to me to the person in the priority seat, so I'm able to sit down. My mind continues to be vacant the entire ride home. I must be in shock. All I can think about is that I *genuinely* could have died. Twice.

The Death card is really coming for me. I'm toast.

I return at twenty past ten, and step inside like a prisoner returning from their break in the yard.

Mum doesn't say anything when the front door shuts behind me, but I sense that she's in the kitchen. I shuffle down the hall and enter cautiously. She's standing by the fridge and peering inside it.

'Hi, Mum.' I wait for her to speak but she still doesn't say anything. 'You okay?' I ask.

'Have you eaten all the yoghurt?' Her head is blocked by the fridge door.

'Um, yeah, it was going off,' I defend.

'Oh,' she replies after a beat. She shuts the fridge and moves towards the dining table, where she sits down. Her hair barely moves as she walks and her spotless beige trousers and cream jumper don't wrinkle as she sits down. How does she do that?

Normally, my heart would beat faster. My stomach would clench. Yoghurty guilt would swirl in my belly and I would try to rationalise it away. The yoghurt was going off. She wouldn't have eaten it. I haven't done anything wrong. It's only some week-old dairy product.

Mum has this way of making you feel *awful* about the smallest of crimes when she's angry about something else. She will guilt me about yoghurt, or the fact I'm twenty minutes past curfew, instead of addressing what she's actually angry about, i.e. the fact I abandoned the party that she organised. Usually I would work hard to try to thaw her; talk to her about her day, make jokes, offer to buy her a replacement yoghurt, until she forgave me. But tonight I simply cannot muster the energy. I'm going to *die*, and she's seriously worrying about a yoghurt?

What if the yoghurt is the thing that gets me? Can you be killed by mouldy yoghurt?

'Mum, I'm exhausted.' My voice cracks. 'Can we talk in the morning?'

'If you like.' She places her hands one on top of the other, on her legs. 'What happened to your jeans?' She eyes the dirty patches on my knees.

'I fell,' I answer, not wanting to talk about it. 'Night.' I retreat.

I make it to my room and collapse on my bed. I know our argument isn't over, but my head is too full of other things right now. Like my imminent death.

I roll over onto my back and stare at the ceiling. The same ceiling I've been gazing at my entire life, minus the time I spent at university. I know every little groove and mark. The years pass but it remains unchanged, just like me. My poster of David Bowie in *Labyrinth* smiles down at me.

Suddenly it feels like the walls are closing in. My familiar bedroom doesn't feel cosy, but stifling. David's smile feels menacing. In that moment I'd rather be anywhere, *anywhere*, but here. I sit up.

Look at me. What am I doing?! Nothing, that's what. But nothing is exactly what got me here. And here is nowhere.

And now I'm going to DIE.

It's funny, but for years, I've *known* I'm not happy. I know this isn't how I wanted my life to be. I want to be successful, in requited love, independent. But I stopped trying to change things.

Take Max. I guess I held onto some hazy belief that somehow we'd find our way back together. Because ending up with the person you love is inevitable, right? But how is that going to happen if I don't tell him? And my job. I always thought I'd find another one day, but I stopped applying for anything years ago.

I think through all the times, even just today, I had opportunities to take action. Okay, so I'm never going to throw milk over Margaret, but why didn't I just resign? Why don't I ask Angie and Dami to talk about something other than their domestic bliss? Why don't I tell my mum that I'm a grown woman who's ALLOWED to drink to excess until I vomit in a toilet and come home as late as I like? Why didn't I grab Max and tell him I would put my OWN pinkie in Ted's bum if it meant we could get back together?!

Why haven't I done any of these things, *ever*?

With sudden, painful clarity I realise that I, Becky Louise Alderton, am a coward. Life is hard so I started lying to people's faces. Hiding my feelings. Avoiding conflict. Going along with things. Taking the 'easy' route. But nothing about where I've ended up is easy.

What if this really is it? The end? If I had died tonight, if those people hadn't hauled me back onto the platform, this would literally be the sum total of my life. And who knows how long they've bought me? Tomorrow I might not be so lucky.

For the first time in years I feel the urge to do something. *Anything*. And fuck the consequences. I pick up a pen from my bedside table and scrabble around for some paper. I can't find anything except my childhood stationery set with dancing llamas on it, but it will have to do.

For the next five hours I write, and write, and write to the people I love. At first the letters start off polite. I write a professional letter of resignation to Margaret, a reserved acknowledgement to Angie and Damilola that I'm sad we've drifted, an awkward suggestion to Mum that I might be too old for a curfew, a lukewarm admission of some 'residual fondness' to Max . . . Then I read back through them and tear them up. Fuck it. If I'm not going to be alive, what will it matter anyway? I'll be too dead to feel any social anxiety. It takes several drafts to get it to the point where I'm not censoring myself, where I'm really letting it all out.

When all of my shameful secret feelings are finally sitting exposed in front of me on the page, I sit back and think about my ticking clock. How long do I have left? A month, a week, a day? And fuck it, am I really going to die here in the UK? If I'm going down, surely I want to do it on a beach, staring at the sunset?!

I grab my laptop and start googling exotic locations. Staring at pictures of places I've only ever dreamed of going. Sri Lanka . . . The Maldives . . . Thailand . . . California . . . Bali . . . I never go on holiday anymore because it's a waste of money when you're trying to save, which is true, but then I ended up spending the money on stupid, smaller things, trying to make myself less miserable anyway. The cost of living is so ridiculous that unless I literally sat inside the entire time, I would never save enough to get my own place. Maybe not even then. I should have just gone on holiday once in a while and bought fewer lattes.

I look outside my window at the rainy London skyline, lit up by people who don't have to be home by 10 p.m. It's been my view for so long that at some point I stopped thinking about the rest of the world. It's taken the prospect of my looming death to remember it's actually out there. How long has it been since I've left the country? Do I even know where my passport is?

I stumble across a website with all sorts of placements across the world, where you only have to cover the cost of your flight, and a host provides food and accommodation in exchange for work. There's a placement at a sea turtle conservation centre in Bali. I scroll through the activities . . . *Help save the turtles while enjoying the turquoise seas and sandy beaches of this paradise island . . . Rewarding volunteer work by day, beach sports and bonfires by night . . .* Basically, it's for people who want to piss around in the sun, in a way that makes them feel sort of good about themselves because they fed a baby turtle.

Saving The Seas . . . There are endless pictures of pools, beaches, bonfires, sand, sea . . . Is this *legit?* Like, this is an actual possibility of a place to be? The whole time I'm here in London, breathing in polluted air, drinking cocktails that cost my hourly wage, eating greasy takeaways in bed, *this* remote, idyllic place is existing at the same time?

I could do that, right? I mean, I've always liked animals . . . I remember that one time Elijah Fallon ran at a group of pigeons in Year Six and I told him to leave them alone. I occasionally stop to move a snail to the side of the pavement. One time, I fed a tired bee some sugar water.

There's a placement creating social media content for an eco-lodge in Thailand, which basically means taking decent photos and filming short videos. One family needs help on a small farm in Sweden. A town in Iceland needs help fishing. A couple in Denmark need assistance running their bakery. There are a million placements, all over the world, that want English speakers to give language lessons to children.

I look through the details of all these placements, but there are no qualifications needed for most of them. I'm just as qualified as the next person. In fact, they seem to have very few requirements at all.

If I'm going to die . . . where would I most like to die? Bali seems like as good a place as any. And there are loads of placements there. Given that the Death card really isn't fucking about, maybe I should just book my flights, write to all of them, and surely someone will get back to me by the time I land?

I look at flights to Denpasar Airport and put one for the day after tomorrow in my basket, so that I have a day to pack. Then I look in my savings. A one-way trip is nearly a thousand pounds and I have just over £2,000.

Two thousand pounds?! I cringe. That's about a month's take-home salary. How, after a year at home, have I saved *one single month's salary*? But then, I think of everything I did even this weekend. I try to keep up with Angie and Dami's lifestyles, even though I make less than them, because I'm embarrassed to ask them to do something cheaper. I go on dates because I keep holding out hope I will meet someone and always pay half. I get wasted with Max at Scintilla because I'm too attached to the memory of us there to go somewhere more affordable.

Well, it's enough: £1k on flights and £1k to tide me over until one of these placements takes pity on me. I click 'buy' before I can change my mind and complete the transaction.

Oh my God. I'm going to Bali. By myself. The day after tomorrow.

That is, if I even make it. What if it's the plane crash that gets me?

I lie awake, thinking about how I might go. Lightning strike? Finally smote down by God? Too narcissistic. I can be a bit of a twat but I'm sure there are people who are much worse than me that God needs to focus on smiting. Will I get hit by a car? What if I'm *very careful* to cross the road from now on? But then if I keep avoiding it, will something else get me that's even more painful? I'd much rather get hit by a car than avoid it and then end up being boiled or something. My list of scenarios gets more and more ridiculous as the night goes on. Impaled by a swordfish? Poisoned by the pungent fumes of Ted's forgotten lunches at the back of the fridge?

What if I don't even make it through the night?! What if I'm gone by morning? What if I never go anywhere and never do anything, and no one ever knows how I really feel?

I spring out of bed and move over to my desk, grabbing the letters . . . Everything I've written feels impossibly vulnerable. I cast my eyes over my mortifying admissions.

I cannot believe I wrote these. I cannot believe everything hidden inside me now *exists in the physical realm*. In that moment I feel it needs to get back to where it came from, where no one can see it and therefore it's basically not real.

And yet.

I can still see that little skull looking back at me, staring straight into the void of my empty life. It probably thought, what's she got to lose, anyway?

How, even in the face of my imminent demise, am I still debating sending these? What hope is there for me if I can't even make a deathbed confession?

Before I can change my mind, I grab the letters, address them and stamp them. I throw a cardigan over my pyjamas and tiptoe down the hallway, careful not to wake Mum. I run down the road to the nearest postbox, where I promptly shove them inside.

Chapter Eight

When I finally fall asleep, I spend a night tossing and turning, having dreams about being pickled to death. The next morning I wake up with my heart hammering in my chest, like when you remember you drank an entire bottle of tequila the night before and accidentally agreed to do karaoke and someone filmed it. I feel exposed and panicked. I cleared out half my bank account booking one-way flights to a country I've never been, where I don't speak the language, where I know no one. I wrote deranged deathbed confessions to all my friends and family.

I remind myself that I'll be dead soon, so it's all okay, as I heave my massive suitcase out from the attic. This morning, I pretended I was going in to work so Mum wouldn't get suspicious, then I snuck back into the house to pack. I spend all morning washing clothes, sorting out admin and deciding what to take. In between packing a tie-dye bikini and a purse in the shape of a turtle, my phone buzzes.

> Hey babe, I'm doing a play in a couple of weeks. It's about our bond with dogs and how they fulfil a deep, innate need that other humans can't because of our superior but ultimately connection-hampering intelligence. There's singing! Want a ticket? Sara x

I reply:

I would have loved to but I'll probably be dead. x

Sara types back immediately.

WHAT?! What are you talking about?

Spellbound Sue said in my reading

That's . . . not a thing!!!

It definitely is a thing. I got the Death card.

No babe! The Death card isn't literal, I promise. I think you might have misinterpreted what Sue was saying?

I stop cold, clutching the turtle purse tightly. No. No. Sue *definitely* said I was going to die. There was no ambiguity. No room for interpretation. But a question starts flickering in my mind . . . What if I *don't* die now? What would I do then? I type:

SHE DEFINITELY SAID IT. x

I start going back over the conversation. I try to replay it but the memories are already a little hazy. Sue said I was going to die when the card came up . . . Or did she? No. I think Sue didn't actually say anything when the card came up. I assumed the Death card meant Death because, well, obviously?! And then I asked Sue if I was going to die and she . . . she asked me what I would do differently if I thought I was going to die and . . . then she said . . . *Well, then . . . yes. I'm afraid so.*

My whole body goes cold as I realise that, thinking back, it's not quite as clear cut as I remember it seeming initially. It was mostly my assumption and then Sue not correcting me. Oh my God. Oh my God. I send Sara a text relaying the whole interaction.

> Lol . . . Yeah, that sounds like classic Sue. She likes to have a little fun with people. Babe, you're not dying. x

This cannot be. This is categorically not an option now. I *have* to die. I've been honest about my feelings! Everyone knows all self-respecting British people would much rather die an agonising death than look people in the eye after that!

Panic starts rising. My chest tightens. I have to know. I google the number for Spellbound and dial in a frantic haze.

'Spellbound, how is your spirit in need today?' I recognise Sue's voice immediately.

'Sue,' I rasp. 'Hi. I was there last night for a reading. The one you said was going to die? I just need to know . . . This is definite, in your opinion, yeah? I mean, how long do you think I have left?'

'Well.' There's a silence. She clears her throat. 'Look, dear, we're all going to die someday, aren't we?'

My heart sinks. My mouth goes dry and a bead of sweat snakes down my back.

'You said it like . . . like . . . I was going to die *soon*,' I protest.

'I didn't, actually,' Sue corrects. '*You* said it.'

'I . . . I . . .'

'Look, dear, something in your life clearly needs to change. I thought letting you believe it might give you a nudge in the right direction. But no harm, no foul, okay?'

No harm, no foul?!

'I . . . I've blown up everything,' I whisper.

'It's the next day,' she breezes. 'How much damage can you have done?'

I hang up the phone.

How much damage can you have done?

I scream 'FUUUUUCK!' very, very loudly.

I can't believe this. Did I really destroy my entire life on the word of a woman who has a tattoo of a nude woman pole-dancing with a broomstick on her left bicep?!

I google 'does the Death card definitely mean death?' To which Google replies:

> *The Death card rarely ever – as is commonly misinterpreted – means physical death. Rather it implies an impactful ending of sorts; the death of a relationship, a friendship, an identity, an era in order that new life can take root.*

I scream 'FUUUUUCK!' again.

WHAT HAVE I DONE?

Six stamps. Six envelopes. Six letters. Words are bizarre things, aren't they? Individually meaningless. But depending on how you put them together, possibly life-changing, earth-shattering, the window into another human being.

That's what I've done. I've given six people – the most important six people in my life – a look at my naked brain. And I'm going to LIVE?

Of course I'm not going to die. That's ridiculous. Laughable. I can't believe a middle-aged woman who thinks she's a witch giving me a card with a giant skull on it had me flying out to the ocean to die like a seagull.

Okay. Plan. Plan. *Plan*. I need a plan. Thank GOD my temporary insanity from last night has passed. I just need to get those letters back, flush them down the loo, rebury all my emotions and desires like a normal person and move on with my life.

I run outside to the postbox. It's possible the letters haven't been collected yet. I try to stuff my arm through the gap but my DAMNED WRIST IS TOO FAT. I go back inside for a screwdriver, a hair pin and various other items to shove into the little keyhole. Nothing works. It turns out picking a lock is NOT as easy as TV shows would make you think.

In desperation I kick it, yelp from the pain and sit back down on the floor, weeping.

I try to think straight. Think of a new plan. Okay, it's okay, all is not lost. It's 2 p.m. Collection time is between 9 a.m. and 5 p.m. They might not have gone yet. I just need to be here when the postal worker turns up and beg them to let me reclaim my letters.

That's three whole hours in which this could all still be saved.

Three o'clock comes. Still nothing. It's fine. It's fine.

Four o'clock comes and goes.

And four thirty. There is a slim, *slim* possibility the postal worker didn't come during the morning. That these letters could still be stopped within the next half an hour.

I sit. I wait. Praying to anything out there that will hear me.

Several people pass me, sitting on the floor by the postbox, tending my bruised knee, and look at me like I might leap up and bite them. Fifteen minutes go by. Then twenty.

Did I really send a letter to Angie telling her that her boyfriend makes me want to wax off my own eyebrows? Did I really tell Damilola I don't like the workaholic person she's become? Did I really tell Max, who has just agreed to move in with his girlfriend, that I love him? Did I make myself homeless and quit my job? Did I just contact my father for the first time in *twenty years*? My head is spinning. If the Death card never really had it in for me – which, obviously, it didn't – I'm now going to have to throw myself in front of a bus anyway.

At five to five I've basically lost all hope. It's getting dark. I'm shivering. I don't even know if it's from cold or nerves anymore.

Five comes. It's over.

Strangely, I feel more relief than anything else. It's out of my hands now. My fate has been decided. There is literally nothing else to do but pack and bolt. I might not be dying but I can still flee the country.

I spend the rest of the evening shoving things into a suitcase and rationalising my decision. This is a good thing. *A good thing*. I wanted change and, well . . . now I have it.

So I quit my job. I don't *like* my job. I've been wanting to leave since the moment I started. Right? And so Max knows I would eat my own hand to be with him . . . I mean, he had to find out at some point . . . Didn't he?

And so I'm moving out of Mum's a bit suddenly. I mean, it had to happen some day. I wasn't going to live here forever. It's better to rip off the Band Aid. And it's probably better that Damilola knows how much work has taken over her personality. Maybe she'll find herself again as a result of my words. And Angie . . . okay, so it's a blunt delivery, but isn't it better that she knows how I really feel about Jacob? I mean, she's been loving him blindly and I have been helping her pull the wool over her eyes.

People might be shocked, mad, upset . . . at first. But we'll have had enough distance between us that it won't be as awkward when I come home. At least six months' distance. Eight thousand *miles* worth of distance. Everything will have improved by the time I get back. I will finally have changed things for the better. Ultimately, I feel confident this is all for the best.

Eventually I go to bed, but I don't sleep a wink. All I can do is picture the letters being sorted by Royal Mail, landing on door mats and being torn open by all my loved ones. When morning comes I'm still lying wide awake, having tossed and turned and sweated all night.

When it's time to get up and leave, Mum's already gone out to meet her morning walking group before she settles in for an afternoon of online chess, smashing opponents in every corner of the globe. I feel a flicker of guilt for not saying goodbye to her face. But I tell myself a letter is *fine*. Totally borderline socially acceptable. If someone sent a text or even an email to break up with your mate you'd be like 'what a dick'. But no one can moan too much about receiving bad news via a letter, can they? It's on *paper*. Someone wrote it with their hand, like Shakespeare or Kate Middleton, so it must be legit.

When my Uber arrives outside, I wheel my cases onto the street and turn back to my house. My house that I've spent most of my twenty-nine years on the planet in. It looks exactly the same but it already feels different; alien and stern, like it senses I'm no longer living in it.

The Uber driver beeps his horn and I take the hint. We load up the car. When we set off, I can't bring myself to look back.

Half an hour later, my phone buzzes. My heart leaps, and I wonder irrationally if it's Angie, Dami or Max having received their letter, even though I know the post won't have been yet. It takes me a second to process Vera's name on my screen.

Hey. Do you feel like doing something this week? We can do it your way this time i.e. inebriated and under cover of darkness. Vx

Shit. I'd completely forgotten about her.

I'm sorry, I can't. Funny story . . . I'm actually leaving the country today! It was a totally last minute thing but I'm not sure how long I'll be gone for. x

It seems a bit short and crap, but really, what else is there to say? She comes back immediately.

> Oh no – gutted I won't get to see you again, but that's so exciting! Well, safe travels and good luck Becky. Have a great trip xx

I'm a bit blindsided by her reply. She's admitting her feelings to a total stranger without it seeming a) embarrassing b) aggressive c) creepy. How does one become like Vera? Can I take lessons? I reply saying thanks and that I really did have a good time on our date. Whether or not I was actually interested in pursuing a relationship with her is beside the point.

I spend the rest of the journey checking the time, wondering if the post has arrived and panicking about whether the letters have been opened yet. I picture them sitting in my unsuspecting friends' corridors. I imagine Fran picking Max's up and handing it to him, having no idea what she's passing on. I see Angie's pinched, disapproving face as she scans the words. AGHHHHHH.

Thank God I don't have to see any of these people for *at least* half a year. Maybe not even then. I'm going to have to stay on the other side of the world *forever*. I can LITERALLY never show my face in the UK again.

What on *Earth* was I thinking?

A few hours later, when I'm through security and waiting at the gate, my phone buzzes again. This time it's a call from Mum.

Oh God. Has she read my letter already? Is she racing after me right now, hunting me down with a crazed look in her eye, my total lack of responsibility having finally pushed her over the edge?!

I don't answer. It's all good, it's all good. Probably just calling to ask me if I want the shell-shaped pasta or penne from Sainsbury's.

Oh God. She's calling again. Bloody hell. I know I'm not going to be able to dodge her calls forever, but . . . maybe just at least until I'm safely across the Indian Ocean.

I let it ring off, when my phone rings *again*. This time it's Gavin. Huh. That's weird. Gavin never calls me . . .

'Hello?' I answer cautiously.

'Were you avoiding my call?' It's Mum. The sound of her voice makes something inside my stomach shrivel and I start sweating. I am so busted.

'No, no,' I say. 'I just, er, I couldn't find my phone in the bottom of my bag, and then . . .'

'Becky,' Mum says. I might be imagining it, but I think I hear her voice wavering? 'I'm . . .' She sniffs.

Oh my God. Definitely not imagining it. She's upset. She's read the letter and she's upset. This is even worse than I thought. I can't remember the last time I heard my mother *cry*. What if she tries to stick her head in the oven, like that one time she threatened to do after I finished her stir-fry sauce?

'Mum, I . . . I'm sorry, I . . .'

She cuts me off. 'Becky. I'm in hospital.'

My entire body freezes.

'You're *what*?'

'I'm in the hospital.'

My blood is running cold. Icy trepidation shoots through my limbs. 'What do you mean?! Why? What happened?'

'I . . .' She clears her throat. Her voice sounds small. 'I took a tumble down the stairs.'

'Oh my God! Mum! Are you okay?!'

'Well, I'm alive,' she says.

'How bad was it? Do you need me to come?'

'Oh, well, the doctors don't know yet. Gavin's here. I'm sure you're very busy.' She sniffs again.

'Uhhhh . . .' I stare gormlessly out the window as an overhead voice announces that my flight is boarding. I'm barely computing what she's saying. My brain has gone blank and, the opposite of just five minutes ago, I feel numb. My brain is deciding what to do, but my heart knows already. There is no way I can get on a flight now. There is no way I can't go to the hospital.

'Becky? Are you still there?'

'Of course I'm coming, Mum,' I say eventually. 'I'll be there in a couple of hours.'

'I'll send you the details.' She hangs up.

I head over to a member of staff to explain the situation and ask how the hell I can retrieve my bags from the plane. As she goes to talk to her manager, I stare out the window and half-watch a plane take off in the distance.

Chapter Nine

The hospital feels small. I have a vivid memory of coming here once before, as a child, when Mum had a minor operation to have her appendix removed, and my mind being blown by the size of the place.

Now, as I wait in the reception area for someone to tell me where to go, I'm struggling to believe that this is the same place. Is it really the same? As I look around the tiny plastic chairs, the low ceilings, the crowded car park, it feels like my world has shrunk.

I guess it doesn't help that an hour ago I was off to explore new horizons and now I'm approximately two miles from where I grew up. But I don't have time to think about that.

'Sandra Alderton,' I repeat to the nurse. I've been sent to three different stations and for some reason Mum and Gavin aren't picking up their phones. I'm trying not to let panic take over, but my mind is filling with all sorts of terrible reasons for their silence. Just how bad is she? What if she's got broken ribs, a collapsed lung, internal bleeding?

An even worse thought keeps nagging . . . What if this was because of me? What if she was so shocked from reading my letter that she fell? *What if this is all my fault?* Because I got carried away by a tarot reading?!

I try to soothe myself. Mum probably hasn't even read it yet and she's probably fine. Of course she's fine.

'Down the hall, room B,' the nurse replies.

'Thank you.' I pause. The nurse senses me hovering over him and looks up from his charts once more. 'I don't suppose you have anywhere I can leave these?' I point at my two huge suitcases. For some reason I'm whispering.

'You can take them in with you,' he says.

'I, errr. I can't do that. It's a long story.'

The nurse raises an eyebrow as if to say, you'd better explain it then, because I don't have time to look after your suitcases without a very good reason.

'See, Dan . . .' I glance at his name tag. 'I was supposed to be leaving the country,' I hiss. 'And, er, I hadn't told my mum and if she sees them . . .'

Dan raises his eyebrow even higher. For a moment I think he's not going to come through, but eventually he sighs and gestures for me to pass them behind the counter. I thank him profusely and hurry off to find Mum's room.

When I see her lying in the bed, I'm immediately struck again by that feeling of being the wrong size. I'm like a giant standing in a dollhouse. Mum looks so small. She's lying in bed, staring at the ceiling. She doesn't look at me when I come in.

'Mum?' I choke. I'm going to cry.

'Hello, Becky.' Her voice is feeble. She keeps staring upwards.

I hurry over to her. She looks so frail. Her expression is drawn and her skin looks deathly pale. Oh my God. I tried to hold it together on the way here but it all starts crumbling. Was this because of me?

I spot her mobile on her bedside table.

'Oh.' I point at it. 'I've been calling you?'

Was she ignoring me because she read the letter? Would she really have been so petty to ignore my calls at a time like this, even if she had read it?

'Sorry,' she whispers to the ceiling. 'I've been preoccupied.'

I relax a little. Of course she wasn't ignoring my calls . . . She called *me*.

'So what happened?!' I pull up a chair by the side of her bed. 'Where's Gavin?'

'He went home to get some of my things. I fell down the stairs,' she says softly.

'Oh no! Mum!' For all that she annoys me, I feel intensely protective. My poor, poor mum. 'How?!'

'I was distracted. I'm getting old and fragile.' She moves to sit up and winces. I lean over and stop her pillow from sliding out from under her.

Guilt clenches my stomach. 'Distracted by . . . something in particular?' I feign innocence.

She makes an indeterminate sound and I relax some more. If it *had* been my letter there's no way she wouldn't have mentioned it yet. I mean, she calls me when I'm at work if she so much as suspects I touched her fancy shower gel. She's not exactly one to hold back.

'Do you know what's wrong?' I ask.

'They aren't sure yet about the extent of the injuries,' she rasps. 'We're waiting for test results.'

Extent of the injuries. That doesn't sound good. Oh my God. Oh my God oh my God oh my God.

We sit in silence but my brain is buzzing. I never really

understood the term 'frantic with worry' before now. Suddenly I wonder how I'm going to get my suitcases home without Mum seeing them. With resignation, I accept that I'm going to have to call for back-up. I open up my contacts, take a deep breath and pray that Damilola hasn't opened her letter yet.

'Mum, I need to make a call,' I say.

'Who?' she asks.

I briefly wonder if people who don't still cohabit with their parents have to answer so many questions about their lives. *I'm popping out to the shop.* What for? *I'm going out this evening.* Where to? *I'll be back later.* What time? *I need the toilet.* Number one or two?

Does the woman need to know *everything*? But if I'm deliberately cagey she'll accuse me of being 'childish' and anyway, now doesn't seem like the time to argue with her.

'Work,' I answer, and she drops it. Of course, she doesn't know I've quit my job yet.

Oh my God. I'm going to have to tell her I quit my job.

I step outside and phone Dami. To her credit, she doesn't say much when I explain the situation to her. She's mostly very quiet, with the odd 'okay?' and 'wow, okay' thrown in.

'So, you need me to . . . pick up your suitcases?'

'Yes.'

'And let myself into your house?'

'Er . . . yes.'

'And put them in your room?'

'I know it sounds mental . . .'

If it were Angie she'd say 'mental doesn't begin to cover it, Becky', but Dami says, 'Wow, okay.'

'I promise I'll explain everything better later,' I plead.

'Okay?' she says. 'Okay. We're coming.'

'We?' I repeat. Oh God. *Please say Phil isn't coming.*

'Angie's here. She wasn't in the gym today. She came to work from mine and brainstorm bits for the new studio.'

No. Nonononono. Not *Angie*. There's a reason why I called Dami! Apart from the fact she works from home on Wednesdays, she Lets. Things. Go. Angie does not. I will never hear the end of this.

'I . . .' I start, but Dami's already hung up. Still, silver linings. If they're both on their way here it means that neither of them have read their letters yet.

Twenty minutes later I grab my suitcases from an eye-rolling Dan and hover outside in the car park. Eventually Dami pulls up in Phil's car. Well, I say Phil's car. It's technically hers too, but Phil chose it, so it's basically Phil's car. It's a giant, fuck-off Range Rover, which Dami never would have considered buying before she met him.

Angie is in the passenger seat, looking like she's chewing on something sour. Dami just looks worried.

'What's going on, Becky?' Dami gets out and moves towards me, putting her hand on my arm. Angie lingers behind her, leaning against the car.

'I'm really sorry, can I explain later? It's just . . .' I gesture at the suitcases, then back at the hospital.

Dami relents and starts wheeling them towards the boot. I stand like a lemon, trying not to make eye contact with Angie, but I can feel her staring at me. She's been silent up until now but I sense I only have moments.

'So, you were going where?' she asks.

'I . . . Bali.' God. It does sound absolutely ridiculous.

'Why, exactly?' Angie says.

'I was going to find work when I got there,' I say.

'Right.' Angie folds her arms.

'I only just decided . . . It wasn't a planned thing. I . . . I had an existential crisis over a tarot reading,' I add. Christ. I am never getting rid of the 'chaotic bi friend' label now.

Dami finishes lifting my case into the car and closes the boot. They both stare at me.

'It . . . told me I was going to *die*,' I add, aware I am sounding more and more unhinged by the moment. Neither of them says anything. 'Obviously, I realised twenty-four hours later I'm probably *not* going to die. At least not now, anyway. But it was pretty scary.'

'Honestly, I'm not sure what to say to that,' Angie comments eventually. 'When were you planning on telling your mum you were leaving the country?' What she really means is, when were you planning on telling us?

'I wrote her a letter,' I mumble.

'A letter?' Dami repeats.

'Isn't that like dumping someone by text?' says Angie.

'No,' I defy, my muscles tensing. 'Categorically not.'

Angie raises one eyebrow.

'I used a fountain pen!' I squeak.

'All right, whatever you say.' Angie smirks. Dami shuts the boot and gives me a pitying smile.

'Look . . . I know I shouldn't have just upped and left but . . . Self-care,' I conclude.

'Oh, Becky.' Dami moves over to me and pulls me into a hug.

Thank the Gods of the twenty-first century for how much

you can get away with if you use the term 'self-care'. 'Sorry I didn't reply to your text. Self-care.' 'Sorry I chose to stay in with my cat rather than come to your child's christening. Self-care.' 'Whoops, I spent all my salary on retinol creams and Domino's two-for-one Tuesdays instead of replacing the hoover. Self-care.'

It's like accusing someone of 'gaslighting' you in an argument. You win, no questions asked, God knows what it actually means.

'Are you okay?' Dami mumbles into my shoulder as she holds me.

'Mmhmm,' I say, basking in Dami's sympathy. Then I remember that soon she's going to be opening her own letter. This might be the last time she's *ever* nice to me. I grip her tightly.

Angie is still eyeing me quizzically from a distance. 'Text us how your mum is, yeah?' she says as Dami pulls out of the hug.

'I will,' I reply.

As I watch them drive away, I think about how that might be the last semi-normal conversation I'm going to have with either of them. I stand outside the hospital for a bit, watching other cars pull in and out of the spot Dami's car was in only moments ago, before heading back inside.

When I get back, the doctor is just leaving. She smiles at me as she heads out and down the corridor. I sprint into Mum's room.

'What did she say?!' I grill her. My heart starts pumping. Then I see the black boot with strips of Velcro fastened on Mum's right leg and the crutches lying by the bed.

'I might not be able to walk for *four weeks*,' she answers breathily, her hand fluttering to her forehead. 'Maybe longer, because of my *age*.'

I can't help but think Mum bites my head off if I ever allude to the fact she's in her sixties, but leans into it when it suits her. Like whenever she wants something down from the attic, suddenly she's Old Mother Hubbard.

I point at the boot. 'So it's broken? Or is it a sprain?'

Mum squints at me as if I'm suddenly standing very far away. 'I don't know, Becky . . . Is that important?'

'Well, yes,' I say. 'They're quite different.'

'Honestly, Becky, I can't remember *everything* the doctor said.'

'It's literally just . . . one thing.' I feel irritation rising. 'Sprain or break?'

She looks flustered. 'Well, if you're going to *bully* me about it, I think it was a sprain, yes. A sprain.'

'Okay.' I nod. 'And . . . did she say anything else?'

She stammers. 'Any . . . anything else? What do you mean?' A puzzled frown crosses her face. Her 'elderly' voice is back.

'I mean, is there anything else? Is there anything else wrong with you besides a sprained ankle? I thought they were running tests on you?'

Mum looks flabbergasted. 'I don't believe so, Becky. I'm sorry, is my being in a cast not satisfactory? Am I not injured enough for your liking? Do I need to be half dead, practically settling into my coffin before you'll come to visit me in the hospital?'

'That's not what I . . .' My brain hurts. But really, honestly, the answer is YES.

I CANNOT BELIEVE I JUST MISSED MY FLIGHT FOR A SPRAINED FUCKING ANKLE.

'Am I interrupting something?' Mum asks. 'Did you have somewhere more important to be today?'

I freeze. Mum doesn't look at me as she says this, fixating on her phone. *Has* she read the letter? Does she *know* I was abruptly moving out?

Surely not. I avoid her question. 'So . . . what do we do now?'

'Gavin's going to be back soon,' she says. 'Turns out he didn't need to get my things after all, so he can take me home. I need rest.'

I look at her properly. She does seem totally knackered. 'Yeah, of course,' I say. Mum is fine, that's all that matters, and my heart swells with joy at the thought of my cosy bed, my slippers, my cracked ceiling. Was I really planning to leave all that behind only a few short hours ago? That seems nuts. 'Let's go.'

'Oh, where are *you* going?' And that's when I know.

She knows.

'Home?' I say weakly. I feel sick.

'I'm not sure where *your* home is, Becky,' Mum replies. She looks me dead in the eye. There's knowing in her fixed, searchlight stare. She brings out a crumpled letter from her bag and waves it in my face. My dancing llamas stare back at me mockingly. 'I found the flight confirmation in your emails. Bali, was it?'

Ughhhhh.

UGHHHHHHHHH.

I falter for a second. Surely she's not going to kick me out, today? I came back for her! I came back for her SPRAINED BLOODY ANKLE. She can't tell me to get lost now?!

Can she?!

'Mum, please, I'll sort myself out tomorrow, I promise. Where am I supposed to go tonight?'

'Mmm,' Mum murmurs. For a moment I think she might be the bigger person. Then she says, 'I'm sure you'll find somewhere. I wouldn't want to infantilise you.' She puts her phone in her bag and finally looks at me. 'Gavin is nearly here, so I'd better go. Would you pass me the crutches?'

I pass them to her and she hobbles out of the room. I watch her move slowly down the bare hospital corridor towards the car park.

And just like that, I'm homeless.

Chapter Ten

I sit outside the hospital on a bench for a while, staring into space and at my phone. How did I end up here? Were things really normal only a few days ago, before I decided I believed in clairvoyants?

I can't help running through the day's alternative timeline. Right about now is when I'd have been deciding what movie to watch on the plane. (Terrible plane movies are basically the best part of a holiday.) Then I'd have been half-watching whatever movie I chose, because I was fretting too much about my friends and family opening their letters.

The letters.

A few hours ago they felt so far away. Now they're catching up to me with immense speed. I can't BELIEVE I said all those things. I can't believe I said all those things WITHOUT A SUCCESSFUL GETAWAY. I can't go away, now. I have about enough funds left for another flight, but what would I do when I got there? I'd have nothing.

I've gone beyond mortification. I barely even feel it anymore. I think I'm hysterical. You have to laugh, really. Don't you? It's actually quite funny. Isn't it?! I start laughing.

My parallel-life self touches down in Bali. My real-life self picks up the phone. I have *extremely* limited time before

Dami and Angie read those letters. Now is not the time to be sitting feeling sorry for myself.

Damilola's phone rings. Just when I think she's not going to answer, she picks up. 'Hello, we left your suitcases under your bed, in case your mum went into your room.'

'Thank you so much, Dami, but she knows now anyway.' I can't help my voice wobbling. 'Dami, I'm really sorry to ask you for yet another favour today, but . . . Could I possibly stay at yours tonight?'

I've got a plan. The plan is: go to Dami's, hide her letter. Hopefully Angie will still be there and I'll ask to come back to Angie's to get a book she borrowed months ago, where I'll hide her letter too, then head back to Dami's and stay in her cosy, comfy spare room and let her feed me Ben & Jerry's while we watch *First Dates*.

There's a silence on the other end of the phone that surprises me. Dami's a people pleaser and incredibly generous, so she usually says 'yes' to everything straightaway, even if you can tell she doesn't really want to. 'Hang on,' she says. I hear her answering her work phone and talking frantically to someone about a campaign that's running behind.

I know I've asked a lot today and I'm highly aware I've been a *huge* pain in the ass, but the fact that she's answered a work call during this conversation stings.

She comes back on the phone. 'Becky . . . I'm sorry,' she says softly. 'I don't think you can stay here tonight. It's a bad time. Can you ask Angie?'

A lump rises in my throat and I barely think before the words are out of my mouth. 'Oh, no problem. Do you have a deadline? I guess that is more important than your best friend's life falling apart.'

There's another silence. 'No, actually.' She coughs. Her voice is very quiet and I can barely hear her. 'But seeing as I do have such limited free time these days – as you've pointed out – I thought I'd spend it with people who actually still like me.'

I nearly fall backwards off the bench. Partially from the realisation that she's read it, but mostly because Dami has never spoken to me like that before in her entire life.

'Sorry,' she adds softly.

'I . . .' I'm lost for words. 'I'm sorry too,' I finally say, thinking back over what I said to her. About work taking over her personality. About Phil making all her decisions. About not knowing who she is anymore. I guess I deserved that.

She hangs up.

Fuck.

WHY IS THE BRITISH POSTAL SERVICE SO FUCKING EFFICIENT?!

I order an Uber to Angie's house. I *have* to get hers before she sees it. I just have to. The magnitude of my words is setting in. If sweet, passive Damilola reacted that badly, then how is Angie going to react when she reads that I compared her boyfriend to a fleshy, murderous blob-on-legs in an Eighties horror film?

My words still didn't really seem tangible until now. They were dream-like, floating in the ether. I was more preoccupied with my imaginary demise. Now they are *real*.

I feel giddy and lightheaded as the Uber pulls up. This entire day, this entire *week*, has been a terrible, terrible dream.

The only thing keeping me sane at this moment is that I know for a fact if Angie had read the letter I'd have heard from her.

From the depths of my long-lost memories, I faintly recall I've got an app that tracks Damilola's and Angie's location. I frantically search for it while sitting in the back of the taxi. I've not used this in *forever,* since uni when we still went out dancing and wanted to make sure each other got home safely from nightclubs. My heart tugs, thinking about how close we were then.

Opening the app feels like opening a time portal. It takes a while to load but eventually I see the little dot that is Angie. Thank God. She's not at home, but she's moving towards it. She must have only left Dami's fifteen minutes ago. She was probably there when Dami opened her letter and they realised my mum wasn't the only person I'd written to. I can see her now, speeding home to find out what hers says.

The race is on.

'Is there any way we can go a bit faster?' I plead with the driver.

He frowns at me in the rear-view mirror. I guess that's a no. So boring. When does that request ever get refused in a film?! 'Follow that car!' 'No, I'm sorry, ma'am, please buckle your seatbelt as we safely and sombrely follow the speed limit.' Has this man never seen *Ronin*? He needs to live a little.

Or maybe he's frowning because there's so much traffic my request is basically impossible.

'Come on, come on,' I will the traffic. I keep refreshing my app and thankfully Angie's progress towards her house seems to be slow as well. She must be stuck in the same jam that I am.

When we get to the junction heading up to Angie's road

I thank the driver, dive out of the car and bolt up the road towards her house. I can barely breathe. My lungs burn. This *has* to be the most exercise I've had since school PE. Running is impossible. I think I'm actually moving more slowly than if I'd walked.

I try to look at the app as I 'run'. Angie's still in the same place. How is that possible?! What happened? Did her car break down by some miracle? Whatever happened, thank the Lord! I'm going to make it!

Then, with a sinking heart, I realise the app's not connecting. It refreshes as my data loads. Angie's little dot slides from behind me, right past me, to her house.

Noooooooooooooooo.
SHE'S HOME.

I keep dragging my lead-filled legs towards her house. She can't read it. What was I thinking?! She'll never speak to me again! I pant, heave, crawl the rest of the way and arrive wheezing at the end of her road.

I make a mad dash up her garden path and bang frantically on the door.

'ANGIE!' I holler.

Angie's neighbour whose name I can't remember – old, bald, bulbous nose, wears a lot of scarves – is approaching his own garden path and eyeing me inquisitively.

I wait on the doorstep, shifting my weight nervously from foot to foot. Her neighbour just *keeps standing there*. Even when I glance back at him and make eye contact. Wow.

Ten seconds later the front door opens and Angie emerges. For a minute I think everything might be OK . . . until I see she's holding the dancing llamas.

FUCK THOSE FUCKING LLAMAS. I SWEAR TO CHRIST.

'Well, you must feel really good about yourself.' She leans against the doorway and folds her arms.

'I don't know what . . .'

'Do you feel better about not having a relationship now you've shit all over mine?'

Ouch.

Angie's neighbour has moved up the garden path so he can hear better. He's lingering by his front door, pretending to fumble for his keys. It's very distracting.

'That's not . . .'

'I'm stupefied, Becky.' Angie shakes her head.

'Look, I'm really sorry, okay?' I say. 'I was having a meltdown. I was convinced I was going to *die*. I didn't mean it. Jacob is . . .' Urgh. I try to think of an appropriate word that will bridge the gap between the ugly truth and ever being friends with Angie again. I can't say that I like Jacob, because I don't.

'A *creep,* yeah.' Angie repeats my words. I wince. 'You think I don't see him flirting with other women? Of course I do! It's *fine*. It's only flirting, God, Becky. We've been together nearly a decade. Being in a relationship doesn't mean you can't ever look at another person. It may surprise you to learn that I find other men attractive too, okay?'

'Sure, yeah, you're right,' I say. I don't mean it – Jacob's behaviour definitely goes beyond finding other women attractive – but I just want to make up and forget this ever happened.

'Yes . . . I am right,' she says, but less confidently this time. Her cheeks are blushing.

'You all right, babe?' says a deep voice from inside Angie's hallway.

Urghhhhhh.

Jacob comes up behind her and puts an arm around her. He looks at me with an amused expression, like he finds this funny. 'Becky.'

URGHHHHHHH.

'Hi, Jacob,' I say awkwardly. How do you act around someone you said you'd rather wax your own eyebrows off than have them look in your direction?

'Look, I just wanted to reassure you,' he starts. For a moment I think it's genuine. 'You don't have to wax your eyebrows for me to not find you attractive.'

BURN. Angie's neighbour, who I'd sort of forgotten about, cough-laughs.

Angie finally addresses him. 'For fuck's sake, Steve. You really need to start watching a soap opera.'

And with that, she closes the door. Steve goes inside too and I'm left completely alone. I keep standing on the doorstep in shock. I can't *believe* I sent those letters. I can't believe I'm not eight thousand miles from here, floating my troubles away on the back of a sea turtle. I can't believe I'm not *dead*.

I crouch down and put my head between my legs. Not for the first time today, I wonder what the fuck I've done. I have hit the self-destruct button on my life and now I have a front-row seat to watch it burn.

Where am I supposed to go?! Damilola and Angie are the sum total of my friends that I can actually ask favours of and they are both, understandably, pretty mad at me. Should I check into a hotel? But how's that going to work? What if

I have to stay for ages? How much money would I end up spending? I'll burn through a grand within a fortnight . . .

What was the point of living at home for so long?! Why did I not save more?! WHY DID I BUY SO MANY TEQUILA TROLLOPS?! Just because you like the name of a cocktail, does NOT mean you should order ten in one night just so you can keep saying it! How am I twenty-nine years old with so little to my name and nowhere to turn?

I breathe in, and out, in, and out. This is all a terrible, terrible nightmare. Yesterday I had a family. Yesterday I had friends. Today I have nothing.

I have one last option. The one person I really, *really* don't want to face. If I could take back one letter out of all six I would snatch back this one in a heartbeat.

I cringe and pick up my phone.

Chapter Eleven

I look up at Max's flat. It's in a modern tower block in Brixton with industrial, cell-like window frames. A lot of other 'struggling artists' live here. When Max's window is open I hear them hanging out on the roof, smoking weed and talking about things like the evils of gentrification or Nietzsche's theory of eternal recurrence. Anyone who lives in a flat like this in London usually prefers the illusion of struggling more than they are really struggling.

I know exactly which window is Max's – third left, second from the top floor – but it occurs to me I haven't actually been here very often, at least not in daylight. We don't generally go to each other's houses. Just hang out in Scintilla, encouraging each other to drink to excess. I guess because I live at home and he lives the other side of London it's just easier for us to meet in Central.

The last of the evening light has faded and I'm starting to feel cold. Obviously, I'm still wearing what I thought was suitable attire to disembark in Bali (I *really* wish I hadn't gone for tie-dye), and all my other worldly possessions are back at Mum's. I feel a flash of emptiness in my stomach as I think of Mum settling in with her evening peppermint tea and *Grey's Anatomy* re-runs before she has a brisk shower, phones Gavin and puts herself to bed. She'll be worrying about how to make it into bed with her gammy foot in time for the alarm beeps, and probably thinking about what a let-down I am.

Right at this moment, I can't say I disagree.

I've been hovering outside for a good twenty minutes, going back and forth on whether this is a good idea. I mean, it definitely *isn't* a good idea, but I'm somewhat running out of friends.

I'm not sure whether I'm dithering because I think he might have read the letter or because I think he might have *not* read the letter. When I think about him having read it I feel embarrassment, fear, anxiety, mortification and sickness to the pit of my stomach. When I think about him having not read it I feel flat and disappointed. Life returns to its usual, dull grey.

Then I think of Angie and Dami and how neither of them is speaking to me right about now. What am I saying?! Of course I hope he hasn't read it! I move towards the building and press the buzzer for flat 59.

'Hello?' That one word carries through the intercom and melts something inside me. 'Becky?'

'Yeah, it's me,' I reply.

The door clicks and I push it open. I enter the stark grey halls, and various drunk memories start coming back to me in flashes. Once, I insisted I was sober enough to walk the entire way up to his flat, passed out on the first set of stairs and Max pulled me over his shoulder and carried me to the lift. Once, I somehow lost Max, got the wrong floor and tried to convince Max's elderly neighbour to let me in. Once, I threw up in that plant pot.

It looks different sober. Surely, I think, I've been here before when sober? Have I really only been here when wasted? In all the years that Max and I have known each other?

I'm still pondering this when the lift opens and Max is standing in front of it. He's wandered into the hallway in his silk dressing gown that he bought as a 'joke' but seems to spend a lot of time sitting around in while drinking whisky.

'Becky! You made it!' He raises the glass of whisky in his left hand. 'Welcome to Max's Home for Waifs and Strays. Sorry you had a bust-up with your mum.'

I instantly begin to analyse his greeting. The look on his face. The raised eyebrow. The smirk. The tone of his voice. Has any of it changed since the last time I saw him? Has he read it or not?

He puts his other arm around me and starts leading me towards his flat. He smells so good and his badly done-up robe is revealing his chest. *Ugh. Calm down, Desperate Becky. Your mum fell down the stairs because of you, and your friends aren't speaking to you. You are not allowed to think about sex at a time like this.*

We approach the door and I quickly ask the question I've been dreading. 'Are you sure I'm not interrupting? If you and Fran had an evening planned . . .'

He waves his hand to silence me. 'Fran's away. She won't be back for a week.'

'Oh.' I try not to let the relief show on my face. 'Where is she this time?'

Fran is away a lot because she works for a humanitarian aid company. It makes it inconveniently difficult to dislike her, so I don't ask about her job unless I absolutely have to. To be honest, I don't usually acknowledge her existence at all unless I absolutely have to.

'Uhhhh. Congo?' He grins. 'I think?'

'It's touching that you pay so much attention to your girlfriend's job, Max,' I say, but I am secretly pleased. He can't tell me what country his girlfriend is flying to but he can tell me Ted's top five favourite episodes of *2 Broke Girls* in order. (Ted really likes *2 Broke Girls*. Max is fascinated by this.)

'Ngeghhhh.' He shrugs. 'I don't know, Becky, she's somewhere, we're here.'

She's somewhere. We're here.

Are those the words of someone who has read a secret love letter from their long-term best friend and is about to declare their undying passion for them?

Or just the words of someone stating a fact?

He closes the door behind us. And does not throw me on the floor and start taking off my clothes. Disappointing. Not that I really thought he was going to.

HAS HE READ IT OR NOT?

I follow him into the living room. It's a large, open space with minimal furniture. There's a sofa, a dining table and chairs, a book case and a plant, and that's it. Max likes to have a clear environment for creative thinking. His bedroom is sparse, too, and the other room he uses as a dark room to develop his pictures. I briefly wonder if things will change when Fran moves in. Then I wonder when she's moving in, but I don't want to ask.

Will she still be moving in if he's read my letter?

Shut up, Desperate Becky.

Max goes to the cupboard and brings out a bottle of tequila. 'The Becky bottle,' he says. 'Just for you. Margarita?'

'Always,' I say.

He gets out a shaker. Max still prides himself on his cocktail-making skills. I could never even get an orange peel to twist in the right shape; it always ended up looking a bit mangled.

'I've got some pyjamas here. And your toothbrush. Well, my toothbrush that you used once after vomming in the plant pot downstairs, so it's your toothbrush now. I'll even let you pick a terrible film.'

My heart liquefies. On some level I'm aware it was probably a bad idea coming here. On another, I knew I'd feel safe and looked after. I know I'll always have a place with Max, whether it's the place I want it to be or not.

As Max busies himself making us margaritas, I glance furtively around the room. *If I were mail, where would I be . . .* I twist around to see the bookshelf behind me.

Bingo.

There are a bunch of envelopes sitting on top of a stack of photography books. I don't have time to get up and investigate now because Max is already pouring. *Must. Not. Look. Suspicious.* If Max hasn't read it yet but catches me trying to retrieve it, I will only stoke his curiosity and he will one hundred per cent prise it out of my hands and tear it open in front of me. And that would be *unthinkable*. Every cell in my body would just . . . stop living.

I'm going to have to wait for an opportune moment.

He sits down next to me on the sofa, proffering the margarita in a proper cocktail glass. I take it and start gulping.

He watches me for a moment, smiling. 'So. Bad day?'

I glance at him from behind my half-empty glass. 'You could say that.'

Max settles on his cushion and observes me. He always does that. He never pushes you to talk, just sits back and gives you the space to do so. I'm not sure if it's my imagination, because I'm paranoid, but it feels as though he's watching me more closely than ever this evening.

Because he now knows I'm secretly madly in love with him? Or as a regular concerned friend because I've shown up at his house out of the blue?

'So, I was sort of supposed to be in Bali right now.'

Max is taking a sip and chokes. 'Bali?' He tries to recover his cool, but it's too late. The coughing has given him away.

'Yup.'

'Holiday?'

'Erm. I was . . . moving? I think. It was a one-way flight, anyway.'

'Interesting,' he says, as though debating a philosophical theory, not receiving news that one of his best friends was about to move to the other side of the world. Without telling him. As much as I know Max cares about me and is just bad at expressing himself, sometimes I wish he didn't keep his cards so close to his chest.

'*Interesting?*' I repeat.

'Yeah.' He nods. 'It is.'

'Is that all you have to say?' I goad.

He pauses for a moment, swirling the liquid in his glass. 'Well, for someone who's lived in the same house her entire life and overthinks literally every single decision except buying Tequila Trollops, it is comment-worthy that person would one day up and leave to live on the other side of the world, no? I mean, if you heard about it from someone else, you'd have a vague inkling of intrigue. You'd remark upon it. You might go so far as to call it *interesting*.' He looks up from his cocktail and grins.

I grin back because I can't not. 'I guess I would. It's because Sara's tarot reader told me I was going to die.'

I know he's going to mock me endlessly, but I want a reaction out of him, and I know this will get it. Sure enough, Max spits his drink out onto his dressing gown. 'I . . . Excuse me?'

I start shaking with laughter. 'Yeah. I used the gift card from Sara and she said I was going to die. And yeah, I just . . . Didn't want to die here.'

Max howls. We both crease up for about five minutes.

'And . . .' Max finally draws a full breath. 'How are you feeling now? Still thinking you're not long for this world?'

'I think, probably . . . I'll survive the night,' I say. 'Yeah. I know it sounds bonkers. I don't know. I think I had some sort of twenty-four-hour nervous breakdown.'

Once we've stopped laughing, Max contemplates me. His eyebrows furrow like he's putting two and two together. If he's opened the letter, is he suddenly realising that's why I sent it? Because I was thinking I'd be dead by the time he read it?

He grabs my now totally empty glass. 'More tequila,' he declares.

He's rattled. I can tell from his vigorous deflection, which is extreme even for him. His movements have become jerky.

There's an edge to his voice. He's upset that I was leaving, or that I didn't tell him, or both.

It's pathetic, but I can't help but be thrilled he cares.

Max makes my next cocktail in silence. I can't think of anything to say either. Changing the subject feels like ignoring the elephant in the room but clearly the conversation about me leaving the country is closed. Eventually he hands my glass back to me and heads for the bathroom.

The time is now.

I put the drink down beside me on the floor and spring off the sofa, towards the bookshelf. I carefully lift the envelopes, trying to preserve the position they were put down in as I rifle through them. Bill, bill, taxes, bill, bill. . . *Christ*. Being an adult is shit. His lamentably dull post makes me want to move back in with my mum immediately. Look at all this laborious admin just for your money to be taken for basic human rights like the internet.

Ugh. My letter isn't here. Then I notice the dates . . . They're all from months ago! Clearly, Max is not a fan of admin either. Where is his *recent* post, goddammit?!

The toilet flushes and I fling myself back onto the sofa.

The bathroom door opens and Max steps out. I try to look 'casual' but have obviously forgotten how human beings sit, because I accidentally cross my arms through my legs like a pretzel. Thankfully, Max doesn't seem to notice.

'I didn't realise how late it was. I should go to bed,' he announces.

I look at my phone; it's ten o'clock. Max is usually up until at least one. 'Since when did you care about how late it is? What about the drinks?' I gesture to the two full glasses sitting out on the table. 'What about the bad film? I was thinking *Sharknado*.'

'I have an important shoot tomorrow,' he says.

'Oh?' I ask.

'Yeah. In Paris. Have to be up early for the Eurostar.'

'Oh.' I'm about to say, *you didn't mention it*, but that would be a bit rich coming from me. 'But what if I'm dead by morning? I hear four hundred and fifty people a year die falling out of bed.'

He doesn't laugh at my joke. He goes into his bedroom and returns with my pyjamas (namely, the 'Live. Laugh. Love.' T-shirt I bought him once as an ironic birthday present) and toothbrush. He hands them to me with a blank expression. Is he annoyed at me . . . or am I overanalysing?

'Do you want the bed?' he offers. 'I can sleep on the sofa.'

'No,' I say. 'No, it's fine. You have a big day tomorrow.'

He nods. *So cold*. I'm not imagining it. I guess he found the whole thing funny at first but now he's processed it a little more, he isn't about to let me off that easily.

We get ready for bed, barely saying anything else to each other. Even though it's tense I can't help but enjoy the sight of us brushing our teeth in tandem next to each other in the mirror. Like we're back together. I catch his eye a few times in the mirror and smile but his face is deadpan.

'Night, dude.' He puts his toothbrush back in the cupboard and pats me on the shoulder.

Dude.

'Night, man,' I reply sarcastically.

I watch his back as he walks away and shuts his bedroom door. I stand for a moment, wondering whether he'll come back out, but he doesn't. Eventually I retreat to the living room.

I spend ten minutes quietly hunting more thoroughly for Max's post, but there's nothing. It could be lying unopened in his bedroom. Or in his post cubby downstairs? But if I slip downstairs now I won't be able to get back in without a key. *Rats*.

Read or unread . . . I won't find out this evening. I give up and lie back on the sofa. I'm none the wiser about whether he's aware of how I feel about him but either way, he knows I was fleeing the country.

Now I'm alone, I can't help but think of everything that's happened today. I think of Angie, Dami, Mum, Max next door, all going to bed furious with me. Even though I'm no longer convinced I'm about to die, the resonance of Sue's reading keeps running through my mind. I think of The Tower card. *A fall from grace, the burning to the ground of what we thought we knew, the destruction of everything we've built.*

I stare at Max's ceiling, knowing I'm not going to get a wink of sleep. I'm going to lie awake all night thinking about how in one day, I've managed to make everyone in the world that I love hate me.

Chapter Twelve

The next morning Max's mood has miraculously recovered. I'm woken up by the sounds of him making pancakes and humming to the radio in the kitchen. It's eight thirty. I only got to sleep about three hours before.

'Made it through the night, Becky?' Max calls as I sit up.

I rub my eyes. 'It would seem so,' I croak. 'I thought you'd be on your way to Paris,' I add, trying to sound more human.

'Train's not for a while. Nutella? Lemon and sugar?'

'Nutella.'

Max plonks a ginormous jar of Nutella on the counter, next to a large stack of pancakes. I sit down at the table and start slurping from a mug of tea.

Max seats himself opposite me, grabs a pancake and slathers it in chocolate. Then he begins ranking the *X-Men* movies in order from one to thirteen; he knows I can't resist rating each movie in a franchise. We haven't actually addressed anything from last night but I'm relieved that the frosty atmosphere has evaporated.

'So what's on the agenda for today?' he asks, reaching for a third pancake.

'Erm,' I say through a mouthful. Trying to rearrange getting to Bali now I know that Mum's okay? I could potentially try to line something up and then go, so it doesn't matter if I spent all my money on flights. But I don't feel as desperate to be sitting on a beach halfway around the world as I was a few days ago. Probably because I'd convinced myself I was going to die. The whole thing feels like a fever dream. Now, having come face to face with all the mess I've caused, it only seems right to stay and try to clear it up.

'Not a lot,' I answer eventually.

What am I going to do now?

Christ. I remember that it is technically a work day. Margaret will have received my resignation by now. She opens all her post the minute it comes in. *Oh God. What did I call her again?*

'You look like you've just remembered you've agreed to some sort of group exercise,' Max comments. 'Did Angie rope you into spinning again?'

'I . . .' I'm about to say *I wrote Margaret a letter*, but I don't want to reference The Letters, in case I can work out whether he's read his from his reaction. 'I quit my job. And . . . I said to Margaret . . .'

Max's face lights up. 'You said to Margaret . . .'

'That she was a blood-sucking sour-faced lemon?' I try to remember. 'No . . . no. That she was a blood sucker and I hoped my blood tasted of lemons. Or something along those lines.'

Max stares at me for a moment as he processes, then howls with laughter. He laughs and laughs and laughs, banging his fist on the table. 'Oh my God. YES.'

'No, no no no. It's bad. *Very bad*,' I say, panic setting in. But I can't help feeling pleased that I made Max laugh so hard.

'No, no, Becky, it's genius. What did the old crone say?'

Interesting, I think. He assumed this was a face-to-face interaction, which suggests his mind hasn't immediately gone to letters, which possibly implies he *hasn't* opened his yet? I make a mental note to search his bedroom, and the post cubby, as soon as he's left the house.

'She didn't say anything. It was . . . via email,' I answer.

'I've never been prouder of you, Becky.' Max puts his hand on his heart.

We stare across the table at each other for a moment. Max doesn't look away. He's observing me closely again. Or *has* he read it? My chest constricts.

The buzzer for the door sounds. Max breaks eye contact.

He goes to answer it and I recover my breathing rate. I can't keep going like this. For a moment I consider just asking him outright. And then I remember I'm British.

I'm so lost in this train of thought it takes me a moment to register Max has been speaking through the intercom for quite a while. Eventually he returns looking bemused.

'Errrr . . . it's for you,' he says.

I blink. 'For *me*?' For a second I'm confused, until I realise it's probably Angie coming to have it out. I thought it was strange I hadn't got a follow-up text or call by now. She's usually one to confront things, not shy away from them. I feel relief flooding through my body. Her turning up to shout at me feels more normal, more manageable, less ominous than her silence. It reassures me that I haven't totally fucked up our friendship beyond repair.

'Oh, I guess I should have been expecting this,' I say. 'Do you mind if me and Ang chat in here while you get ready? We'll be quiet. Actually, I can't promise it will be quiet . . .'

'It's not Angie,' Max interrupts. 'It's your . . . sister?'

I swear to God, I do an actual cartoon double-take. Out of all the people I might have guessed, I wouldn't have got there on my own. I would have sooner guessed Margaret. Or Ted. Even Jessica. Even the woman who cleans the We Work, You Win second-floor bathrooms would have been a more likely bet than my sister.

My *sister* is here?

My dad had another child after he and Mum split up. She's ten years younger than me. Her name is Leila. That's all I know.

All right, that's not *all* I know. From the *occasional* online stalk, I know she has long, dark hair and a nose piercing. She has a pet guinea pig. (Such a useless pet. Not as lively as a cat or a dog but not as small and cute as a hamster. What do guinea pigs even do?) She likes a lot of bands I've never heard of that make me feel old. She goes to a lot of clubs that make me feel old. She lives in Manchester with her mum and my dad. Her dad. Our dad?

She's *here*?

'Becky. Becky.' Max waves his hand in front of my face. 'You've been staring into space for *quite* a long time. What do you want to do?'

'I don't know?' I squeak. 'I can't deal with this?'

'I pretended I didn't know you and that I'd check with my flatmate. Do you want me to say my imaginary flatmate has no idea?'

The temptation to have Max send her away is *incredibly* inviting. In all honesty, I've never even thought about meeting my sister. It sounds odd because I always knew she was *out there* in the vague, hazy way you know that Flat Earthers and Scientologists are out there. You know they exist in theory but you're probably never going to have lunch with one.

And now she's *here* and I can't cope. I'm right in the middle of a million other things I have to handle. I have to check up on Mum, talk to Angie and Dami and somehow find out if Max knows about my mortifying undying love for him. How am I supposed to factor a sister I've never met into the equation?

No, no, she'll have to go. I simply do not have the time for this today.

THERE IS NO TIME.

'Yes, yes, tell her I'm not here,' I ramble. 'You don't know me. You've never heard of me.'

'Becky who?' Max shrugs.

I hear him mumbling through the intercom. He returns looking triumphant. 'Sorted,' he declares. 'One unwanted family member *dispensed with*.'

I nod and smile weakly.

He leans down next to me so our faces are level. His arm is draped around my chair protectively. 'How are you doing? Are you all right?'

I nod again but don't say anything. I feel immediately guilty about having sent her away. The aim of the letters was to start confronting things – albeit because I wouldn't be around to deal with the consequences – but here I am, just the same old Becky, hiding away from her life. Should I go after her?

'I think maybe I should . . .' I say.

'Hey, you're okay.' Max tilts my chin up and smiles at

me. Our faces are almost touching. I can count his individual eyelashes. All other thoughts dissipate.

Letter-writing Becky was an idiot. She wanted things to change. Who needs change when I can count the freckles on Max's cheekbone?

There's a knock at the door.

Max and I both turn our heads. 'Is that her? How did she get upstairs?' Max whispers.

We stay still and silent. The knock sounds again and Max glances at me with a hint of hysteria. For a moment, I have this strange feeling we're like naughty schoolchildren secreted in a den, being told that playtime is over and refusing to come out.

'Becky?' a young, female voice sounds. 'Becky, I know you're in there.'

Max shakes his head and gets up. 'Becky, get down,' he whispers.

I hesitate. Am I really going to *literally hide*?

Max points behind the sofa and I give in to all my worst instincts. I crouch behind a piece of furniture to avoid my only sibling who, presumably, has travelled all the way from Manchester to see me.

I hear Max open the door. 'Uhh, can I help you?' He sounds genuinely confused.

'As I said before, I'm looking for my sister, Becky.'

At the sound of her voice I feel a huge rush of intangible emotion. I'm not sure if it's fear, joy, shock, or just being very weirded out by being in the same room as this blood relation for the first time. Maybe it's all at once.

'Don't know her,' says Max. He's putting on his 'arrogant'

voice, kind of like how he sounds when he's arguing with Angie about the economy.

There's a deep sigh from the other side of the door. 'Okay, sure. Do you know if she's gone to work?'

Obviously I've never heard her talking before in my life, but something about the way she speaks is oddly familiar. The cadence, the tone maybe. I can't quite put my finger on it.

'Like I said . . .' Max replies.

'Yeah, yeah, you don't know her.'

She sounds exasperated. I feel even more deplorable for crouching on the floor.

'Well, if you do happen to meet her, can you please tell her I opened her letter?'

The mention of the letters lights something in me. I'm not sure if it's resentment, because that letter wasn't for her, it was for my father, and the thought of her reading it makes me feel like I did the time Ted found my old Tumblr account of emo song lyrics and sent it around the whole office. (He genuinely thought he was being nice because the songs 'moved him'.) I'm not sure if it's bravery, because I'm reminded again of how much three-days-ago me genuinely wanted to move forward. Even if it was only because I'd lost my mind and convinced myself I was departing this mortal plane. But something compels me to stand up.

Max and Leila both look in my direction and, for the first time in my life, I'm face to face with my real-life sister.

Chapter Thirteen

'How did you find me?' I ask. We're sitting on Max's sofa. As soon as I announced myself he slunk off awkwardly to his bedroom. Leila is wearing bright red sparkly boots, flares and a denim jacket. It's a bold look.

'I went to your mum's house. She said you only have like, three friends, and she gave me all of their addresses. It didn't take very long to track you down.' She shrugs and drapes her long, dark hair over her shoulders. 'I went to your friend Demi's?'

'Dami,' I correct.

'Yeah, I went there first. We looked you up on her friend-finding app.'

That's how she was so sure I was here. Ugh. And I *hid*. She shoots me a disappointed look, like a weary teacher with a misbehaving student.

I look at her and try to find something of Dad in her face. I can't find any trace. I figure she must look more like her mum. I guess I don't exactly know Dad's face that well, though. I've seen it mostly in photographs. I bet there are all sorts of subtle ways she, or maybe I, are like him that I wouldn't be able to pick up on. The sound of a laugh, the lopsidedness of a grin, the mannerism of a gesture.

'Dami seems nice.' Leila's comment snaps me out of studying her features. 'Your mum seems scary.'

I can't help but laugh. Leila doesn't even crack a smile. It's like she was making a comment about the weather. My heart swells for a moment, thinking of my nice friend and my scary mum.

'So, are you staying here?' she asks.

'Uhhhh . . .' I realise I haven't established that with Max yet. And he's leaving for Paris soon. 'I don't know.'

'Right, well, where will you go if not?' she presses.

'Uhhhh . . .' I say again. 'I don't know?'

'Right.' A sceptical look crosses her face, mixed with vague curiosity. I can't believe a nineteen-year-old is wondering how I could be so disorganised.

She's right, though. If I don't stay here, where *am* I going to go?

'Excuse me,' I mutter, standing up. I cross the living room, knock on Max's door and slip inside. Max is folding things into a canvas bag. He looks up as I enter. I close the door behind me.

It's strangely intimate being in his bedroom. Obviously I used to be in his bedroom all the time. Back when we still lived in our dingy flat-shares we barely spent time in any other room. We'd sleep, eat, have sex, watch movies all in Max's tiny, freezing-cold box room. But grown-up Becky and Max don't hang out in each other's bedrooms. For obvious reasons. Namely, that grown-up Max has moved on and just sees grown-up Becky as a friend.

I would give anything for one of those movie marathons in this bed. It looks so comfortable. What would he do if I just climbed into it? Right now?

'Becky?' The sound of Max's voice brings me back to reality.

'Yeah, uh. I'm really sorry, is it okay if I stay here while you're away? It's just . . . I kind of . . . Well . . .' I tail off.

'You have nowhere else so you came slumming it to ole, reliable Max. Yeah, yeah, I get it. It's not Bali, but needs must.' Max shoots me a bitter grin. If only he knew how deeply untrue that was. That there's nowhere else on planet Earth I'd rather be than wherever he is. 'I'd kind of assumed you were staying.'

My tense muscles loosen a fraction. At least I'm not totally homeless for now.

'Hey, sorry if I made things more awkward for you.' He gestures his head towards the door, beyond which Leila is sitting. 'I was just trying to help. You've got a lot going on. I didn't want you to feel overwhelmed.' He rubs my shoulder protectively.

'Thanks, Max.' Cosy warmth prickles all the way up my back. Max is always looking out for me and never judges me, no matter how much of a mess I make of things.

His hand stays on my shoulder for a second longer than normal before he takes it away. I wonder, for the millionth time, if he's read the letter. He hasn't commented at all on Leila's mention of my dad's letter. Is he avoiding the subject of them altogether because it's too awkward? If he *hadn't* received his, wouldn't he have asked about Leila's? But then, Max has never been one to pry.

'I'd better get back out there,' I say. 'I have an estranged sister sitting on the couch and all.'

'That you do,' Max agrees, and goes back to packing.

I remain for a second longer, hoping time might just stand still in this moment where I'm near Max in a small, safe space, but there's only so long one can linger in a corner staring without bordering on creepy. Eventually I slip back outside.

'I'm staying here,' I announce as I walk over to Leila. She's scrolling on her phone.

'Okay, good,' she says flatly, barely looking up.

I sit next to her and observe her tapping away at her screen. A bit like with dating apps, it's odd to meet someone in the flesh that you've only ever seen pictures of. You can never account for their manner, voice or vibe until they're right in front of you. I stare at this girl, wondering, like I have many times through a screen, about all the experiences she's had that I didn't. She *knows* our father. She knows what it's like to be put to bed by him, to eat breakfast with him, to go on holiday with him. She knows what music he likes, what jokes he finds funny, whether he's a cat person or a dog person (or a guinea pig person). She knows what it's like to have a dad.

I'm swept away by a wave of untamed jealousy and try to ride it out. *What is she doing here in front of me? Why isn't she still behind her screen?*

When she doesn't stop looking at her phone, I cough awkwardly. She puts it down in her own sweet time.

'Can I ask, I mean . . . Not to be rude but . . . Why are you here?' I ask lamely.

She reaches into her handbag and pulls out an envelope. My insides shrivel.

Leila clears her throat and unfolds the paper. 'Dear Dad . . .'

'What are you *doing*?' My face burns.

'Don't contact me, etc, I'm sorry that you missed out on knowing me. . .'

I snatch the letter out of her hand. This is even worse than Tumblrgate. I'd perform all those songs about tying my dead, blackened heart to a brick and throwing it in a lake, on national television, if she would just stop reading. 'This wasn't addressed to you.'

'That is my address.' She points to the envelope.

'It's not your *name*,' I retort.

'It's kind of nice that we're bickering already.' She nods. 'I thought we'd have to wait at least a few years before we got to that stage.'

I genuinely can't tell if she's joking or not. Her face is placid.

'Why are you here? You're not Dad.' I place my finger on his name again to make my point.

'You told Dad never to get in touch with you, bold *and* underlined. Even on his deathbed.'

I open my mouth. I close it again. She has me there. 'I didn't mean Dad *should* be here. I just meant . . . you shouldn't be here either.'

'Okay, well, what did you want to gain from sending this letter?' Leila cocks her head to one side. It doesn't feel like she's being confrontational, it seems like she just genuinely wants to know.

'For him to leave me alone,' I say.

'You haven't spoken in, what, twenty years?' She shrugs. Again, she's not saying it maliciously, she's just stating a fact. But I can't help feeling wounded.

'I want him to know that it's off the table now. That it's my decision too,' I explain. 'I'm not abandoned anymore because . . . I'm abandoning him.'

There's a moment where she seems to see me properly for the first time. Her eyes scan my face, considering this perspective that seems like brand-new information to her. Maybe it never occurred to her that I felt abandoned. Maybe she thought I had no interest in our father. Maybe she's just never thought about it before, full stop. 'Oh,' she says softly.

A lump rises in my throat. Leila sees the tears in my eyes and looks away awkwardly. God, this is beyond mortifying. Here I am crying about the father who deserted me to the girl who grew up with that father. Fathering her and such. He probably plastered her scabby knees and did up her shoelaces and boiled her eggs.

God. This can't be happening. Whatever happened to small talk?

'I'm sorry,' Leila says to the wall. As if reading my mind she adds, 'I should have started with small talk. My mum says I need to be less direct. She's Dutch. I get it from her.'

I don't know what to say to that. I'm still working very hard on trying not to cry and I'm glad she's still looking at the wall. I make a mental note never to go to Holland.

'What do you do?' she asks. 'For a living?'

'I'm in marketing at a recruitment company.' *Don't cry don't cry don't cry.*

'Oh. Is that . . . interesting?' I can tell she's trying hard to be polite. It doesn't come naturally. She's not at all how I expected her to be, from her Instagram or her red sparkly boots. I expected her to be . . . fluffier? She's quite abrupt.

'I mean, it's . . . There's a lot of . . .' I run through all the things I'd say to people when I started at We Work, You Win. *There's such fulfilment in helping people find jobs they love . . . Satisfaction in growing the business and increasing enquiries from top companies . . . Creativity in developing brand awareness . . .* I'm sure all those things are interesting to some people, but not me. 'No,' I say finally.

Leila snorts.

'But I quit,' I add. 'The other day.'

'Oh, that's good. Well, what do you want to do next?'

'God, I don't know.' Familiar panic starts flooding through me at the mere thought of trying to figure that out. Flying somewhere far away in the face of my imminent death was easier. Now I'm back in London, everything is weighing on me again, piling up around me so I can't move. Before I can elaborate she moves on.

'And you live at home?'

'Yep,' I say. 'Well. I did. What about you?' I ask. 'Are you at uni?'

'No,' she says. 'I'm taking a gap year. Saving up to travel, working in a bar. I'm not sure I want to go to uni anyway.'

'Working in a bar, when I was just a bit older than you, was the best time of my life,' I say mournfully.

'What was so good about it?' Leila asks.

'Err . . .' I met Max. Everything was possible. I hadn't failed yet. 'I met lots of people.'

'Don't you have three friends?' Leila finally turns back to me, clearly sensing the danger of me crying has passed.

'What is this, an interrogation?!' I yelp. 'Jesus. Yes, I have three friends. And two of them I met at school. All right? Are you happy? I just liked the bar.'

'Sorry,' Leila says. There's a silence while I recover. 'I *really* need to work on my chit-chat,' she adds thoughtfully.

'It might be an idea,' I say through gritted teeth.

At that moment Max's bedroom door opens. He's got his rucksack strapped to his back and his camera bag in his hand. He looks adorable. I wish he wasn't leaving.

'Are you going?' I say.

'Obviously.' Leila nods at his bags. I'm beginning to find her irritating.

'Yeah.' Max is trying to edge towards the door as quickly as possible and avoid looking directly at Leila, after lying to her about not knowing me earlier. 'Bed's made. Food is in the fridge. Spare keys are in the bowl.'

'Such a good boyfriend,' Leila comments.

'Oh, err, we're not . . . I mean, we're just friends,' I correct her. I can feel a blush creeping up my neck. Leila stares at my reddening skin. Then she stares unabashedly between Max and me with obvious confusion. Can someone teach this girl to read the room?

Max doesn't react. He's probably too busy thinking about getting to St Pancras to notice my face is on fire. 'Nice to meet you, Leila.' He waves. 'See ya, Becky.'

I get up and follow him into the hallway so we can have a moment to ourselves. He leans against the front door, smirking. 'And here we have living proof of nurture over nature,' he whispers. 'I can already tell you're polar opposites. You should be studied.'

I can't help but smile. 'She's half-Dutch,' I explain.

'Right, well, enjoy.'

We lean in to hug. And then *something* happens. Something that has not happened in five years. Instead of putting his head to one side, like in a normal hug, he tucks my head directly under his chin. When we were going out we always used to laugh that I was a whole head shorter than him and he'd hold me in that exact position, my face buried in his chest, before we'd kiss.

The smell of his aftershave, his warmth, his arms around me, my head under his. I'm twenty-four again. We've stepped back in time to 2019. I might be disappointed by the *Game of Thrones* finale, but my best friends and I still have time for each other and talk to each other about things other than kitchens and overflowing inboxes. I don't want to kill my mum. I love Max and he loves me. I have prospects and life feels like it's going to be easy.

Too quickly, present Max pulls away and coughs awkwardly.

'Bye, Becky,' he mumbles, without looking at me, and leaves. I stand with my arms still slightly raised, staring at the closed door.

And I know, like I always know with Max without him actually saying the words.

He read the letter.

Chapter Fourteen

I'm mortified. I'm elated. Did that really just happen?

I turn around and Leila is standing in the corridor behind me. She's watching me with her arms folded.

'I thought he wasn't your boyfriend,' she remarks.

'He's not,' I answer.

'Then what was that?' She points behind me to where we were just standing. I guess she saw us.

'We used to date,' I mumble, pushing back past her into the living room.

'No shit.' She follows me.

I sit on the sofa and bury my head in my hands, trying to make sense of the past five minutes. Of the past twenty-four hours.

'What's wrong?' she asks.

All normal social conventions are out the window between us and by this point I couldn't care less. 'He's not my boyfriend, but . . . I want him to be,' I moan through my hands.

'So, seems like he could be.'

My head springs up. 'What do you mean?' I can't help hoping as much, after that hug, but I don't want to get too excited. It's possible that years of yearning have driven me insane and I'm reading too much into it. Like the time he gave me his last piece of gum and I talked about what it might mean for a month. I need someone else to validate me.

Leila surveys me from across the room, obviously sensing my emotions are heightened again and wary of coming too close. 'I mean, my friends don't hug me like that.'

Sweet validation. I could kiss her!

'He has a girlfriend,' I say.

Leila shrugs. 'Things end.'

'I broke up with him. I broke his heart.'

'Mistakes happen. People forgive each other.'

I get the sense that Leila sees everything in black and white. It's very jarring. Back in the day when I still shared this kind of stuff with Angie and Dami we'd be analysing every detail of the hug. Or, as it would come to be known, The Hug. We'd analyse what we suspected Max was feeling. We'd analyse how *I* was feeling. We'd analyse what my next move was and whether that was okay given his relationship with Fran and how to go about it sensitively. (Or, at least, so I wasn't literally standing outside his window playing Avril Lavigne's 'Girlfriend' on a boom box and dancing around in my underwear.)

'It's a bit more complicated than that,' I defend.

'Do you want to be with him or not?' Leila asks.

'Obviously.'

She shrugs again. 'Okay,' she says, as if there's nothing else to say.

I am bewildered by this tall child showing up in my life, acting like she has all the answers and bossing me around. I didn't ask her here. I didn't ask for her opinion. We don't even know each other. And I'm the older one. Why is she the one giving me advice? Does she think she knows better than me, will be able to do life better than me, just because she had a well-balanced upbringing with two sane parents and I had . . . well . . . my mother?

'Look, I've actually got to go. I have . . . things to do.' I stand up.

She purses her lips. 'Didn't you quit your job?'

'Other things. And er, I need to go . . . yup, now,' I add, moving towards the kitchen counter and reaching for the keys Max left in the bowl. 'I'm already late. Late for an important date.'

Late for an important date?

'Okay, can I use the bathroom first?' she asks.

I look at my wrist. There isn't a watch there. I rub the back of my hand as if I was just inspecting a freckle. 'I've really got to get cracking, but you can let yourself out.'

Get cracking?

'Oh, okay, bye,' she says.

I know that I'm behaving like a crazy person, but I need to get away from her and her cold, logical take on my life, which she has walked into without invitation, commented on without permission and has no idea about. I have to start putting my life back together and she is not helping. She's making my brain feel even more scrambled.

'Bye,' I say more softly. I add, 'It was good to meet you. I'm sorry you came all this way but . . . you came at a bad time.'

'Yeah,' she says. She might be about to add something else but I turn too quickly. I practically run to the front door and into the hallway. When I get into the lift I realise my legs are shaking.

First things first, I've got to check up on Mum. I dial her number.

'Becky, you're up early,' Mum says.

It's ten o'clock. I ignore this.

'How are you?' I ask. 'How's the foot?'

'I'm very drained of energy. It's tiring just trying to move about.'

Even though she kicked me out, it's not like I'm not helping her by choice, I feel bad.

'Can Gavin stay with you?'

'I'm managing,' she says.

Mum and Gavin have been together years now, but you wouldn't know it. He comes to big events and obviously, he was at the hospital yesterday, but they're not actually hugely involved. They see each other once or twice a week to go to the cinema or for a coffee. Mum claims that she 'doesn't like to rely on him', and it feels like they've been in the early stages of dating since they first met. It's never struck me as being strange until now. I guess I've never seen her actually need help before.

'Mum, I know you're very independent, but this is an unusual situation. Gavin loves you. I'm sure he'd be happy to . . .'

'Honestly, Becky, I'm fine.'

I don't push it. There's a silence. I'm not sure what else to say, since neither of us wants to reference the conversation we had yesterday.

'Did your sister find you?' she asks. She unsuccessfully tries to keep the curiosity out of her voice.

'Yeah. She did.'

I don't volunteer any further information. It will be killing Mum that she can't be nosy about it. It's bizarre to think that, for once, she has no idea where I am or what I've been doing. Part of me is satisfied. Part of me wants to run home and never leave the house again. Maybe offer her a tracker she can put around my ankle.

'Okay, bye then, I guess,' I say, unwilling to give her any insight into my present state of being but unsure what else to say.

'Bye.' She hangs up and I feel a pang of homesickness. Which is ridiculous, given that I'm only on the other side of the Thames. The lift opens onto the bottom floor of Max's building. Sunlight penetrates the long, almost floor-length windows and London waits for me outside. What does an unemployed twenty-nine-year-old woman with no friends or funds to speak of do on a Thursday morning?

The answer is painfully obvious.

She gets a job.

I make my way through the throngs of people, leaving Leila behind as fast as I can. I pace towards Brixton tube station and down underground, even though I have no reason to hurry anywhere . . . It's just how one moves in London. Once I get to Oxford Circus my feet take over on autopilot, leading me up the escalators, past the tube poster of the Soho Theatre production with the actor who looks like Angie if she were a bloke, out the far right barrier, past the man who sells me Extra every week and says, 'Someone's got a hot date.'

I've been doing this commute every day for *five years* and I've never once felt out of place while travelling it. These are my frantic Londoners with their heads down, my grotty tube station walls, my gum-covered floor. I've never once questioned whether I belong here. But today I feel like an outsider.

Somehow the Becky that showed up for work on Monday isn't the same Becky who's here today. I don't think I changed in less than a week. I think somehow, slowly, I've been changing bit by bit, every single day, only it took me a while to notice. But now I've noticed it, I can't just slot back into my familiar surroundings.

I shake my head. I don't have a choice.

When I arrive outside We Work, You Win, I'm suddenly unsure of what to do. I've still got my building pass, but can I just walk in? Am I technically still an employee? Margaret probably hasn't even had time to process my resignation yet. Maybe I could just breeze straight past and sit at my desk like usual and pretend to know nothing about any letter?

It's only been a few days and yet, as I step inside the bright, shiny reception, it feels like years have passed. There's no way I can just walk in. I head over to the reception desk, which I haven't visited since my first week working here.

'Can I help you?' One of the guys ushers me over, looking me up and down suspiciously. I glance at myself in the mirror behind him and remember I'm wearing Max's tracksuit bottoms and *Adventure Time* hoodie. Fuck.

I start taking off the hoodie and then see the Live. Laugh. Love. T-shirt underneath.

Fuck.

What's a better look to go begging for your job back? A cartoon for mid-thirties stoners or a motto considered to be motivational and life-affirming by people who live in Essex?

I try to see myself through Margaret's eyes. She is more shocked by slovenliness than fake tan or giant lips, so I guess I should opt for the second. I continue taking off the hoodie.

'Can you call Margaret Robson and tell her Becky Alderton's here? She's at We Work, You Win, fifth floor, extension 117.'

'Do you have an appointment?'

'She'll know what it's about,' I say.

He considers me for a moment before calling, but does pick up the phone. 'Hi, I've got Becky Alderton downstairs. She said you'd know what it's regarding. Okay, I'll send her up.' He puts the phone down and gestures towards the barriers. 'The guest entrance is on the far left. Margaret's on floor five.'

My hackles rise. I already told him which floor it was. I know this building inside out. I consider using the employee entrance with my pass just to make a point, but you're supposed to hand them in when you quit and I don't want them to notice that I still have it and confiscate it. I'm weirdly attached to my pass.

I wait by the *loser* guest entrance until he remembers to buzz me in. In amongst feeling annoyed by the know-it-all receptionist who's probably worked in this building ten minutes, I'd forgotten to feel nervous about facing Margaret, but as I get into the lift I start bricking it.

What am I planning to say to her? Mine and Margaret's relationship is one of zero confrontation. I do the ludicrous things she tells me to do without arguing and she's perpetually disappointed in me for losing my youthful enthusiasm. We've survived this way for years and now we're about to be forced into a situation where we absolutely cannot ignore the elephant in the room, i.e. that I don't really want this job but I need it.

Floor three.

WHY did I think this was a good idea?

Floor four.

And why didn't I prepare what I would say on the way here, instead of listening to *Who Shat on the Floor at My Wedding?!*

Floor five. The lift doors open and I frantically hit the ground-floor button. *I need more time to think. Maybe I can just ride the lift up and down while I strategise . . .*

Before the doors close again, I see Margaret standing by the noticeboard. She catches sight of me and it's too late.

Chapter Fifteen

I step out of the lift. Margaret nods towards her office, which I take to mean she'll meet me there in a second.

I start the walk of shame across the main floor. Oh my God. Everyone's going to stare. News of my abrupt departure has probably got around already. People wondering why I left so suddenly and who the department's going to hire to replace me. I really wish I was wearing something normal.

I walk past Bill, Leanne and Karim, who are making their morning tea, involved in a heated discussion about the best kind of pastry. (Leanne votes Danish, Karim votes almond croissant. God, they couldn't have an original conversation if they tried. But also, it's clearly a pain au chocolat.) I move nice and slowly, so they'll catch sight of me and we can get the inevitable onslaught of questions out of the way, but they're too involved in their pastry talk.

That's odd. Did they see me? Maybe they don't recognise me in this T-shirt? I move towards Margaret's office.

I've stood outside this glass door a million times, watching Margaret sipping the tea I made her through pursed lips, or brushing a stray hair from her pristine camel garb. Today I almost feel like I'm truly observing Margaret for the first time. I think of her getting up in the morning, picking out one of her indistinguishable outfits, pinning her hair in its tight bun and thinking how smart it looks, complimenting herself on 'running a department' even though to this day I am not entirely sure what it is that she actually does.

It's strange, isn't it, how when you see someone every day you can stop seeing them at all? They're just *there*, more impression than human. But Margaret is a real person. A real person who *really* loves camel.

She spots me lurking outside and ushers me in.

I enter and wait to be told to sit down. She doesn't invite me to sit, though, so I hover awkwardly in the corner.

'Becky,' she says. Her voice doesn't give much away. It always sounds brittle and tense, so she could be in a really good mood for all I know.

'Margaret,' I answer apprehensively.

'What can I do for you?' she asks. 'Shall I get out my cheque book?'

'Hmm?' I'm confused for a moment. Then I remember. *Oh*.

'How much was it? £55.45?' She bares her teeth at her little joke. 'Or would you rather a Pret card?'

'Hahaha . . .' My laugh sounds unnatural. 'That, er, that's fine . . . Won't be, er, necessary. Look, er . . . About that . . .'

Margaret raises her eyebrows and folds her arms expectantly. I realise, for the first time, how much Margaret reminds me of my mother.

WHY did I not think about what I was going to say when I got here? What did I POSSIBLY think I could say in this situation?!

'We've, er, we've worked together a long time . . .' I say finally. No idea where I'm going with this, but let's roll with it. 'Five years. Five years is a *long* time. I could have loved and lost a healthy pet guinea pig in that time.'

Margaret wrinkles her forehead.

'A *whole* guinea pig's lifespan,' I continue. 'We have been a team. You and I. I've seen many employees come and go . . . I've seen the company go from strength to strength . . . I've seen, er, many a stunning outfit . . .' I gesture to her fur camel hat.

Margaret raises a hand to silence me. She looks as physically pained by hearing my words as I am by saying them. This is why she stopped letting me pitch for new clients. 'What is it that you want, Becky?'

'I want my job back, please,' I squeak.

Margaret lets out a troubled sigh. She sits back in her chair and regards me. I might be imagining it, but I think I see her expression soften just a fraction.

'I'm sorry, Becky, I can't help you,' she says.

'Oh . . . I . . . Okay.' I don't know what I was expecting, and yet somehow I'm hurt. How can my job, that I had for five years, have disappeared so quickly? *Poof?* 'Have you already hired someone else?' I needle her. I want her to look me in the eye and admit she simply doesn't want me back, because there's *no way* they've hired someone new already.

'We've redistributed your role,' she says.

I let the words settle. They've *redistributed my role?*

They're not even replacing me?

'What do you mean?' I goad, giving in to the self-destructive urge to torture myself. It would save my feelings not to interrogate this further, but now I have to know more. Sort of like if you see someone's phone open and your own name on screen. You're not going to *not* look, are you?

'Jessica and Ted will be taking on a few additional responsibilities,' she clarifies. 'The intern will be buying my sandwiches.'

A few additional responsibilities for Jessica and Ted and an intern buying groceries. Is that really all my presence in this place amounted to? They don't even need a whole person to cover me?

I'm not a person. I'm a few extra responsibilities and a sandwich. I've never felt so insignificant.

We sit in silence for a moment. Margaret's face is impassive, as usual. I can't tell what she's thinking at all. I know things had become strained towards the end of my time here, but it occurs to me that I'm surprised by how cold she's being. I guess I thought underneath it all she was a little fond of me.

'Well, it's nice to know five years holds so little value,' I say.

I know I'd lost my way towards the end, but I was here for so long. How can that mean nothing?

'Time itself doesn't hold value, Becky, it's what you do with the time that counts,' she answers, like she's Mahatma Gandhi or something.

Well, what I've done with my time is waste it here, at boring, meaningless We Work, You Win. And it was all erased so easily. How fragile everything seems.

'I know it feels bad right now, Becky,' she says. 'But I think one day you'll look back and see I did you a favour. I had high hopes when you first started here, but I think we both know this isn't where you want to be.'

It isn't, but . . . I have nowhere else to turn. I've never felt so low. I'm officially at rock bottom. But I suppose, if I'm really honest with myself, I can't blame her.

'Right, well, thank you for everything, Margaret,' I say, my lip wobbling. 'It's been . . .' I choose my words carefully, wanting the last ones I say to her to at least be genuine. 'A fashion inspiration.'

She gives me a grave nod. 'Good luck, Becky.'

I step out of her office, thoroughly humiliated and ready to dive into my trusty toilets for refuge. Then I remember I don't work here anymore, so that would be weird, and head for the lift instead. En route I smack right into Jess.

'Oh, hi Becky!' She waves.

'Hi, Jess,' I say, my heart sinking at the prospect of having to put on a fake smile and endure her zest for life and genuine passion for the company, when I feel like I'm about to cry.

'I like your T-shirt,' she says sincerely. 'I have it in blue.'

'Thanks,' I say.

Here we go. I ready myself for probing. *What happened? Are you okay? How long had you been thinking of leaving? What are your plans?*

'Are you here to pick up your stuff?' she asks.

'Yeah.' I nod. She doesn't say anything else.

Wow. Is that really all she wants to know?

I stare into her wide, round blue eyes framed by her perfectly intact ponytail. She's not even *pretending* to care that I'm leaving. Outrageous. Does she really think I care about pictures of Leanne's baby that looks uncannily like Bruce Forsyth? No. Of course I fucking don't. But I give my cursory smile, my 'ooh' and 'ahh', and I try as hard as I can to refrain from referencing *Strictly Come Dancing*. I play by the rules because if we don't then society fucking collapses and we'll all just be going around *saying what we actually think* and then where will we be?

God, I'm *fuming*.

DID I EVEN GO HERE?

'We put it in a box for you on your desk,' she continues, when I keep standing in front of her. 'I think there was just a stress ball, and . . . a Hijingo cap?'

My hangover cap. I won it at office Hijingo night, back when I first joined and still went out and had fun with my old team.

'Thanks,' I say, and move on.

I walk back past Bill, Leanne and Karim, who still don't look up from their conversation. This time I stop right in front of them and clear my throat VERY LOUDLY. They look towards me with trepidation. There's fear in their eyes.

'Hi, Becky,' says Karim hesitantly.

'Hello,' I reply petulantly. 'Hello and GOODBYE.'

I storm towards the lift, half wondering if they'll follow me. They don't. I remember my Hijingo cap on my desk, run over to get it and then run back to the lifts.

Tears are streaming down my face as the floors decrease in number. Ugh. Why did I go begging for my stupid job back?! That was so degrading and I didn't even want it. It's like when you go on an awful date with someone you wouldn't sleep with for a million pounds and a free trip to Hawaii, and then they text you, saying 'sorry the spark wasn't there'.

I'm rushing out of reception when I hear footsteps behind me. 'Becky, stop,' sounds a raspy voice.

Usually I wouldn't be pleased to see Ted. But right now it's comforting that any human being on the planet notices my existence.

I turn to face him and don't even bother to try and hide that I've been crying. He politely avoids staring directly at me and looks at the floor.

'We just wanted to check you're okay,' he breathes.

'We?'

'Yes, Leanne and Karim told me you were here picking up your stuff.'

'Oh, so they did notice me, then.' I'm aware I sound like a toddler, but I can't help it coming out that way.

'Yes, uh, they did,' Ted says.

'Right, because it didn't seem like they did.'

'Well, uh, you're not normally one for a chinwag, so . . . I suppose they assumed . . . Well . . .' He pauses, then carries on. 'I mean, you never come to the pub, or . . . I mean . . . even the Christmas party? So I guess they just assumed . . .' He trails off.

I guess they just assumed you wouldn't care that much about saying goodbye, I finish for him in my head.

My cheeks prickle with shame as I pick up on what he's politely trying to tell me. This isn't about people not noticing me; my co-workers obviously see me more clearly than I thought. I honestly didn't think they had registered my contempt for this place. Humiliation burns as I think of everyone recognising my apathy and lofty condescension.

Of course they aren't bothered that I'm leaving. Why would they be? Why would they rush to talk to me, when I've spent every day ducking out of conversations with them as quickly as humanly possible? Ted's right; I stopped showing up to everything I was invited to. I just . . . I was just so bitter about feeling stuck there that engaging with it or trying to make the best of it made it worse, somehow.

Margaret was right not to let me back. All my colleagues were right not to care. God knows why Ted still gives a shit that I'm leaving. He's too sweet for his own good. If only I had died after all. Then they would have at least had to pretend I was a beloved and dependable colleague at my funeral.

I look at Ted, still staring at the floor, trying to comfort me even though I've been such a dickhead. 'I'm sorry, Ted,' I say, and I actually mean it. 'Tell the others I'm sorry about my outburst, okay?'

'Righty-ho, will do.' He salutes me. 'Good luck with everything, Becky, it's been a pleasure.'

I can't imagine that it has, but it's nice of him to say it.

'And er, I cleared your internet history before IT got to it,' he whispers theatrically behind the back of his hand. 'All traces of Netflix and Amazon Prime totally removed. By the way . . . what's *Xanadu*?' he asks.

I laugh, thinking about how to begin explaining Olivia Newton-John and Gene Kelly in the world's most bizarre musical fantasy movie. 'Uhhh . . .' I say.

'Don't worry, no spoilers,' he says. 'I'll check it out. Bye, Becky.'

I watch as he heads back into the building. It was never going to be my dream job, but for the first time in my life, I wonder, was it really *that* bad here? Would I have got more out of it if I had just kept trying a bit harder? Maybe then

I'd have received a leaving card at least, some friendly well-wishes and clichéd platitudes. A hug or two. *Something* to commemorate five years of my life.

I stand on the street and stare up at We Work, You Win, feeling, if possible, more lost than I did this morning.

Chapter Sixteen

I return to Max's place with my tail between my legs. The prospect of looking for a new job looms over me with more dread than when I thought I was going to fall down a manhole or be taken out by a flying champagne cork. I can't bear to return to that place of giving job applications everything I had and never cutting it.

It doesn't help that I went for a walk to clear my head and ended up passing Spellbound Sue, waving a crystal skull around some bewildered-looking man's head in circular motions. Even she has a job. Somehow, we live in a world where Spellbound Sue is more employable than I am. Life simply isn't fair.

I sit on Max's sofa, pull out his laptop and open Google. I take a breath.

What do I type?

What job do I even want to do?

A flash of foreboding flies through my chest as I stare at the screen. *This*. This is what I've been avoiding for so long. I feel so validated. Confronting not knowing what I want to do is every bit as awful as I thought it would be. Why do I still not know what I want to do? Do I even have a soul?

Maybe I did belong at We Work, You Win.

I'm distracted by a gentle thud in the other room. For a

moment, I'm relieved. An intruder is *definitely* more pressing than sorting out my career. No one could blame me for procrastinating finding a job if I was being attacked by a burglar. I might even be able to put it off for another six months while I deal with the trauma of the incident. Especially if they have a knife or something. I could say sorry to Mum for making fun of her elaborate alarm system and she could lock me in the house until I recovered.

Then I remember to actually panic. *Fuck. There's someone in the house.*

A second later Leila emerges.

'Bloody hell,' I say. 'You scared me!'

'Really?' She yawns. Her hair is all mussed up from resting on Max's bed. Clearly she's made herself at home. 'You don't look very afraid. You're lazing on the couch.'

'I was about to grab a chair or something,' I grumble.

I wasn't.

'Interesting,' Leila comments. 'You don't seem to have fight *or* flight responses.'

'Why are you still here?!' I demand, ignoring her observation. 'Taking a nap in my house?'

'It's not your house.' Leila frowns.

'Oh, you know what I mean.' I close the laptop and put it on the table. God, she's annoying. But on some level, I am pleased that she ignored my request to leave and is still here.

She sits down in the armchair across from me and hugs her knees to her chest. 'I don't have anywhere to go,' she admits. For once, she doesn't sound like she's reading the news. Vulnerability has cracked its way into her voice and her posture.

'Oh,' I say. 'Oh. What about your . . . parents?'

I avoid mentioning Dad directly.

'I was living with my girlfriend,' she says.

She seems a bit *young* to have been living with a girlfriend. I'm nearly thirty and the thought of moving in with someone still gives me the feeling you get before going down a tunnel slide. It's dark and scary and fuck knows what you're going to find in there or whether you'll make it out the other side.

'And you're not anymore?' I ask.

'Obviously.'

'But can't you go back to your parents'? You must have been there to get my letter.'

'I wasn't staying there, just visiting. Mum wasn't happy about me moving. Apparently I was *too young*.' She puts air quotation marks around her words. 'I don't want to prove her right.'

Well, you kind of have, I think, but I don't say it. Then I think, why not say it? She's been free with her opinions about my life. But she looks so defeated I don't have the heart. I watch her hugging her knees to her chest, sitting in some stranger's living room with nowhere else to go, and it dawns on me that her self-assurance is just bluster. This nineteen-year-old doesn't have the answers to everything any more than I do. She's just immature enough to believe that she does.

Suddenly, having her here doesn't feel as overwhelming as it did this morning. Even if she was fathered by my absent father. Having a father clearly doesn't mean she's got the magic key to life, either.

'So can I stay?' she asks.

'Yeah, all right.' I smile.

She smiles back at me. 'Did you do all the things you needed to do today?'

'Uhhhhh . . .'

'I take it, no?'

'Well, I tried to get my job back. It didn't go well.'

'Wait.' Leila sits up in the armchair. 'The job you hate? Why would you want it back?!'

I shrug. 'Needs must.'

'But there are a million other jobs out there. You finally quit. If you went back you probably would have stayed for *another* five years!'

'That's not . . .' I don't finish my sentence. She's right. It made no sense to go running back to a job I only just worked up the confidence to leave. But it doesn't make any sense that she's hiding out here instead of telling her parents she split up with her girlfriend, when she's going to have to tell them eventually. People do things that don't seem to make sense all the time.

'I think . . . I think when moving forwards doesn't work out for me, I go backwards.' I'm only just beginning to see this about myself. The only reason I even took the job at We Work, You Win was the crushing disappointment of missing out on jobs that I actually wanted and didn't get, and I'd interned at WWYW, so I knew the commute and where to get good coffee from. 'It's instinct.'

Leila nods. 'It's the wrong instinct. Driven by fear.'

I burst out laughing. Leila's a little like Angie in how she doesn't mince her words, but with less awareness; she's not trying be catty, she's just saying what she thinks. My heart tugs thinking of Angie. I wonder what she's doing. Maybe she's working out with clients at the gym, planning for the wellness centre, texting Dami, cooking some kind of healthy meal at home for Jacob. I long to hear about her day.

'So is that what Max is?' Leila asks.

'Huh?' I say, still half-thinking about Angie.

'Moving backwards because moving forwards didn't work out? I mean, he's an ex-boyfriend, right?'

'Oh . . . *no*,' I say. 'No. Very different situation.'

I had a lot of fledgling relationships that didn't work out because the dating-app scene is a nightmare, sure, but I was always in love with Max deep down.

She nods and says wistfully, 'I think I'll always be in love with Polly.'

I have the impulse to laugh. To tell her that's not true. That she'll definitely get over it and meet someone else. This declaration of undying love sounds so ridiculous coming out of a teenager's mouth. But it didn't happen for me, did it? Guiltily, I think that I'm the least qualified big sister to give advice ever.

'Shall we get drunk and order shit tons of Chinese food?' I say instead.

'It's four o'clock,' she comments, to which I shrug.

'I like your style,' she says.

Suddenly, I could not be happier for her company. Her obvious loneliness speaks to my own and I'm grateful she's here. I'm filled with the urge to connect with her, to get to know her, and forget about everything else.

Two hours later Max's booze cupboard has been almost entirely raided. We have been laughing, and swapping stories, and I believe 'bonding', all the while carefully avoiding the mention of our mutual life-giver.

'The gin! The gin is *gone*!' cries Leila. She's hanging upside down off the armchair, with her legs over the side. She's peering into the bottle.

'AH!' she shouts. 'I got gin in my eye!'

'So the gin wasn't gone,' I comment.

'Now it's gone.' She clutches her eye.

We both laugh hysterically. In that moment Leila pouring volatile flammable liquid into her eye is the funniest thing I have ever seen.

'So do you stay here a lot?' asks Leila, after we've calmed down. She flails her arm, wildly gesturing to the room.

'Noooooooo,' I say. 'No no no no nooooooo, sir.'

'Why not?'

'I don't know,' I answer honestly. Why not?! Why NOT? I wondered the same thing when I got here, but it had never crossed my mind before. 'It's just easier to meet in Central, I guess.'

'Is it Max's girlfriend? Would she mind?' Leila's face is turning red and her features are indistinguishable from this angle. She looks like a squishy, bloated toad.

'I don't know,' I say again.

'You don't know much,' Leila says.

'Nope.' I knock the side of my head with my knuckles. 'Empty.'

'What's she like? Can I see her?'

I nod and open Instagram, typing Fran's name in the search bar. I don't usually stalk Fran. It never occurs to me. *She* never occurs to me. I know she exists in theory but more as like, a fence between me and Max that stops me coming too close, not as a person.

Leila pushes herself up from the floor and takes my phone. 'She looks nice.'

This is a stab in my vulnerable, drunken stomach.

'What are you saying? That I'm *NOT* nice?!'

'Wooooooooaaahhhhhh.' Leila raises her arms defensively.

'How does one even look nice? How can you tell?!' I yell. 'It's not a physical feature. That's like saying, oh she looks . . . *conscientious*. Oh, she looks *impulsive* . . . Oh, she looks *parsimonious*.'

'Parsimonious?' Leila wrinkles her nose.

'It means frugal. I'm not going to show you if you say stupid things.' I snatch the phone back. I start scrolling through Fran's profile myself. There's a picture of her grinning in a field, petting a goat. There's an action shot of her playing football with a group of children. There's a snap of her out for drinks for her co-worker's birthday . . .

Fine. She *does* look nice. I bet Fran would get a card when she left her company. Her colleagues probably adore her.

Leila moves to sit next to me, peering at the screen. 'You can totally tell.'

'Ugh!' I wail. 'I don't enrich the lives of any children or goats!'

I throw my phone away. Leila catches it deftly. She looks at it for a second as I sit stewing. I'm in a foul mood now. Where can I get hold of a goat to stroke?

'Er, Becky . . .'

'*What?!*'

'The heart on this one is red.'

'Huh?'

She points at a picture of Fran standing on some bridge

in front of a river and a beautiful sunset. The little heart underneath it is red. The picture is from three years ago.

'Did you like it on purpose?'

Nooooooooooooooo.

'What?!' I jump up and peer closer. 'No! Did I do that just now?'

'I don't know.' Leila shrugs. 'Do you usually like her pictures?'

'No!' I say. 'I don't.'

'Okay, don't panic.'

'LEILA!' I panic.

'There's a chance you liked it three years ago.'

'Maybe.' I start sweating. 'It's *impossible* to remember!'

'Think, Becky, think. Cast your mind back to three minutes ago. Did the little white heart come up? The one that comes up when you click?'

'I don't know,' I wail. 'I'm too drunk, *I don't know*!'

Leila leans away from me and observes me like you might a wild animal. 'Maybe she won't get a notification. Sometimes I don't get a notification every time someone likes something.'

'I can't pin all my hopes on that!' I cry. I click on the picture again to unlike it. 'Will that help?' I ask desperately. 'Will that make a notification less likely?'

'Er, I don't know,' says Leila. 'But I did just think of a way we could check.'

'HOW?' I could kiss her. 'DO IT!'

'We could have looked in your recently liked posts to see if it's there. But you've unliked it now, so that won't work.'

'LEILA!' I howl.

'Look, it's okay . . .' Leila soothes.

I close my eyes, awaiting her comforting words of wisdom.

'If you *did* like it, she'll probably just think you're a bit sad.'

I open my eyes and turn to her slowly. 'Is that supposed to make me feel *better*?'

Before Leila can respond, we hear the sound of keys in the door.

'Is that Max?' Leila whispers.

'No . . . No. He only left this morning. He would have told me if he was coming back.'

'Oh.' Leila glances at Fran's profile in my hand. '*Oh*. You might want to close that.'

'Yes, thanks, oh sage one,' I hiss at Leila, putting my phone away.

Chapter Seventeen

The door clicks open and footsteps sound in the hallway. I feel as if I'm being caught somewhere I'm not supposed to be. Almost like Fran's walking in on Max and me in bed together, or something. Which is ludicrous. Ostensibly, I'm just a friend who's crashing. I'm allowed to be here. She can't know that I inhaled Max's clean laundry or that, this morning in the very same hallway she's now standing in, Max put his chin on my head. And neither of those things is exactly incriminating, anyway. Who doesn't like the smell of freshly washed clothes? And what is one friend's chin on another friend's head, really?

The footsteps get nearer. 'Hi, Fran,' I shout out, before she turns the corner into the room.

Fran springs back in shock, then doubles over laughing in relief. 'Oh my God. Becky! You jumped me.'

'*Surprise!*' I call. It's meant to be 'lighthearted' but I'm so tense it comes across more 'axe murderer'. Especially when I wave my arms around madly.

'I didn't know you'd be here.' Fran stands up straight.

'I didn't know you'd be here,' I reply. Again, going for 'laidback' and achieving 'accusing'.

'I live here.' Fran sounds confused. 'Didn't Max tell you?'

Her words land a painful blow. She's moved in? *Already?* I thought that wouldn't happen for ages. If I'm really honest with myself, I don't think I'd properly engaged with it happening at all. At least, I did when he first told me, and then somehow the news got swallowed by the black hole of denial that lives in my brain and gobbles up anything I don't want to acknowledge. The same hole that blanks out the *Gilmore Girls* revival.

It's a very convenient method of dealing with distressing life events. Except I *did* waste what felt like hours of my life watching Lorelai do *Wild*, and Fran *is* living in Max's flat.

'He mentioned it.' I try to make it sound as if it isn't major life-altering news that I didn't react to by leaving my own birthday party in a blur of tears and vomit. 'I just thought you were away.'

'I was in Zambia,' she says. 'But they had more volunteers than they thought so it was more useful for me to head up the UK team this week.'

Ha. Zambia. Not Congo. Max doesn't even know where you were. He always knows where *I* am. (All right, so it's not that hard to keep track of my movements, but still.)

'Right,' I say, like her flying around between continents and having a cool job don't impress me. 'Sorry to scare you. Didn't Max tell you I was staying?'

'No,' she says. 'But of course you're always welcome. Hi, by the way.' She acknowledges Leila. 'I'm Fran.'

'Hi, I'm Leila. I'm Becky's sister.'

'Oh.' Fran falters. 'Did I know you have a sister, Becky?'

'This is the first time we've ever met,' Leila says cheerfully. Leila and I look at each other and burst out laughing. We're still drunk. And being around each other is still slightly absurd.

Fran's eyebrows rise a million miles. 'Oh gosh,' she responds. She looks deeply uncomfortable. I bet Fran has siblings that she knows and likes. I bet her parents are still together and *get on* and do sickening things like hold hands while driving, threatening the lives of others like old, grey deviants because they're so in love. I bet they all play boardgames as a family without having any petty arguments. 'I'll go hang out in the bedroom. I don't want to intrude.'

'What? Why?' asks Leila, brandishing a bottle. 'We have gin! Oh wait. I guess it's yours. Sorry. You have gin!' Then she remembers the bottle is empty and starts laughing. 'And whoops, it's actually gone. SORRY.'

Fran smirks. Who knew offering someone their own gin, that you already finished, could be charming? It is, though. I realise, with some surprise, I've warmed to Leila.

'Oh, you must have a lot of catching up to do . . .'

'We've been catching up all day,' Leila says. 'Sit with us!'

'Okay.' Fran smiles awkwardly. 'I'll just put my things down.' She disappears off into the bedroom.

I take back my positivity towards Leila. I have the urge to take off my sock and stuff it in her mouth. 'What are you doing?' I hiss. 'Why are you encouraging Fran to hang out with us?'

'I'm curious.' She shrugs.

Oh, she's *curious*. She thinks it's fun to mess with my life because she's curious. I flick the side of her forehead. She frowns.

'Did you just *flick* me? Are you twelve?'

Fran comes back into the room. She's put her coat away and she's wearing straight-leg jean dungarees underneath.

She's quite fashionable. I tried wearing dungarees once and they just made me look like a giant baby.

She sits down on the armchair Leila was hanging upside down off a few moments ago and awkwardly smiles at us.

'So Fran, *what* do you *do*?' Leila's words slur and she's putting emphasis on random words in a way that makes her sound quite mad.

'I'm a communications officer for a humanitarian aid company,' Fran says.

'What *does* that mean?'

'I coordinate internal communications around the projects, so I'll tell the various volunteers what they'll be doing, make sure staff are informed of developments. Sometimes I'll be on site and publish content for our website.'

'So you get to travel a lot?'

'Not for every project, but yeah.'

'Oh coooooooool!' Leila crows. 'I bet that's *amazing*!'

Traitor.

'It's pretty great,' Fran agrees.

'Did you always *know* you wanted to do that?!'

'No. I mean, I knew I wanted to help people and do something in the charity sector. But not a communications officer specifically.'

Ugh. She helps people. Because she's a *good person*. Why don't I have the urge to help people? I'd settle for even a glimmer of interest in anything that was a feasible career. Deciding I wanted to become a grandmaster after watching *The Queen's Gambit* doesn't count.

'What about you, Becky? How is your job hunt coming? I

hear you quit recruitment.' Fran directs her attention to me. I feel hot under the spotlight.

'Errr yeah, not bad,' I say. 'Got a couple of interviews lined up.'

'Really? Where?' Leila side-eyes me.

'Errrr. The London Fire Brigade.'

The London Fire Brigade?

I've said it now.

'Oh gosh.' Fran's eyes widen.

'Yup,' I continue. 'I guess I've always wanted to . . . save people's lives, you know.'

'Oh gosh, I thought you meant support staff. So you're going to be an actual . . . firefighter?'

'Uh, yeah.' I keep digging my hole. 'Yes. I want to be on the front line, you know. I guess I've always been drawn to danger. Jeopardy. *Peril.*'

Fran is lost for words. Leila is shaking her head slowly. No one speaks so I keep going.

'I can't wait to risk my life by entering a burning building,' I add.

'Okay!' Leila claps her hands together. She widens her eyes at me as if to say *be normal.* 'Who wants tequila?'

I proffer my glass and she says, 'Not you. You've clearly had enough.'

No one asks me any more questions about my potential future career as a firefighter.

Rude.

'So where were you living before you moved in here?' Leila asks Fran, pouring her a tequila.

'Dalston,' she answers.

'Dalston?' I repeat. I always had Fran pegged for more of a Kensington kind of girl. She once accidentally pronounced 'apple' like 'ahpple'.

Fran nods.

'Have you always lived in London?' Leila continues.

'I actually grew up in Hong Kong.' Fran sits back, eyeing her neat tequila suspiciously. She politely takes a sip.

'Hong Kong?' I repeat.

'Yep. My mum's company relocated her there when I was six. We moved back when I was fourteen.'

'Like . . . *Hong Kong,* Hong Kong?' I say again.

'Yeah, I went to an international school.'

Huh. I always figured Fran probably grew up somewhere like . . . Canterbury.

'Oh,' I say.

'You guys have met before, right?' Leila jokes.

Fran laughs timidly. The fact that we're both involved in Max's life, but not in each other's, hangs awkwardly in the air. 'How long *have* we known each other now, Becky? A year? I think I'd been dating Max around a year when we met. Was it at Sara's birthday, when she made us all dress as sexy politicians?'

'Yes,' I say. I was Tantalising Theresa May. It was the first time Max – dressed as Devilish David Cameron – brought Fran to anything. I got so upset I tripped over my sheaf of wheat and smacked my head into a cupboard. 'So . . . yeah. Must be about that,' I say. Once again I'm shocked by my complete lack of timekeeping. A year? Did I really meet Fran a whole year ago? I feel like that only happened the other day.

'That is *so* Sara!' Fran laughs as if she knows Sara really well or something. It briefly occurs to me, after two years, I guess she might. Then I feed the thought straight back into the jaws of my trusty denial monster. Of course she doesn't know Sara. Every time Max sees Sara and co, we see them together. Max barely brings Fran to anything and she's away a lot. Up until this spontaneous and frankly reckless decision to move in, Max and Fran really weren't all *that* enmeshed in each other's lives.

'Her next one should be easier, at least,' Fran says.

'Her next one?'

'Yeah, nuns and popes. I've already ordered my Mother Teresa habit.' Fran laughs.

My throat closes up. Nuns and popes? What?! How does Fran know what Sara's next theme party is going to be? My mind whirs. Sara didn't say anything about it at my birthday, I don't think? I was so focused on the news of Max and Fran moving in together that I can't remember. But . . . no. No, she definitely hadn't decided at my birthday, because Angie asked her and she said she was still thinking. So she's decided at some point between my birthday party, just under a week ago, and now? And somehow Fran knows about it? Did they see each other?

No. Surely not, I rationalise. *You're being paranoid.* In what world would there be a group thing that Fran was invited to and I wasn't? This is *my* friendship group. We only manage to get together a few times a year. Plus, Fran's been away anyway. Sara must have messaged Max about it and he told Fran. I start to breathe more easily. Of course, that's what happened.

'Right, yeah. OBVIOUSLY,' I say. 'Silly me. I'm going as . . . Hildegard von Bingen.'

Fran smiles and nods. I must say, I am impressed with my own quick thinking. Any old fool knows Mother Teresa, but Hildegard? That's next level. I wonder if Fran is intimidated by my vast knowledge of famous nuns.

'She is, after all, one of the best-known composers of sacred monophony,' I add. 'Did you know she experienced visitations from God her whole life? One she described as a *fiery light of exceeding brilliance that inflamed her whole breast like a warming flame.* Imagine that.'

Ha. Bet you wish you didn't have a meaningful job now, eh Fran? Who's the one who has all the time in the world to sift through the cavernous depths of Wikipedia, researching interesting facts about notorious medieval saints?

'That's interesting, Becky,' Fran says.

Leila starts shaking her head at me again and her reaction helps me picture myself objectively. My flash of smugness dies as quickly as it rose. In the five minutes since Fran arrived I have both pretended I'm becoming a firefighter and quoted *Hildegard von Bingen* in an attempt to . . . what? Impress her? Win? What exactly am I winning?

Leila asks Fran another question about herself and I try not to interject. I clearly cannot be trusted to speak. I sit quietly and observe my estranged sister making conversation with the love of my life's girlfriend and wonder, yet again, how on Earth I ended up here.

Chapter Eighteen

As the evening goes on I feel worse and worse. I've never spent any proper time with Fran before and it's bizarre, like having a conversation with a mythical creature. Usually, when Max and I spend time together it's alone. Our group events aren't frequent, because it's so difficult to get everyone together, so people don't necessarily bring their partners. Obviously we've met at the occasional party, exchanged a few words, but we usually end up sitting at opposite ends of a table or I get so upset by her presence that I become too drunk too quickly and go home.

She's always felt more like a concept than an actual person. But now, sitting here in front of me, talking about plummeting fertility rates and who was robbed on the Man Booker shortlist and how she desperately needs a haircut and the spa trip she's going on with her auntie, she is unavoidably real.

Fran has an *auntie*. She didn't just appear out of a vortex one day like a big, witless, life-ruining plankton. She lived in Hong Kong until the age of fourteen and she reads smart novels and has opinions about them and she cares about things in the news and she has split ends.

Fran has an AUNTIE.

I stare at her gormlessly as she talks, trying to put Fran back in her denial box. But it's too late; thanks to Leila she's escaped. Several times I want to message Angie and Dami before remembering I can't. Several times I freak out about missing the last train back home or getting in before my curfew, before remembering I don't live there anymore.

By the time Fran decides to go to bed I've well and truly sobered up.

'Well, I should turn in, it's been a long day,' she says, getting up. 'But it's been lovely.' She looks at Leila, not me. 'Night, it was great to meet you. Night, Becky.' She finally looks at me and gives me a brief, shy smile.

It occurs to me that now she's here she will obviously be getting the bed and Leila and I will be sharing the living room. Well, I know which one of us is sleeping on the floor.

Fran goes to find us the roll-up mattress, then retreats. I look daggers at Leila as Fran closes the bathroom door.

'I hope you're happy.' I cross my arms.

'What? I thought that was nice.' Leila seems genuinely puzzled.

'Nice? *Nice?*'

'I mean, you were a bit weird.' Leila shrugs.

'Yes, because you invited my . . .' I try to think of an appropriate word for what Max is to me. There isn't one. 'Max's girlfriend to spend the evening with us.'

'You're in her house!' Leila presses her fingers together in disbelief.

'This is Max's house,' I correct.

'It's their house, Becky, she lives here. What were you going to do, banish her to her bedroom all night?'

She has a point and I know that logically she's right. I don't know what I was intending to do. Since the letters, I haven't had a plan. My plan was to get strangled by my own scarf or exploded by a stray firework before I had to deal with any of this. But I don't need some superior teenager telling me that.

This whole situation is farcical. I wrote those letters for closure with my dad and Max, and I've somehow ended up trapped in a confined space with my father's daughter and Max's girlfriend. *Getting to know* them? Learning about their taste in books? As if Leila popping up out of nowhere wasn't bad enough, now she has me practically holding hands and skipping with Fran?! Why doesn't she just bust out the friendship bracelets and suggest we braid each other's hair?!

Leila puts her hand on my arm. 'Becky, Fran seems really nice. Do you think—'

The overfamiliarity of her gesture makes me feel like I can't breathe. And whatever she's about to say, I don't want to hear.

'Look, I don't even know what you're still doing here,' I snap. 'You're getting on a train first thing in the morning.'

Leila seems taken aback. *Good*, I think. She finally gets the message. She doesn't belong here. What was she thinking . . . That we were going to just be sisters now? It's been nineteen years. We missed our window. We can't ever get that time back. This whole evening was a delusion.

'I told you, I have nowhere to—'

'It's not my problem,' I say. 'I didn't ask you to come here.'

Leila is silent. I sense I've said enough but for some reason words keep coming out.

'I'm sure it was wonderful, growing up with a father who adores you. I'm sure you think that everyone in the world must feel the same. I'm sure you expect to have a warm welcome everywhere you show up. But guess what, the world doesn't give a crap. *Welcome to adulthood.*'

I mean what I'm saying, in one way. But you know when, despite meaning something, you also know it's totally irrational bollocks, coming from a place of insecurity and wanting to hurt someone as much as you're hurting, rather than actually *meaning* it?

The bathroom door opens and Fran steps out in her pyjamas. 'I've brushed my teeth so the bathroom's yours. Sleep well.'

Neither of us says anything.

'Night,' Leila whispers sadly.

Fran steps towards the bedroom then turns around. 'So rude of me, sorry, would you two like the bed? It would make more sense for me to sleep on the sofa.'

Fran seems to notice there's something wrong and glances between us awkwardly.

Leila coughs. 'That's kind, Fran, but we'll be okay out here.' Her voice is small.

'Okay, well, see you in the morning.' Finally, Fran leaves.

Leila moves to the thin roll-out mattress on the floor and pulls a blanket over her shoulders. She doesn't say another word to me and I don't to her. For what feels like hours I lie awake, listening to the sound of her breathing, feeling a mixture of emotions. I still can't quite accept I have a real-life flesh-and-blood relative, filling and emptying her lungs of oxygen right beside me. For a while I continue to think, *how dare she come here and barge her way into my life and make me think more about Dad deserting me than I have done in the past twenty years and acknowledge Fran as a real human being?*

But a little while later, I mainly just feel awful for the way I spoke to her. It's not her fault that she grew up with our dad and I didn't. It's not her fault that Max is with Fran.

I must eventually drift off, because the next thing I know there's light creeping in through the windows. I pry my weary eyes apart and, for a moment, expect to wake up in my own bed. It takes a millisecond to remember where I am. Flashes of the previous night return to me. Oh God.

Did I really say I was applying to be a firefighter?

My head feels like it's been repeatedly slammed against a brick wall and my mouth tastes like a badger took a shit in it. What strange concoctions were we consuming last night? Did I drink any water at all?!

I see the empty roll-up mattress next to me and with an awful, gnawing lurch, I remember everything I said to Leila. I sit up on my elbow. 'Leila?' I croak. 'Leila?'

Fran emerges from the bedroom. 'You're up,' she says brightly, like she's been awake for hours.

'Just about. Is Leila here?'

'She left this morning. I gave her some money for the train,' Fran says.

She left. She actually left. My little sister.

SHE'S ONLY WEE.

I'm older, I'm wiser . . . I should know better. I should look out for her. But I took my frustrations out on her. I feel hollow. Fran's eyes search mine and I look away.

'Is everything okay with her, Becky?' She hesitates before she says 'with her', like she really means 'with you' but doesn't want to say it.

I think of her leaving the flat this morning. Putting on

her stupid sparkly boots. Wiping her smudged eye make-up. Deciding not to say goodbye. Closing the door. Staring out the window on the train back to her own life, wondering why she ever came here.

'She's fine,' I say. Of course she's fine, probably. That's her whole thing, isn't it? She's a bit clueless and pretends to know everything because she's nineteen and that's what you do at nineteen, but ultimately *she's okay*. She has her mum and dad to fall back on. She'll be a bit embarrassed when she admits she broke up with her girlfriend but they'll take her home with loving arms and spoil her. She'll lick her wounds and feel fine in no time. I've never been a part of her life before, so why would she miss me now? We never belonged in each other's worlds. She'll forget about me, just like Dad did.

'How much was her train?' I ask.

'Don't worry about it.' Fran waves her hand.

'No, really.' I can't bear for Fran to be sweet to me. I can barely look her in the eye. 'I'll pay you back.'

Fran bites her lip. 'It was eighty.'

I cringe. My money is dwindling fast. WHY did I order so much Chinese last night? And, God, all that extra booze on Deliveroo?! Pay day is in ten days and I should still get paid for this month . . . But it won't take me long to run out entirely.

'Cool, no problem,' I say unconvincingly. 'Message me your deets.'

'Okay.' Fran nods. She leans against the doorway, as if she's too uncomfortable to come into the room. Which is stupid. It is technically her flat.

Oh God. *I'm alone with Fran.* No long table to sit at the

other end of. No other people to duck behind. No booze to impair my capacity to connect. There's no way I can hang out here all day.

'Anyway.' I scramble up from the sofa and start pulling on my socks. 'I'd best be off. I've got lots to sort out.'

Not a lie. I just have no idea where to start.

'Okay, cool.' Fran folds her arms like she's hugging herself.

I grab my Live. Laugh. Love. T-shirt and pull it over my head. I hastily grab all my belongings that are strewn across the room and start picking up stray bottles.

'Don't worry, really.' Fran holds out her arm. 'I'll do that.'

'Okay, sure,' I say cheerily. 'All right, well, bye then.'

'See you, Becky,' Fran says. 'Good luck with your . . . various job applications.' The corner of her mouth curls in amusement, not unkindly.

'Thanks.' I grimace. Thank God she's too polite to bring up the London Fire Brigade. ''K bye.'

And with that, I am out the door.

Chapter Nineteen

As soon as I've left Max's, I realise I have absolutely nothing to do. Nowhere to be. No one to visit. Purely because the alternative is *literally* wandering the streets, I'm forced towards doing the thing I've been hiding from basically since leaving university.

Deciding what I actually want to do with my life.

No biggie, I tell myself . . . Maybe it will be easy? Maybe if I put my mind to it, it will only take me one afternoon? Maybe all those years of procrastination were completely unfounded and the answer will come to me straightaway?

I head to the library near Mum's house. I can't remember the last time I came in here, but I'm still technically a member. There are two rows of ancient computers with a shocking internet connection and you have to log on and off every hour to restart a session.

I sit down.

Okay. I can do this. *I can do this* . . . Or maybe I should go buy a coffee first? Or shop online for a new phone case? My one's broken. I've been thinking for a while that I should probably research new hairdressers because my one's a bit slow. Or learn how to do it myself on YouTube. I mean, how hard can it be? I've actually got lots of little bits of fluff stuck to my jacket, maybe I should find some Sellotape and get those off . . .

No. Focus, Becky.
FOCUS.

Okay . . . Here we go. Seeing as I have no idea what I'd like to do I keep it broad and search 'jobs'. Maybe I'll be inspired. I start going through random listings on *The Guardian* website.

Teacher? Hmmm. I don't really like kids. HR? I don't really like people. Therapist? I'd have to pay patients to take my advice. Fundraiser for a charity? Sounds very wholesome. They'd probably be able to sense the vast amounts of money I've wasted on clothes and booze over the years instead of helping others and ward me away from the building with salt and garlic. Tax manager? I'd be begging We Work, You Win to take me back in minutes.

Urgh.

This is hopeless.

What if I'm too old for this?! What if I do find something I want to do and inevitably just get crushed again? Can I really start over somewhere new, at the bottom? But then, I'm literally never going to be any younger than I am in this moment. Current me is the youngest possible me I have left.

I sit back, ready to quit already. I mean . . . I looked at *five different job listings*. I basically deserve a trophy.

I get up to go, when I am suddenly struck by fear. Fear is not an unusual sensation for me, but this feels different. The fear of not finding anything I want to do is nauseating. The fear of finding something I want to do but being rejected again is crushing. But, for the first time, the fear of not even *trying* to do all those things hits me harder. If I walk out of here, where am I going to go? I don't have my familiar, easy routine and comforting pay cheque. I don't have a place to live. I don't even have any mates.

I have no other options but to sit back down and keep looking. So I do.

For the rest of the afternoon I languorously comb the internet. Five or six times I end up arbitrarily switching seats with some teenagers doing their A-level homework. But somehow I get more done in one day than I have in seven years. I can't remember focusing so much since final uni exams.

I trawl noticeboards for jobs. Any jobs. I take tests. SO MANY TESTS.

What job should you do?
What skills do you have?
What's your personality type?
What scent are you?
What flavour are you?
What are you like?
What do you want?
Who are you?

IF I KNEW THE ANSWER TO ANY OF THESE THINGS I WOULDN'T BE HERE.

About sixty per cent of the quizzes tell me I should be a waitress. One tells me I am a 'seahorse' and have 'deep, magical qualities' that might make me suited to a role in hypnotherapy, conveyancing or sports coaching.

One quiz gives me results in the form of a voice recording. The soothing female speaker spends a long, painful fifteen minutes outlining every detail of the problem. About how I cannot get on the right path because I wouldn't recognise that path if I was on it. About how I can't find work I enjoy because I don't know *what* I enjoy. About how I don't know what role would suit me because I don't know myself. It likens me to a fly trapped inside a house, slamming against a window over and over, able to see the outside world but not access it, not moving direction but repeatedly bashing its head against the glass and hoping for a different result. About how I've been that fly for so long I'm almost scared to try a different escape route because not trying and failing is easier to take than trying and failing.

Yes, I think. *Yes. This is me.* Finally, someone knows what I'm talking about. I am SEEN.

Then it says, 'so how do you break the curse of the trapped fly?'

Yes, I think. Yes, yes, TELL ME!

The voice proceeds to recommend that I stop trying to see the end goal and 'take small steps'. It suggests I use 'measurable methods with specific aims' rather than daydreaming.

Yes, yes, go on . . . ! I wait eagerly for clarification of these small steps and specific aims.

It then recommends daily high-intensity workouts, breathing exercises and buying their step-by-step career guide.

Is that IT?!

It spends fifteen minutes ripping me to shreds, tearing down what little self-esteem I have remaining, comparing me to an insect with a brain the size of a poppy seed, and then suggests BREATHING EXERCISES?

The sad thing is I felt so low after listening to it, I probably would have bought the career guide if it wasn't priced at £74.99 and that wasn't such a large percentage of what I have left in my bank account.

I even watch motivational videos. But when I get to a guy dissecting a grapefruit by segment in order to demonstrate the components of a satisfying career, I decide enough is enough.

I leave the library feeling quite broken and no less clueless than at the start of the day. All I achieved was applying for one job that I liked the look of and am definitely not going to get, because I am not at *all* qualified. But I do feel better, because I did *something*.

It's five o'clock and the sky is still light. The days are getting longer. Usually that's a comfort, but at the moment I'd really rather my days be as short as possible. Still, I suppose I shouldn't complain in case I have to sleep on a bench tonight. It's a very real possibility.

What do I do now?

I walk around the park in circles for a while. Past the swings where Mum used to push me. Past the tree I once insisted on climbing and ripped my trousers on, then refused to come down for two hours because my butt was showing. Past the bench where I used to make out with Wotsits Walter (he really liked Wotsits and his name made for convenient alliteration). Past the bushes where Angie, Dami and I tried our first joint. Past the bin that Dami threw up in afterwards. There are memories in every corner of this park. I sit down on a bench and think, *in ten years I'll probably look back on this as 'where I sat and moped after alienating everybody I loved and ruining my life'*.

A group of kids playing behind the bench flee when they see me sit down. They can probably sense my inability to set myself bitesize goals blocking my path to my ideal role in hypnotherapy and are running off to play nearer someone more aspirational.

I stare across the grass and up at the clouds. Only the other day I was detonating everything, deliriously certain that I wouldn't be around to clean up the mess. It's like trying to clean up a nuclear spill with a mop and bucket.

There's so much to think about. How much can one brain handle? I try to separate one issue at a time and work out a plan for each. Leila: was never supposed to be in my life and we'll both be better off not knowing each other. Dad: now that Leila's gone, I can keep the door closed on him like I intended. Mum: Ugh. Can I come back to her later? Okay, that's family.

Max: *might* still have feelings for me? I just need to find out? Somehow, without humiliating myself in case he was just sniffing my head because he likes the smell of my shampoo? Fran: Ughh. I hate that Fran is now crossing my mind! She's not real . . . She's a unicorn! Unicorns don't have *feelings*. They gallivant across the world doing charity work and saving children and they dress in edgy wide-leg jeans and crop tops to make others feel like lesser beings but they DON'T HAVE FEELINGS.

Dami and Angie: can't stay mad forever. I just need to apologise.

I can't believe I'm even thinking this but, as I sit on this bench, contemplating the tangled web of hurt feelings I've weaved amongst my loved ones, one of the motivational videos I watched this afternoon crosses my mind. It said the best way to get things done was to 'do the thing you're dreading the most, first'. Okay so the guy who made it also suggested I 'show self-compassion by hugging myself twice a day' so he's clearly not entirely sane, but that particular piece of advice did resonate.

I get up from my sad little bench. It's time to talk to Angie.

Chapter Twenty

The next day, I walk up the road to Angie's house feeling like I might vomit. I tried to call her last night but she didn't pick up, so I spent another night on Max's sofa – Fran texted me to say she'd be out for the evening – and decided to just show up today.

She still hasn't reached out to me at all, which is unfathomably unlike her. But I'm hoping that she'll be more open to my apology now she's had a couple of nights to cool off and because Jacob won't be around. I know for a fact Jacob plays football on Saturday afternoons.

I reach her front door.

I breathe in. And out. Breathe in. And out.

Angie's never been one to keep her anger inside, so I'm expecting a full-on *EastEnders*-style confrontation, but once she lets it out the storm usually passes pretty quickly. I just need to get it over with.

With a shaky hand I knock.

I hear footsteps.

'Hi.' I cough, as she opens the door. Not for the first time this week I'm highly aware of my Live. Laugh. Love. T-shirt. Angie's in her tracksuit bottoms and cropped top that shows off her toned stomach. Her make-up is perfect, as usual, even though she's probably been working out.

She looks at me like I've seen her looking at kebabs, or unkempt facial hair, and steps aside. 'Come in.'

I enter her pristine hallway. Everything is white, cream or beige in Angie's house. Apart from the special navy 'Becky blanket' she gives me to sit on since the Unfortunate Pesto Incident.

'Ang, before we talk about anything, please can I borrow some clothes? My case is still at my mum's and . . .' I gesture to my T-shirt.

She nods and I gratefully rush upstairs to her room and pull out a normal top to change into, before coming back down to the kitchen.

Angie is already at the espresso machine that I can never remember how to use, with two giant mugs. I sit down on a stool at the island in the middle of the room and take in the gleaming grey tiles and standing column wine rack she agonised for hours over when she moved in. At Angie's I always feel like a kid visiting their posh babysitter's house. She and Jacob bought this place together; he's a finance bro, so pretty loaded.

Angie presses a few buttons and the machine whirs. The comforting sound of hot coffee pouring fills the room.

'No Jacob?' I check, just to make sure.

She shakes her head. 'No. You can relax.'

Thank God. I'm unsure how I can ever be in the same room as him again.

Angie passes my beverage across the counter but doesn't sit down opposite me. She remains standing on the other side of the island.

'Dim,' she says and the bright, stark lighting softens. She

puts her mug to her lips and takes a delicate sip. I do the same and swish it around my mouth, which has gone dry with nerves.

'Angie,' I say, finally. 'I'm sorry.'

As soon as the words are out of my lips I know just how much I mean them. I've never meant anything so earnestly. Now I'm here, I allow myself to feel just how desperate I am for her forgiveness.

'Sorry for what?' Angie asks.

'Err, the letter,' I reply. Does she have amnesia?

'Yes, but why? Sorry for what you said because you didn't mean it? Sorry because you could have phrased it differently? Sorry you wrote it in a letter instead of saying it to my face?' She delivers the lines coolly and I can tell she's been practising them in her head. I wish I'd been more prepared with my answer.

'Er . . . all of the above,' I croak. My mouth is dry again already. I take another slurp of coffee.

'So you didn't mean it?' She folds her arms. 'You *don't* think Jacob is a creep?'

Uhhhhh. Oh God. 'No?' It comes out like a question.

'His presence doesn't inspire the urge to wax off your own eyebrows?'

'No.' I feel a smirk coming on. *For the love of God, whatever you do, do NOT laugh.* I bite the inside of my cheek.

'Not even slightly convincing, Becky.' Angie shakes her head.

'Okay. I guess . . . I meant it a *bit*,' I admit.

'Say that then,' she says. 'Say what you mean. Lying hasn't got either of us very far, has it?'

This conversation feels very Angie and yet not at all like Angie at the same time. I'm used to her being a bit brutal, but something has shifted. Her snark has dissipated. Her comebacks aren't as caustic. I notice that behind her make-up she has dark circles.

'Is everything okay, Angie?' I ask.

She takes a breath. 'Jacob's gone,' she answers.

'Gone?' I repeat dumbly. 'Like, gone out?'

'*Gone* gone,' she clarifies.

'What do you mean?!'

'He's moving out.'

I nearly fall off my chair. I was *not* expecting to hear this. Angie's obsessed with Jacob and their life together. They've been a couple since forever.

'What happened?!' I press.

'I found out some stuff,' she answers vaguely. *Some stuff.* Angie rubs her eyes and my stomach twists into a huge, lumpen knot. She looks knackered. I've daydreamed about them breaking up a million times and imaginary me has always clicked my heels together with glee. But seeing my beautiful, headstrong friend struggling is heartbreaking.

'Do you want to talk about it?' I continue. 'I mean, we don't have to.' I realise I may have lost the right to ask too many questions.

'Well, it was because of your letter, really,' she says.

Even though I think this will be a good thing for her, my heart sinks in the knowledge I've caused her pain. I shuffle uncomfortably in my seat.

'The night you came over . . .' she carries on. She still

hasn't sat down. 'All I could think about when I went to bed was how mad I was at you and how unreasonable you were. Jacob was all, *don't let her get in your head, babe*, and saying you were just jealous of me.'

I know Jacob is an asshole, but I can't help but feel a wave of indignation at him accusing me of being envious. I can't fathom anything worse than spending every waking moment thinking about house decorations and grown-up dinner parties and whether there are enough polenta appetisers for the vegans you had to invite but don't really like or how far away to sit Pervy Uncle Bill from Booby Aunt Carol.

'But . . . I don't know. I couldn't stop thinking about what you'd said. And I couldn't stop thinking about how if you thought it, whether everyone else secretly thought it as well. When I woke up, something possessed me to look at his phone. I know it's a bit, well . . .' she adds hurriedly, like I'm going to judge her. 'But like, with what you'd said . . .'

'Ang,' I reassure her. 'I get it.'

She looks relieved. 'Well, anyway . . . I found some weird messages from his friend Mark.'

I frown. 'This has taken an unexpected turn.'

She laughs. 'I *wish* he was screwing Mark. No. The messages didn't sound like Mark at *all*. They had kisses and were talking about missing files. He and Mark don't even work in the same department.'

'Oh,' I say.

'Yeah. He'd saved some girl from the office as "Mark" on his phone. There was nothing incriminating, exactly. But . . .

they'd been to the pub when he told me he was working late. And the messages only started three days before, so he'd been deleting them.' In true Angie style her voice remains steady and confident, but she can barely keep her disappointment out of it.

'God,' I say. 'What then?'

'I asked him about it.'

'What did he say?'

'Oh, you know. That he'd saved a colleague called Delith as "Mark" so I wouldn't get unnecessarily jealous if her name flashed up . . . That he didn't mention the pub for the same reason. All the stuff I'd been expecting him to say, really.' Angie swirls her coffee. 'Then, I don't know. I felt so confused. Like, is he sleeping with someone called Delith? Or is she really just an innocent co-worker and he didn't want to worry me?'

Angie forcefully places her mug down on the counter, getting more wound up as she talks.

'But anyway, when I didn't immediately accept his answer, he changes tack, starts almost blaming me. Saying there was nothing weird about his behaviour and that I was just as mental as you.'

I snort. Jacob is *unbelievable.*

Angie shakes her head. 'Anyway, he went off to work and I thought about it all day. And the next day. I'm not convinced he's been banging Delith in the office toilets or anything. Maybe. Or maybe they really did just go to the pub. But, the more I thought about it, the more I thought maybe that's not even the main issue. The point is . . . how could I ever *know*? His immediate response was to gaslight me about it. I don't know . . . I had a really hard, honest look at our relationship, and asked myself whether I could trust him. And the answer is no, I can't. And I asked myself, do I really want to live like that? And no, I don't. So when he came back last night I asked him to leave.'

We're silent for a moment. Angie's looking at the floor. It occurs to me that, for the first time, we may have used the word 'gaslight' correctly in a sentence. But now doesn't feel like the right time to point that out.

'Ang, you must be gutted,' I say. I can hardly believe she really asked Jacob to go . . . Because of my letter. It's not like I put those messages on his phone, but guilt gnaws at my stomach anyway. 'I'm sorry . . .' I begin, but Angie holds up her hand to cut me off.

'Don't be,' she says. 'It's good that this happened.' She sounds a bit like she's convincing herself, but in time I think she'll truly believe it.

I'm flooded with relief. Angie is okay. It's raw right now, but in the long run, everything that's happened will be for the best.

It all turned out all right. Angie will forgive me. Now we can start moving past it and everything will go back to . . .

'But what I'm still wondering, Becky,' Angie disrupts my train of thought, 'is why you sent that letter?'

I lean back in my chair, stumped. I wasn't expecting that question. Up until now I had thought this was going pretty well. She's annoyed at me, clearly, but the focus was all on Jacob. Angie seems sad but she seems content with her decision and with him being out of her life. For a second, just for a blissful, foolish second . . . I thought that might be it. No such luck.

'Why?' I repeat. 'Isn't it obvious?'

'Not really.' Angie folds her arms.

'Well . . . I've never trusted Jacob. I felt like you should know.'

'So you said it purely for *my* benefit?' Angie doesn't sound convinced.

I don't quite know what to say. I knew she'd be mad about the letter, I just wasn't expecting this particular line of questioning. 'Of course,' I insist. 'Why else would I?'

'I don't know, it just seems odd. You could have spoken to me about it. Why write a letter like this?'

'What about all the stuff you just said?!' I can feel my voice rising an octave. 'About his secret messages from "Mark"?!'

'Yeah. But you don't get let off the hook because things *happen* to have worked out. What if you'd stirred the shit for nothing?'

'Well, it's still better that you're warned, surely?!' Another octave.

Angie steps across the kitchen, opens a drawer and retrieves a little piece of paper. My stomach plummets.

YET AGAIN THE LLAMAS COME BACK TO HAUNT ME.

She unfurls it and begins reading. 'Dear Angela. Do you remember how grossed out you were by the alien in *The Thing* when I made you watch it? How you said if it touched you, you would shower until you had no skin left? Well, that's how I feel about Jacob.' She folds the paper back up and looks at me. My face heats up. I thought it was funny when I wrote it. This time it doesn't sound so hilarious.

'Okay, maybe my delivery left a little something to be desired . . .'

'You can say that again, Becky. It doesn't exactly sound like a concerned friend. It sounds . . .' Her voice cracks with exhaustion. 'It sounds spiteful.'

I splutter. 'I mean, I *was* concerned—'

'And why now?' she interrupts. 'I mean, you could have chosen any time over the last eight years to bring this up. Why now?'

'I thought I was going to die,' I squeak. It sounds so lame.

'Right, sure.' Angie rolls her eyes. 'You thought you were going to die, uh huh, even though you've literally never believed in tarot before. Come on, Becky.'

'I did believe it!' I protest.

'I think you did, in a way,' she concedes. 'But I think, on some level, that you *wanted* to believe it. I think you were looking for an excuse to send these letters. You're angry with us. About Dami's wedding. About my business. For having jobs we enjoy and relationships we care about and homes we take pride in.'

Does she think I'm that petty?

'I don't care that you have jobs, and partners, and homes,' I snap. 'It's that you never stop *talking* about your stupid jobs and partners and homes!'

'There it is.' Angie's mouth twists like she's tasted something unpleasant. 'Stupid. Our lives are stupid.'

'I didn't say that, I . . .' I stumble over my words. She's distorting everything. All they've talked about for months now is Dami's wedding and Angie's new bathroom and somehow I'm the bad friend? 'Do you think it's easy for me, listening to you going on for hours about floral arrangements, and renovations, and business plans, when I don't even have a relationship that's lasted more than a few dates . . .'

Angie sighs. 'Oh please. Don't get me started on *that*.'

'What?! Go on. Enlighten me. What does Angie, someone who's never even had to use a dating app, have to say about my romantic life?' I don't know why I'm encouraging her. I don't want her to say any more hurtful things. But I'm fully engaged in self-destructive mode now and I can't stop.

'Romantic life?' Angie scoffs. 'You don't *date*, Becky. You go out with strange people and have a terrible time and come back with a funny story for Max. Or if you do meet someone you like, you don't allow it to develop. Like Vera. I mean, why did you go at all? Why waste your time *and* Vera's time?'

Even though I'm wounded by her words I can't help but crack a smile at the name 'Vera' being used in a serious context. 'What . . . should I not try?' I defend.

'You're not trying,' Angie mutters. 'I mean, on paper you're trying, but you're not really trying.'

I take a breath. God, I hate her sometimes. She's talking to me like I'm a child. *Not trying?!* Is she serious?

'What?!' My voice is pure disbelief. 'I've been on loads of dates! How many do you want me to go on? Should I get one of those bots that sends out automated replies?!'

Ugh. Angie has NO idea. She thinks I've not got anywhere because I'm not *trying* . . .

'You used to,' she says. 'But you barely go on any dates anymore. When you do, you expect it won't go well, so it doesn't.'

Is she right? Did I stop trying? In amongst all the shit dates, the let-downs, the disappointments, did I stop opening myself up to the possibility of letting someone in and start going through the motions?

No. She's *not* right. I go on fewer dates now, sure, and with less enthusiasm than my early twenties, yes, but I still go. This is ludicrous. 'You're saying I haven't met anyone on purpose? I'm alone on *purpose*?'

'I'm saying, it's hard out there, and you gave up. You don't give anyone decent a chance. You'd much rather the date was shit so you could make a spectacle of yourself for Max's benefit.'

This is insane. Angie has well and truly lost it. Months of staring too hard at The Folder have eaten away her brain. 'Well, by the sounds of it, Max is the only person in the world who actually likes me,' I say.

'Oh here we go,' says Angie. 'It's always *you and Max against the world* and *he's the only one who understands you*, like I'm some different species because I have a mortgage. Well, guess what, Becky? So. Does. Max.'

I don't understand what she's implying, but I know I'm not going to like it. 'So?'

'Max has a job he cares about!' Angie waves her arms around. 'Max bought a flat. Max has *moved in with his girlfriend*. Compare me and Max on paper, and you and Max, and me and him come out looking a *lot* more similar than the two of you.'

Resistance flares up in my stomach. My immediate response is *she doesn't know what she's saying. She doesn't get it*. She and Max are not in the same universe.

'Who you are is about more than those things. It's about a mindset, Angie. Sure, Max has a flat, but he didn't spend an entire week choosing which lasagne dish would best go with the kitchen counter.'

Angie folds her arms. 'Oh, because you're so much fun, and I'm so boring, right, Becky?'

'That's not what I . . .' I don't finish because, yes, that is a bit what I meant. 'I just meant that you don't have to agonise over every little decision. Sometimes can a lasagne dish just be a fucking lasagne dish?'

Angie tilts her head to one side. 'And Fran moving in? Do you think Max thought about that decision?'

'No,' I say quickly. 'Not properly. I mean, maybe a bit. But he's impulsive . . .'

She's got me. She's rattled me. She knows it, too. She sees in my eyes that her point has finally hit home. No amount of denial, no matter how hard I've been trying, can cover up the fact that somewhere along the line Max did decide to make a colossal commitment to another woman.

'You're the only one who's been acting like a kid, Becky,' she says finally. 'Just you.'

Her use of the word 'kid' reminds me of the first card in the tarot reading that started all this. Six of Cups. *Overgrown. She's wearing a fairytale costume that no longer fits, living in the past.*

'If you don't change,' Angie carries on. 'You're going to alienate everyone worth having in your life for good.'

It's the worst thing Angie's ever said to me. My throat begins to close up. She must be wrong, she must have it all wrong. Except, everything she's saying about my dating behaviour is eerily similar to what Margaret and Ted said about me at work, and they were totally right.

I'm too choked up to speak. It feels like I've swallowed a golf ball, but I can't think of anything else to say to defend myself anyway. I put my mug down, pick up my bag and head to the door. Angie doesn't stop me.

Chapter Twenty-One

I stand on the street outside Angie's house, trying not to cry. I tell myself that she's not right, that she's got everything twisted. I fire off a message to Max, looking for validation.

> You won't believe what Angie just said to me

I pause, wondering how much of the conversation I can relay without including any of the stuff about him.

> She implied that I am jealous of her lasagne dish

Not exactly, but close enough.

> She is dead to me
>
> DEAD
>
> We are over. Finished. We will never speak again!!
>
> . . . Please reply soon because I am quickly running out of friends

I'm not sure why, but I get on the tube. I have no idea

where I'm going. Without thinking, I head to the Piccadilly line. Maybe I'll finally ride it all the way to the end and learn what's in Cockfosters.

As I sit aimlessly on the train, watching people get on and off around me, all with places to go and jobs to do and people to meet, my argument with Angie plays on a loop in my mind. Each time I find some new part of it to obsess over.

I'm not sure how long I've been on the train staring into space for when my phone buzzes in my pocket. It's Max. I'm desperately relieved at the sight of his name. I get off at the next station so I can have consistent wifi, press the green button and cradle the phone to my ear.

'Becks?'

'Max.' I lean against a wall.

'Where are you?'

'Uhhh . . .' I open my eyes and look around. 'Arnos Grove?'

'Where the fuck is that?'

'Uhh . . .'

'Why don't you go back to the flat?'

'Because Fran's around today and I really didn't want to impose. Honestly, it's okay, thank you so much for everything, but I'll find somewhere else.'

I expect him to tell me to go back to his place, that I'm being ridiculous, that Fran doesn't mind, that it's no imposition. But he says, 'Come here.'

I close my eyes. Am I dreaming? Being at a random station in the middle of North London makes this conversation feel even more surreal. 'Come *here*? You mean . . . Paris?'

'Yeah.'

I splutter. 'I mean. I don't really have the money . . .'

'I'll get you a ticket.'

'Max, that's generous but . . . I can't accept that.'

'Ngeggggh. Sure you can. Work are paying for my accommodation and food, so everything else is free. You can stay with me. I'll sleep on the sofa.'

Max is such a good friend. The *best*. He's always there when I'm having a shit time, distracting me and looking after me. But can I really just . . . go to Paris?

'It sounds like you've had a rough day,' he carries on when I don't say anything. 'Come on. We'll have fun. Bitch about Angie over some snails.'

I laugh. My gut instinct is *no, this is wild, who does this?* I have next to zero funds and no job and I'm hopping on a train to France? It's irresponsible, it's reckless. I can practically feel my mother's judgement breathing down my neck. But then the freeing thought hits me . . . *she won't know where I am*. No one will. No one else except Max *cares* where I am.

'I don't know . . .' I say. 'I was finally going to see Cockfosters.'

Max laughs. 'No one sees Cockfosters unless they live in Cockfosters. You can't just go around flouting sacred London rules.'

I smile. 'Okay,' I say. 'Okay. Yeah. I'll be there.' There's nowhere I should be, nothing I need to do, no one I owe anything to.

'I'll send you the tickets and the directions to the hotel. Keep an eye on your emails.'

Max hangs up and I stare at my phone. Did we really just have that conversation? Is this really happening?

I can't help the little voice whispering at the back of my

mind... Is he asking me purely as a friend or is this a romantic invitation? A little part of me dares to hope the letter has made him see the light and he's broken up with Fran.

My head is spinning with logistics. I don't even have my clothes... Or my passport?

Shit. My passport. Definitely going to need that. But everything is at Mum's. There's no way she'll let me be so irresponsible...

Then I shake myself. What sort of self-respecting adult turns down a free trip to Paris with the love of their life because they're too afraid to ask their Mum for their passport? I don't have to have her permission. Even if I'm not dying tomorrow, I am *not* going to cower in a corner and let my life pass me by anymore. I begin the journey home.

When I arrive outside, I wonder about the etiquette here. Can I let myself in? I have my keys, but technically I don't live here anymore. I guess I have to ring the bell?

I ring the bell. I already know Mum will be startled. She thinks anyone arriving after 5 p.m. is a burglar.

'Hello?' Her suspicious voice sounds over the intercom. 'Who is it?'

'Mum, don't worry... It's me.'

There's a shuffling. The intercom clicks off. For a moment I think she's going to ignore me and leave me on the doorstep but then I see her big black boot and crutches appear through the window. She slowly makes her way to the front door and opens it.

I step inside. The familiar smell of home hits me like a comforting blanket and I breathe in deeply. I can hardly believe that just over a week ago I still lived here.

We both don't say anything for a moment. Mum's got her arms folded to keep her big cardigan wrapped around her.

'Well,' she says eventually. 'I'm not happy with you, but there are clean towels in the bathroom and crumpets in the freezer. Why don't we talk in the morning?'

It takes me a second to compute what she's talking about, then I realise . . . *She thinks I've come back*.

'Oh, no, Mum,' I say quickly. 'I'm just here for my stuff.'

Her face drops. She looks crestfallen, but she pulls it back. 'Oh,' she says. 'Fine.'

'I thought I wasn't *allowed* to stay here?' I remind her. Only Mum would say I couldn't come home and then get annoyed with me for not coming home.

'Well, I'm not going to leave my only child on the street, am I?' She tuts.

No. I guess not. I suppose I knew on some level that if it really came to it, Mum would let me back in. I knew deep down that I was the one staying away.

'I need my passport, too,' I say, knowing it's back in the safekeeping drawer after instructing Dami and Ang to replace it.

'Whatever for?' Mum raises her eyebrows.

'I . . .' I start panicking, scrabbling for an explanation. Then I remind myself I don't *have* to tell her anything. I don't live here anymore. And even if I did, I'm a grown woman and really, we both know Mum needs to stop tracking my every move. 'I just want it,' I finish. It feels so wrong, but so good.

Mum's face tightens but she doesn't say anything else. She goes to the drawer where we store all our important bits and pieces and I take my cue to head upstairs.

My bedroom is just as I left it a few days ago. I take a moment to look around the room. My garish yellow walls, my *Labyrinth* poster, my albums, my fluffy toys. Every relic of Becky through the ages stares back at me and I can't work out if they're drawing me in or warding me away.

It's quite convenient that I've got a suitcase ready and waiting to go. I pull it out from under the bed and think fondly of Dami and Angie shoving it under here for me to hide it from my Mum.

Not wanting to linger too long in my room, I pull the suitcase to the door. I turn around for one last look and stare longingly at my bed. I mean, I don't *have* to go. I could tell Max it's too late, I changed my mind . . . Maybe I could even go tomorrow? I could just tuck up in my bed and . . .

My phone beeps. It's Max with my tickets. My train leaves in three hours.

That's that, then.

Downstairs Mum is waiting by the door. I know it's killing her to not ask where I'm heading. As I leave I pull her into a big, deep hug. She's stiff at first but then she softens and pats my back.

'I love you, Mum,' I say. Then, still half-regretting leaving my bed behind, I step out into the night and begin my journey to King's Cross.

Chapter Twenty-Two

On the train journey I am a mess. I'm so hyped and jumpy that I buy food and I can barely eat any of it. I just pick at my bread roll until it looks like it's been ravaged by a bird. When the guy comes around with the bin, I avoid looking him in the eye lest he remember my face as one who wastes pasta.

Later on, I spill my water all over myself. I try to read a book but my eyes are just scanning the page. I try listening to music but everything is too noisy. In the end, I just stare out the window.

I try to calm down by telling myself that I'm reading too much into it. That this is just a friend visit, that of course Max hasn't broken up with Fran, that he just feels bad for me and didn't want to impose on Fran and he felt less weird inviting me to hang out than offering to pay for me to stay somewhere alone. Maybe we'll just have a normal evening getting pissed in the bar, except we'll be in France rather than England. Really, it's not THAT far. And everyone speaks English anyway. It's *basically* like going to Birmingham.

Oh God. Or what if he wants to tell me he's thought about it and it's Fran that he wants? That he's sorry but he thinks we should have some distance? Maybe he wants to be noble by telling me to my face or something? This sort of situation is precisely why I should have been squashed under some poorly constructed scaffolding by now.

Except, deep down I know something has shifted. I know that hug meant something. If he didn't want me he wouldn't have held me like that. If he was going to reject me then it would make no sense to invite me to a different country to tell me.

Whatever happens, by sending those letters I've laid my cards out on the table and changed everything. We can't go back.

I'm still nervous when I step off the train, but I'm instantly swept away by the city waiting for me outside. It's not a world away from London; a big, grey European city, beautiful buildings, busy Parisians and tourists hurrying past. But the atmosphere in the air is something else. There's a man playing the accordion right outside the station. I'm probably imagining it but I feel like I can smell crepes. I hear an old couple shouting at each other in French and smile.

I begin the walk to Max's hotel along the Seine and it's so, so pretty. I stop for a moment, gazing across the river, breathing in the crisp, night air and letting the unfamiliar beauty of a different city settle over me.

I haven't left the country in years. I don't remember the last time I travelled with friends. Angie, Dami and I used to go somewhere exciting on the cheap every year until we were in our mid-twenties and then the trips dropped off. Angie and Dami started saving for other things: houses, cars, weddings. If they were going to have a trip somewhere, they'd prioritise going away with their partners rather than me. Travelling alone never even occurred to me until Bali. I let the lack of having someone to see the world with stop me from seeing it.

Paying London rent, it was difficult to afford it anyway. Then, when I moved back in with Mum, I was supposed to be saving for a flat . . . Even though that felt like it was never going to happen, and probably, I might as well have spent my money on an experience that meant something to me instead of trying to keep up with my bougie friends. I make a promise to myself, there on the Seine, that even though Bali didn't work out, I'll make other plans.

I drag my suitcase along the dark, cobbled streets. It's nearly two in the morning. This whole thing is surreal. I imagine what Angie and Dami would say if they could see me. If Max hasn't broken up with Fran then they'd probably shake their heads in pity that I went all the way to France for a reminder of my friend-zone status. If he has broken up with Fran, Dami would probably say it was 'romantic but unhinged' and Angie would deem it 'a laborious booty call' and say that 'I must be hard up if I'm willing to do international travel for sex'. I can't help but feel that, either way, they'd both have encouraged me to stay in the UK, but I quickly bury that thought. I'm here now.

Max's hotel is cute. It's white with rows of traditional Parisian shutters. There's an archway with a revolving door surrounded by planters and lanterns. Instead of going in to ask for him at reception, I loiter on the corner and call him.

'Hello?' Max answers.

'*Max. I'm outside.*'

He laughs. 'Ah, sweet. Why are you whispering?'

'*. . . I don't know.*'

He laughs again. 'It's the first floor, room twenty-four. See you in a sec.'

I start rolling my suitcase through the lobby towards the lift, with my head down. I know I'm allowed to enter a hotel late at night with no questions asked, and no one on reception knows who I am or cares, but somehow I feel like a teenager sneaking into a boy's room and hiding from his parents.

When I get to Max's room I take a huge breath and knock on the door. He predictably answers wearing a hotel dressing gown with a bottle of wine in hand.

'Becky, you made it!'

I instantly relax at the sight of him. The familiar in the unfamiliar.

'I did,' I say lamely.

'I'm impressed.' He welcomes me in. 'I must say I had my doubts. Thought I'd probably lose you somewhere along the Channel.'

He's trying to gently sound out whether I regret coming. Is he regretting asking me?

'That would have been difficult once I was on the train, given there were no stops. I guess I could have flung myself out the window.'

'It was that bad with Angie?' he jokes.

I wheel my suitcase inside and the door closes behind us. The room is cute and cosy and we're in pretty close proximity. My eye flits over the bed. And the sofa, which looks pretty small. Is he actually intending to sleep there? He'd have to curl up into a ball. I perch on the edge of it and take off my jacket.

'It was that bad.'

'Well, I'm glad I could offer you refuge.' He sits down next to me, opens the wine and takes a swig. Then he passes it to me.

'What happened?'

'It was awful.' I take a huge gulp of wine. 'You know I can't handle confrontation. Remember how upset I was when Margaret accused me of taking her stapler?'

Max smiles. 'You *did* take her stapler.'

'Yeah, and she should have done the normal, decent thing and pretended not to notice. Anyway, I'm traumatised for life.'

I'm making light of it, but I'm genuinely shaken by my fight with Angie. Every time I think about it I feel sick.

'What did she say?' Max puts his hand on my knee. It's distracting.

'Uhhhh . . .' I say, unsubtly looking down at his hand. He doesn't seem fazed.

'She . . .' I try to get my brain to connect with my mouth but it's hard with the hand-on-knee situation. I can feel my vagina reacting. Thank God I'm not a man and he can't tell. 'She said that I think she's boring because she likes kitchenware a lot.'

Max grins. 'She got you there.'

'She said . . .' I swallow. My heart starts hammering as I think of all the things she said about Max and how to phrase them. 'That I don't give the people I date a chance. That I'm subconsciously alone on purpose, or something.'

'Are you?' Max stares at me intensely. I look away and take a very long drink from the bottle. When I look back he still hasn't turned away.

He takes the bottle from my hand and leans over me to put

it on the table behind us. There's tension. So much tension. It feels bizarre to be hanging out with Max in this way. There's always *some* kind of sexual tension when we're together, obviously, but safe sexual tension hidden behind a very big wall that neither of us would ever climb. Now the wall has come crashing down and I'm looking it right in the face.

If there was any doubt left in my mind that he read the letter, there's no doubt now. But this isn't the outcome I expected. I expected him to awkwardly back off for a while. We'd avoid each other until I was over it and maybe he'd got a pet with Fran and then we'd safely and respectfully become friends again when I could bear to look him in the eye. I didn't expect him to break up with his girlfriend and invite me to Paris.

How many times have I imagined sleeping with Max? How many times have I fantasized about him throwing me down on a bed or onto the floor or over a table? How many times has he followed me into some public toilets at an event because he can't keep his hands off me? How many times have we secretly done it with people in the next room? How many times did he show up at We Work, You Win to strip naked in Margaret's office and put on one of her camel fur hats? (As a joke, not because I'm into that.)

Now we're in Paris. Alone. In a hotel room. And it isn't in my head, it's real.

Max leans in and kisses me. Muscle memory takes over and it is the *strangest* feeling, because I remember kissing him years ago. The feel of his skin and the pressure of his lips all come rushing back and in one way it's like no time has passed, yet everything's changed, everything's different, this is nothing like it was then. It's not like my memories and it's not like any of the times in my head either. This is its own bizarre reality.

We keep kissing, getting used to each other's movements. Half the time I'm thinking more *about* what we're doing than focusing on the action itself. *I'm kissing Max. This is happening right now. Max is touching my arm. Max is unbuttoning my shirt.* It's almost like I'm watching it happen rather than taking part in it. I mentally shake myself. *Stop it. It's finally happening and you're MISSING IT. Pay attention, Becky.*

I'm topless now and so is Max. We break for breath, taking in each other's bodies. He kisses me again. I am determined to stop overthinking and be present in every single second of this.

I close my eyes, running my hands up and down his back. He presses his chest against mine and my arms are all full of him and then I'm lying back on the bed and he's on top of me. This is Max. *Max.* My Max. Max is mine. He's always been mine. This is right. This is good. This is the way it was always supposed to be. What have the last five years been about anyway? They were stupid, stupid years. Wasted years. Years we will look back on and wonder what the hell we were doing.

He's kissing my ear and biting the lobe. His hand is trailing down my stomach to my jeans. The button pops apart and he pulls on the zip, kissing down my neck. I wonder if he did that to Fran's neck?

My eyes spring open.
Fran?

NO, FRAN. You are not welcome here! You are definitively not invited! Get out! Get out get out get out!

I close my eyes again, trying to clear Fran from my mind, but suddenly she and her stupid dungarees are imprinted on my eyelids. What's she doing right now, as her recent ex-boyfriend unbuttons my jeans? Sitting at home in his flat, what had just become *their* flat, thinking about him? Trying to read the latest Donna Tartt novel but feeling too upset? Maybe messaging her auntie?

This is all Leila's fault for humanising her.

I open my eyes again and send up a silent apology to her. *Look, I'm sorry Fran, I really am. I feel bad that you were caught up between two people who belong together but because of stupid pride were playing games and dancing around each other for so long. But you'll meet someone else. Another charity worker or something. Someone much nicer than Max. Max is not that good a person. It never would have worked out between you anyway. You were always too good for him. Max is kind of irresponsible and pretends to be poor when he's privileged and makes fun of people and . . . doesn't seem that upset about breaking up with his long-term girlfriend?*

My kisses become less fervent, my heart sinking as a horrible option that I hadn't considered nudges its way into my consciousness. *No. Don't be stupid. Of course he did. He wouldn't be doing this if he . . .*

'What's up, Becky?' Max sits up and looks at me with searching eyes. Shit. He noticed my head was elsewhere.

'I'm fine,' I say breathlessly.

'Are you sure? You seem distracted.'

I'm ruining it. I'm killing the mood. This is the moment I've been waiting for. This is what I've wanted forever and I am officially fucking it up. *Don't fuck this up, Becky.*

'I'm fine, honestly,' I promise. 'Are you? You good?'

'Yeah,' he says, sitting back. 'I'm good.'

But he isn't. He's not looking at me and he's pulled away.

'It's just . . . I . . . Is this okay?' I ask. 'You only just broke up with Fran.'

He's silent and not making any eye contact. Through the window I hear the sound of some French people walking down the street laughing. And I know, then, that I have misunderstood. He didn't break up with her.

'Oh,' is all I can think to say.

'I am going to speak to her,' he replies quietly. 'Obviously. I just haven't, yet.'

He cheated on her.

No. That's not fair. My mind scrambles to make his actions seem justifiable. He's not a *cheater* cheater. It's not like he'd go out to a random bar and have sex with just anyone. We're best friends. We're in love. We always have been. It's not proper cheating if it's fate, right? He *is* going to speak to her.

But reality has set in. We're now both thinking about Fran. Her name looms over the room unspoken, like Voldemort, and the moment has passed. I pick up my top – which is crumpled on the floor – and start getting dressed.

In the end, Max does sleep on the tiny sofa.

Chapter Twenty-Three

The next morning, I wake with a deep, painful longing to call my mother. I reach for my phone immediately, then stop myself. What would I say? Plus, I feel like somehow she'd be able to tell I wasn't in the country just by the sound of my voice.

Light is trickling in through the shutters but I have no concept of what time it is. After our heated moment last night we put our tops back on, drank wine and watched French TV, never again referring to said moment. Ostensibly, we hung out like we normally would, with a giant elephant sitting in between us. Max's jokes were a little try-hard. My laugh was a little forced. We went to sleep and Max pretended being crumpled up on the tiny sofa was comfortable.

Max is in the bathroom and I'm grateful for the second it gives me to collect myself before coming face to face with him. I hastily wipe the sleep out of my eyes and mentally prepare myself.

I can't believe . . . I came all the way to Paris and didn't even get an orgasm out of it because of my stupid conscience.

Why are you showing up now, Conscience? Where were you when I thought it was a great idea to copy Gemma Lee's maths exam in Year 12 and ended up getting stuck in the mathletes? Or when I was supposed to be babysitting little

Freddie Patterson and his parents came home to find him locked in his room while I made out with Fit John on their bed?

WHERE WERE YOU THEN?

But of course, I know that I was right to stop it. Even if on some level she must know it's over, given that it's clearly over for Max, it wouldn't be okay to do anything before he's spoken to her. There will be plenty of time for us once that's happened. We don't need to rush anything . . .

The toilet flushes. There's the sound of taps running and he emerges. He's already dressed, which makes me aware of how little I'm wearing.

'All right, Becky.' He flashes me a quick smile and moves towards his camera bag, crouching down to rummage for something.

'Are you off?' I ask.

'Yep, got to be on set in half an hour.'

'Cool.' I don't really know what to say. 'Big day?'

'Yuh.' He's still rummaging. 'What are you gonna do?'

'Oh . . . I'm not sure. Wander around. Buy a baguette. Stare at some French people, working out how to hold said baguette in a way that seems natural.'

'They'll love that.' Max laughs.

'What time do you think you'll be finished?'

'Not sure,' he says. Max has never been good at specific time commitments. I guess that's why being a photographer suits him. His schedule is all over the place and he's never quite certain how long a job is going to take. It's usually fine because he'll just message me for a drink on days that he finishes early enough and check whether I'm still in town. But the prospect of sitting around in a strange city with nothing to do but wait for him, without being sure what time he'll be able to meet me, feels different.

'Oh,' I say, wanting to pin him down but not wanting to seem like a nag.

'I'll message you later?' Max adds.

'Okay, yeah.' I smile. I'm being stupid. It's not like Max isn't telling me because he doesn't want to. How is he supposed to know?

I smile at how much we sound like a regular couple. It fades when I remind myself that we're not. We haven't been a couple in years and Max has a different girlfriend at home who he just moved in with. Guilt starts clawing its way into my stomach again. I wonder if Max is feeling guilty?

Ugh, shut up, Conscience. WE HAVE HEARD ENOUGH FROM YOU. It's fine. Nothing happened. He's going to speak to her when he gets back to the UK.

'All right then.' He stands up, hooking his bag over his shoulder. He hesitates before moving towards me. It's only for a second, but it's there. Max never likes to seem wrong-footed by anything but I can tell he's unsure how to behave around me, unsure whether to act like we're together or not. He leans over the bed and . . . pats me on the shoulder.

'See you, Becky.'

'Bye,' I reply quietly. He strides quickly out of the room.

Did he just . . . *pat me on the shoulder?*

The door closes and I am alone. I don't usually mind Max's inability to express himself. I pride myself on my ability to read him. But in this moment, sitting in my pyjamas in a hotel room in a different country with no one I can call, the fact that I have no idea what he's thinking leaves me feeling profoundly lonely.

What am *I* thinking?

I sit in the bed, trying to work it out. Only, it's difficult in the void of knowing how Max is feeling. If I knew he was planning on breaking up with Fran this evening and declaring his undying love for me then I'd be on top of the world. I'd do a little dance along the Seine. If I knew he was feeling confused or, worse, like inviting me here was a huge mistake . . . Well, then I'd probably want to fling myself *into* the Seine.

Oh God. Is that a possibility? That I'm a *mistake*? I replay every interaction between us this morning. He didn't wake me. I'd assumed it was because we went to bed late and he wanted to let me rest, but what if he was trying to avoid me? If I hadn't woken up would he have said goodbye or slipped out without a word? He wasn't holding eye contact . . . It was all brief, short glances. I'd figured he was preoccupied and focused on getting to his shoot, but what if he just couldn't bear to look at me – the giant, lumbering mistake lying erroneously in his bed? What if he only kissed me at all because he was confused by the letter but now he realises it's Fran he loves? Oh God.

I breathe. The kiss. He *kissed* me. I did not ask to come here . . . He invited me. Of course I wasn't a mistake. Mistakes are made with random people in a bar, or a colleague you barely know and drunkenly snog at the office Christmas party. You don't make *mistakes* with people you've known and loved for seven years.

He was hesitant, but of course he was; you're hardly going to start acting like a happy couple when you haven't broken up with your girlfriend yet, are you? That wouldn't be right. He must be feeling terrible, but of course he does. He might regret the *way* it happened, but it doesn't mean he will regret it happening. You can feel guilty about the way lots of things happen . . . like . . . buying a book from Amazon. I might hate myself for giving my money to Jeff Bezos but it doesn't mean I don't want the book?!

I think about last night. The way his lips pressed against mine hungrily, kissing softly and biting fiercely, his hands exploring foreign yet familiar territory. It was so natural.

That is . . . until it wasn't. But that's *completely* understandable under the circumstances. It will feel normal once he's broken up with Fran and we're not in this weird situation anymore.

It's okay, I tell myself. I am not The Other Woman. I met Max first, so, I categorically cannot be The Other Woman. I have always been here and he met Fran way after me. If anything *Fran* is The Other Woman. That's just how time works. And who are we to argue with the mighty nonspatial continuum measured in events that succeed one another from past through present to future?! Look, I don't make the rules.

I check my phone. Twenty minutes have passed since Max left. He hasn't messaged me. No one has. Not for the first time in the past week I *long* to hear what Angie and Dami would think. My fingers itch to tell them what's happened but, with the bitter aftertaste of my fight with Angie still lingering, I remind myself they don't want to hear from me right now.

I decide the best thing to do is not overthink the situation any more than I have done and try to just enjoy the day in Paris. I mean . . . I'm in *Paris*, after all.

I order a huge breakfast to the room. I get an omelette AND croissants because, why not? Thank you, Max's boss.

I get dressed and head out into the sunshine. I don't make a plan and just meander through the streets to see what I might stumble across. I find a quaint little bookshop and spend ages rifling through its shelves. I buy a coffee from a cute little café and rich, dark chocolate raspberry profiteroles from a chocolaterie. I window-shop all the fancy stores on the Champs-Elysées and wish I had enough money to buy something.

I start off having fun, or at least, I'm doing things that seem like they would be fun. But I can't help constantly checking my phone to see how much time has passed and whether Max has messaged me yet. My feet get tired from the constant walking, but I don't want to sit for too long in case I think too much. The day feels slow and time seems to inch by.

Then I begin to fluctuate wildly between feeling giddy, like I'm possibly having the time of my life, and feeling lower than the sewer rats running beneath the city. I am like an unmoored boat that's drifted out to sea, being battered around by feelings coming in random waves. I can't decide if I'm excited and free or pointless and lost.

At around four I sit down on a bench outside the Louvre beside a cluster of pigeons. It crosses my mind that things don't feel all that different here than they did two days ago, sitting on my childhood park bench beside London pigeons. Then I roll my eyes. Of course things are different . . . What is wrong with me? This is what I wanted. I am in Paris. With Max. Something finally happened with him, like it was always meant to. He's going to speak to Fran. I message him, 'Hey, do you think you'll be finished soon?'

But as the day drags on and Max still doesn't contact me, it gets harder and harder to hold onto that positivity.

Eventually, when it gets to 6 p.m. and Max still hasn't replied, I decide to head back to the hotel to get my things. It's starting to get dark and there's a chill in the air and I don't care if I'm in an exciting new city or not, I'm hungry and tired and lonely and bored.

When I find my way back, they won't let me in the room because I'm not on the booking and I don't have a key. It's a massive, humiliating hassle involving multiple staff and managers, but eventually someone is sent to the room to retrieve my case for me.

I walk super slowly to the station, checking my phone every five seconds. There's a faint ray of denial still glimmering. Maybe he got caught up? Maybe he left his phone somewhere and he can't message? Or it ran out of battery? He wouldn't leave me wandering around Paris alone for this long without a good reason, would he? Surely if he had a working phone on him he would at least keep me posted?

The train is pulling back into London before my phone lights up with a message from Max. It says, 'Hey, sorry, where you at?' By that point I've gone beyond caring. I'm full of warm relief at the sight of my familiar city welcoming me home.

Chapter Twenty-Four

When I get off the train I know exactly where I want to go, and thankfully, this time she agrees to see me, even though it's past ten on a Sunday night.

Damilola's flat is almost the polar opposite of Angie's house. It's a small, cosy loft conversion full of homey knick-knacks and contrasting patterns. It's warm and sweet, like she is. Climbing the stairs to her hallway I'm filled with affection, until we enter the living room and I see the huge TV that's too big for the space with every single games console imaginable piled underneath, the exercise bike blocking the bookshelf and the dartboard ruining her wall. The presence of Phil's out-of-place things marring Dami's snug lounge always bothers me.

I sit down on her squishy green sofa in my usual corner. Dami sits next to me and looks at me kindly, stroking my hair from the side of my face. Every muscle in my body relaxes and it's like I suddenly feel just how exhausted I am. I fall forward onto her chest. She puts her arms around me and squeezes and we sit like that for a long time.

Eventually I sit back and we cross our legs and face each other, like we're twelve-year-old girls at a slumber party.

'Talk to me, Becky,' she says.

'I'm sorry,' I murmur.

'I know.' She gives me an understanding smile and reaches for my hand.

I don't say that I didn't mean what I said in the letter, because we both know that I did. But I am sorry for upsetting her.

'I'm sorry too,' she says. 'I know I bang on about my job and I'm always late and distracted because of my overflowing inbox and that's so boring, when you're twiddling your thumbs waiting for me. And I'm sorry that Angie and I got carried away talking about my wedding. I know it's dull and probably feels lonely when you're not dating anybody. And I'm sorry for talking so much about houses and cars and . . . *fridges*. We should have been more mindful.'

I feel myself welling up. It's so freeing to hear Dami acknowledge how I might have felt over the past few years. So much that I could sit here all night and talk about Phil's new toastie maker with fifteen different settings if she wanted to. I realise, hearing her apologise, maybe it's not that I find those things as dull as I thought I did, but maybe I just needed recognition from them that they understand that's not where *I* am.

'I mean, you can't *not* talk about your job just because I hate mine,' I say. 'Those things are your life. And they're important. I do want to hear about them, I promise. Maybe just . . .'

'Maybe just not spending half an hour explaining our new compulsory cybersecurity training?' Dami laughs awkwardly.

'Well, maybe,' I admit. It was actually over half an hour. I timed it.

'Look, I'm genuinely sorry about how preoccupied I've

been.' Dami squeezes my hand. 'I didn't even realise how out of control it had got. But then I showed your letter to Phil, expecting him to disagree with you, and I could just see from the look on his face that he thought you had a point. I think he was too scared to bring it up with me himself. We talked and . . . well . . . I know that things need to change. I'm going to really try to stop checking emails constantly and be more present. So all in all, wording aside, I don't think your letter ended up being a terrible thing . . . !'

I smile. Dami's sweet to let me off the hook so easily. I'm pleasantly surprised to hear that Phil agrees with me on this and that he was afraid to broach it with her. Phil's so loud, I assumed he always made his opinions known.

'Becky.' She rubs my fingers with her thumb. 'I can agree to cut back on how much I talk about all kinds of things . . .' She pauses, looking uncomfortable. I sense that she has something she wants to say to me and is struggling to get the words out. She finds confrontation more hellish than I do.

'But?' I encourage her. 'It's okay. You can tell me.'

Her voice practically drops to a whisper, as if the low volume will soften the blow of her oncoming reality check. 'But sometimes, well, sometimes it's hard to know what you *do* want to talk about. It feels like you stopped sharing anything with me and Angie a long time ago. We ask you about how things are going and get a monosyllabic answer . . . Or you stuff your face full of potato and nod. Sometimes it's like you show up physically but you're not really there. It feels like you cut us out.'

I'm horrified. Do they really feel like I cut them out? 'No,' I say. 'No, it's not that at all. It's . . .'

Dami waits eagerly for my explanation. I can tell from her face that this is a sensitive subject. I can't quite believe that my not wanting to talk about anything has actually been hurting her feelings. I thought they didn't *want* to hear about my life. I feel terrible.

'Nothing in my life changes,' I mumble, burning with familiar shame. 'There's only so long you can bitch about hating your job without leaving it. Or be in love with an unavailable person before everyone loses sympathy.' I realise that's the first time I've ever described Max as unavailable, which is ironic, given that we just kissed. 'It's . . . embarrassing. I'm just so aware that I ran out of credits a long time ago.'

Dami shakes her head emphatically. 'Babe! You *never* run out of credits with us.'

I laugh bitterly. 'I don't know, I'm not sure Angie would say the same right now.'

Dami winces. 'Well . . . she'll forgive you. I'm sure of it. Maybe just . . . don't send us any more letters, okay? If you have something to say, just say it.'

I smile regretfully, thinking of how differently I could have approached the situation to stop it reaching boiling point like it did. I could have set small boundaries and asked for what I wanted, instead of keeping everything to myself and letting resentments build and build until they exploded in a fit of anger. I think of Angie's choice of word. I hadn't thought of the letters as angry up until now, but how obvious it seems now that they were.

Mostly with myself.

'I promise,' I say. 'I will try to be much more honest in a far less aggressive manner in the future. And you must promise to call me out if I'm behaving like a sullen teenager.'

We both laugh. 'Deal.' We shake hands.

'So, in the spirit of sharing,' I begin, thinking of everything that's happened in the past week that I've been dying to tell her. I talk about Leila showing up at my door, about begging for my job back, about being unable to avoid Fran for the first time in two years, about Paris, about Max.

Dami sits wide-eyed and open-mouthed for most of it and mostly says 'Ooh' and 'Wow, okay'. She probes me about how I'm feeling but doesn't express any firm opinions, for which I am grateful, particularly when I get to the Max bit. I squirm with how wretched I feel, but she listens to me attentively and she doesn't seem to judge me at all. I wonder why I had expected her to. It feels like the first proper conversation we've had in years and, with a stab of guilt, I realise clearly I've been more to blame for that than I thought.

It's the middle of the night by the time we decide to turn in. Dami tiptoes in to join Phil, who fell asleep hours ago, while I tuck up in their comfy spare bed with a hot water bottle and a cup of hot chocolate. I get the best night's sleep I've had in what feels like years.

Monday morning I'm woken by the sound of pans clanging and loud singing. Phil is doing his own version of 'SexyBack' in opera-style baritone. It is *way* too early for this level of volume and enthusiasm.

I pad sheepishly into the kitchen, highly aware that I'm asking hospitality from people whose relationship I condemned a mere week ago.

'I'm bringing Sexy *Beck* . . .' Phil sings when he sees me. He winks and throws a tea towel over his shoulder.

I'm relieved it doesn't seem like it will be awkward. Phil is the kind of guy who will roar with laughter at something you said that isn't very funny and tell long, rambling stories with no end point or talk in great detail about something you have zero interest in without caring that you're not listening. One time he slapped me on the back so enthusiastically I spilled my drink all down Angie's dress. He's overly friendly and a lot to take, but today I'm grateful for it.

'Bacon?' Phil calls.

'Uh, yes please.' I sit down next to Dami at the table, who I note happily is reading the paper instead of checking her emails. How she can read with this level of noise going on, God knows. Maybe long-term relationships are basically just mastering the art of tuning each other out.

'How did you sleep?' Dami puts her paper down and strokes my shoulder across the table.

'Like a cat,' I say. 'Thank you so much for letting me stay.'

Damilola opens her mouth to reply but before she can say anything, Phil calls, 'Oh don't be silly, Becks, we love having you, don't we, Dami?'

I can feel the familiar vexation flaring in my chest at his speaking over her. I try to hang onto all my goodwill from last night and remind myself Phil is letting me stay in his house after I insulted him.

Except that it's Damilola's house. And his noise and his belongings are crowding it.

'Gives me a chance to make my famous bacon sarnies,'

he carries on. 'You are getting The Royal Treatment this morning, ladies.'

Dami smiles. 'I get the royal treatment every morning.'

Phil honks with laughter. 'Yeah, not gonna lie, it's true, it's true.'

He sets the bacon sandwiches down on the table in front of us and leaves the room.

'Are you not having one, Phil?' I call after him.

'I'll be having mine to go!' he hollers from next door. He reenters in his shoes and jacket and grabs one. He kisses Dami on the forehead. 'Bye, babe. Bye, Becky!'

'God, are you off already?!' I ask. 'It's early!'

'Gotta get all the way over to Epping, don't I.' He fiddles with his collar.

'Oh,' I reply. I knew Phil was in insurance. I had no idea he worked that far away. 'Do you always work in Epping?' I ask.

'Yeah,' he says. 'Bit of a nightmare commute but it's not too bad, only one change then you just ride the Central line all the way. Going opposite to the flow too, so nice and empty for most of it!'

Dami puts her head in her hands. 'I feel awful. We'll move somewhere in the middle eventually. I just have so many late nights . . .'

'Babe, babe, we've been over this. Doesn't bother me!' Phil beams. He kisses her on the forehead again. 'See you tonight. Oh, what do you want for dinner?'

'Whatever you like,' Dami says absently. She's automatically picked up her phone to check her inbox. Then she remembers herself and puts it down.

'Becks?' Phil looks at me. 'You're our guest.'

'Uhhh. Oh! Hmm. Well, it's been a while since I had your egusi stew, Dami?'

'Ah, blast from the past. I remember that.' Phil kisses his fingers. 'Delicious. But as La Head Chef around here I'm not sure I could do it justice, Becks. I was thinking lasagne or a spag bol?'

'Sounds good.' Dami's fingers are twitching as she attempts to leave her phone on the table. She's obviously seen something in there that's agitated her.

'Sounds great,' I agree.

'Okay, laters.' Phil finally heads out the door. I hear it slam and his loud footsteps as he plods down the staircase.

I'm upset that Phil hasn't had her stew in a while. She used to make it all the time. Back when we'd visit her at uni Angie and I practically lived off it. She was like the mother hen and we the poor, desperate baby chicks begging for her stew lest we live off Domino's, run out of money to pay for Domino's, then starve. I mean, I assume she's expanded her repertoire since then, but still.

'Blast from the past?' I comment.

Dami doesn't respond. She might have resisted her emails for the majority of the duration of breakfast, but her brain is obviously still engrossed in the tasks that lie in wait for her. 'Huh?'

'I said, blast from the past? Egusi stew? I never thought I'd see the day you went longer than a week without eating it.'

'Oh.' Dami blinks. 'Yeah, I just sort of stopped having time to cook, to be honest. Or clean. I work so late. Phil does most of it. Well . . . all of it, really. It's bad, I know.' She grimaces.

'I should do more. But Phil doesn't mind. He leaves his job at the door and I, well . . .' She gestures to her phone.

I go to say 'makes sense' automatically, and stop myself, because I question whether it does. Didn't I just promise myself I'd stop concealing problems? Didn't Dami agree that things need to change?

To be honest, if I was Phil, I'd have an issue about coming back from my hour-and-a-half-long commute to someone who worked from home three days out of five and had 'stopped having time to cook'. But he didn't seem annoyed about it at all. He seemed to accept his chef duties jovially. God, I think to myself. Did I really just think something complimentary about Phil?

I find I don't want to keep quiet in this conversation. I don't want to end up sending her another letter in ten years' time, telling her I think she's wasted her life and taken all her relationships for granted being buried under a pile of papers.

'So . . . do you work late *every* night?' I ask.

'I mean . . . not *every* night. Most nights.'

'And you never cook? Or clean?' I ask.

'No. Oh God, you think I'm a terrible person,' she flaps.

'*No*,' I reassure. 'No. I just wonder if, even if Phil doesn't mind, if that kind of imbalance is good for anyone. Do you and Phil get any time together?'

Dami winces. 'Sometimes. Not as much as I'd like. You know, the nights I am free, I'm just so tired . . .'

I nod. 'Dami, in the spirit of what we were talking about last night, I just want to be honest with you. I wonder if maybe things need to go further than not checking emails when you're eating breakfast or out with your friends. I wonder if you need to have a serious conversation about your workload. It doesn't seem fair on you, or Phil.'

She thinks for a moment. 'Maybe. I guess I could do that.'

I have no idea whether she actually will, but surprisingly, it feels good to have told her what I really think, in a non-judgemental way, and to have her listen and accept it. I feel like we've had more real communication with each other in the last twenty-four hours than we have throughout most of our twenties.

'Maybe we could cook for Phil tonight, together? I can go to the shops and get stuff and help with the prep.'

Dami smiles. 'Okay, yeah, that's a great idea. Thanks, Becky.'

Now that we're finished speaking, she goes back to her phone and I munch away on the bacon sandwiches Phil made. I've always looked at Phil like some big, lumbering interloper in Damilola's flat, drowning her out and taking up all her oxygen. Probably hoovering up all her food and leaving his shit lying around for her to clean up. I guess I kind of assumed that part of the reason she had no time outside of work was because she must be doing all the domestic chores and making time for Phil, too. But him doing all the housework so that she has enough time to do five jobs in one, and them barely getting to hang out, doesn't exactly fit with that image. I take another bite of my sandwich and wonder what else I've managed to misinterpret.

Chapter Twenty-Five

The stew turned out to be a more emotional experience than any of us anticipated. It was waiting on the table for Phil when he got home, and he was so grateful he welled up and hugged me in his vice-like grip for a quite frankly socially unacceptable amount of time. When Dami saw this – and how stressed Phil must have been without letting on – *she* welled up. And then once Dami tasted it, it nearly set her off again, because she couldn't believe she'd gone so long without cooking it.

Dami and Phil agree I can stay a couple of weeks while I figure out my next move, which is incredibly generous of them. Being so up close to their relationship, over the next few days, I realise more and more just how mistaken I was about them. It transpires that Phil isn't as keen on a giant wedding as I thought; he was just trying to be accommodating because he knows that Nigerian weddings are traditionally quite large. Not to mention, being around Dami's family so much of the time – because they're heavily involved in the planning – must take a lot of energy, but he never complains about it. And the only reason Phil moved into Dami's tiny flat was because she wanted to keep living here. It puts a new spin on all his shit cluttering up the place, especially when I learn he'd given up his original Pac-Man arcade game because it wouldn't fit anywhere. That's true love.

This agreement had been reached *before* she routinely worked from home three days a week, but Phil had never made her feel bad about it, claiming he gets 'time to listen to a podcast' on the way to work and 'time to clear his head' on the way back. After the Intense Stew Incident, Dami insisted she would put moving into a new place back 'on the table'.

As I spend more time with Phil, rather than dodging his booming voice at parties that I inevitably leave early to go and hang out with Max, I see that I was right in some ways but not in others. He *is* very different to Dami. He is loud where she's quiet and rough around the edges where she's dainty and elegant . . . But I was wrong about him shouting over her. He makes a lot of the obvious decisions like what car they drive and what they watch on TV. But he's the one driving the car most of the time. And he's the one watching a series while she's finishing up Teams meetings with the US five hours behind us. So fair enough? He's made a huge effort to slot into her life, and seeing what an incomplete picture I had makes me feel pretty idiotic.

It doesn't take long staying with them to see Phil makes Damilola happy. I wonder how I've managed for so long not to see that. I don't think it's that I wasn't paying attention, as such. Technically I was watching and listening. But I wonder if I've been choosing what sticks, forgetting things I didn't want to see, and building my own reality because it was easier for me to believe my friend's relationship was terrible.

I have this overwhelming sense of something unravelling

and not being able to stop it. Like when you've snagged a jumper and there's no way to sew the fabric back together and you know, eventually, the hole is going to get so big you're not going to be able to hide it. At the back of my mind, possibilities stir; what else have I been blinding myself to? Every now and again Angie's words cross my mind. Her accusations about my selective memory have taken root and started to blossom.

Max messages me a couple of times. I sent a short reply to his 'Hey, where you at?', saying I was back in London staying at Dami and Phil's and he just said, 'I'll pray for your ears.' I assume relating to Phil's general volume. I wasn't in the mood to make fun of the people who'd generously taken me in, so I didn't respond.

His next message, the following day, says, 'Did you know that koala fingerprints are so indistinguishable from human ones they've been confused in crime scenes? Mind blown.' I automatically type out a witty reply like I normally would, but when I go to send it I find that I can't. How can we be talking about koala fingerprints when we kissed and haven't even mentioned it? When he said he would speak to Fran and I haven't heard from him since? When I went to Paris to see him and left without saying goodbye?

When I don't reply, the next day he texts, 'It is possible to put a frog into a trance by lying it on its back and gently stroking its stomach.'

This is Max's version of hounding me. Two messages in a row with random animal facts that he knows I love, left out in the cold. But for the first time in years I feel underwhelmed with his attention. I don't *want* to read into what this means and what he's really feeling. I just want to talk to each other like normal people. I want to know how he interprets what happened and how we're going to deal with it. Is he still with Fran? Or has he told her? Is he going to tell her? Does he want to be with me or has the whole thing made him realise we're just friends and it's Fran that he loves? I can't get any of that from talking about hypnotising frogs.

For the first time, his not saying what he's thinking isn't intriguing me . . . it's *boring* me. And I'm surprised by it. I've never once thought of Max as dull. Max is *fun*. He's unpredictable, you never quite know what he's going to say or do next, he's a fountain of interesting knowledge. But right now his behaviour just leaves me feeling deflated. I leave him on 'read' again.

Instead of spending my mental energy decoding whether or not Max's messages about hypnotising amphibians mean 'I love you, Becky' or 'I'm confused, Becky' or, indeed, really are just about frogs, I help Dami and Phil with cleaning, and cooking, I binge watch *The Sopranos* with Phil while Dami's working late at the office, I take long baths, I search for jobs.

On the Wednesday after I arrive, Dami finally sets up a meeting with her boss about her workload. The following two evenings, she puts away her laptop at 7 p.m. It's not going to be some miraculous overnight shift – she still works until ten thirty the other nights – but I can see that even getting a couple of nights free of Dami's emails is making both of them happier.

Unfortunately, or maybe fortunately, Phil takes an overly involved interest in my job application process. Every night he asks me what I've discovered that day and I find the lack of anything to answer so humiliating that I eventually start applying for stuff just to get him to leave me alone. In the week that I've been here I must have sent off nearly thirty applications. I'm not sure I'm interested in most of them and even less certain that I'm qualified, but at least I'm doing something.

On Sunday evening, Phil and I are just about to play season 2 of *The Sopranos*. He's trying to be 'helpful' in that annoying way people do when they tell a nervous person to 'not be nervous'. He's in the middle of pointing out the obvious, like suggesting job sites I've tried a thousand times and generally making me want to hit him over the head with something very large and heavy, when he accidentally says something useful.

'So, what *are* you qualified to do?' he asks, after I've shot down three suggestions of things I was wildly unqualified for, including skydiving instructor.

'Marketing,' I say through gritted teeth. 'But the point is that I don't want to *do* marketing . . .'

But he's already pulled up the computer and is googling jobs in marketing. 'Brand marketing,' he booms. 'Product marketing. Publishing and media marketing. Entertainment marketing.'

'I don't . . .' I dismiss. Then I back up. 'Wait, entertainment marketing?'

'Uh huh.' Phil clicks. 'There's a job on this entertainment site at a *leading marketing agency that works with production companies, studios and networks to create global campaigns that build, engage and entertain audiences.*'

'So like . . . movies and stuff?' I repeat brainlessly.

'Yuh. Their website is so cool, check it out! They're hiring!' Phil nods eagerly and ushers me over. I click through all kinds of programmes and movies that I've seen and loved.

My heart starts hammering. I like films. I *love* films. I've watched them all. From action to horror to romance to mystery, from old to new, if there's anything I can do it's sit back and enjoy a film. Is Phil telling me there is an actual job out there that sort of combines my skills and my one, singular interest in life, i.e. being entertained while shoving snacks in my face? Someone out there is actually employed to market *television*? I'd completely dismissed marketing because I'd assumed all marketing jobs were like mine. But I guess, of course that's rubbish. You can probably market all sorts of stuff. Books. Hair products. Clothes. FUN stuff.

I'm so excited I can barely pay attention to the TV for the rest of the evening. There is a job in existence I genuinely like the sound of and might be able to do.

When Phil's finished watching, I get the laptop out and begin crafting my application. It's like my own personal *Iliad*. I take care over the structure of every sentence and nuance of every word. I try to strike that balance between confident and cocky. I try to sell every single one of my skills without making it sound like a long, boring checklist of things I can do. I try to convince them of my passion for cinema without overdoing it.

There is one fly in the ointment . . . The dreaded reference section.

When I get to it, I feel any small drop of hope drain out of me. Having only had one job, the only person I can ask for a reference from is Margaret. And having called her a 'cog' in a 'soul-guzzling corporate machine', I'm not sure she's going to be in the mood to talk me up.

UGHHHHHH.

I try to tell myself it doesn't even matter whether I get the job. I have *identified something I actually want to do and might actually be able to do*. That's progress.

By the time I'm done it's nearly midnight. I must nod off on the sofa, because the next thing I'm aware of is Dami covering me over with a blanket.

'Oh, sorry, I didn't mean to wake you,' she whispers.

''S okay, I should move,' I murmur into the edge of the couch. 'Did you just get in?'

'Uh huh.' She grimaces. 'Emergency in one of our key accounts.'

I nod and push myself up. She sits next to me, putting her hand on mine. 'Your phone lit up a minute ago,' she says. 'It was Max.'

'Oh,' I say.

'Some diagram about the best way to eat an alligator?' Her inflection rises at the end of her sentence. Dami and Max never saw eye to eye in their sense of humour.

I can't help but laugh. Because it's funny, but because it's pathetic too. Pathetic that we can't seem to have a conversation like two grown-ups. Apparently we're going to be forever exchanging memes and loaded glances.

'Becky, I hope you don't mind me asking,' Dami says softly. 'But how do you want your future to look? Do you want to be with Max?'

'Yes,' I say, although with more hesitation than I would have said it a few weeks ago.

'What is it that you like about Max?' Dami asks.

'Um . . . he makes me laugh,' I say.

'That's good.' Dami nods. 'What else?'

I think for a moment, surprised by how difficult I find it to answer the question. I don't often analyse *why* I like Max. I just do. Like, why do old people suddenly decide they like bird-watching and Werther's Originals? Because the world has ordained it to be so.

'I . . .' I search my mind. 'He keeps things interesting. I'm never bored.'

'But what makes it interesting?' Dami probes.

'Well, it . . . You know. I guess, never really knowing when he's going to show up, but knowing that he will. Or not quite knowing what he's actually thinking . . . it feels like anything could happen.'

What I don't say is that actually, recently I *have* been finding that aspect of his personality less interesting. I thought once the veil was lifted on the fact we still have feelings for each other, we could have a real conversation. But this thing has happened between us and we're exactly the same as ever.

'And what about when you're with him? Do you like yourself?'

'That's hardly a fair question. I rarely like myself,' I answer.

'What is it that you don't like?'

Is Dami considering a career change into therapy?

'Um, I guess . . . I spend too much money on stupid shit. I spend half my life drunk. I don't have anything I really care about. I stopped putting any effort into things and started making fun of people who do.' I feel myself getting choked up as I say that last part. It's something I only realised when I went back in to We Work, You Win, and after the reality check from Angie.

'And does Max facilitate those things?' Dami says.

'I mean . . .' I think through every usual interaction with Max. Sitting in dingy Scintilla, bitching, wasting my money, wasting my time. 'Yes. But that's not on Max,' I add.

'No, that's not on Max,' Dami says. 'But he doesn't help anything, does he? He doesn't encourage you to move forward.'

'No, but . . .' I feel a reflex defensiveness. 'That's because he likes me as I am. He doesn't need me to change. That's a *good* thing, right?'

Dami looks thoughtful for a second. 'Personally, I think couples should take the bad with the good. I don't think they should relish the bad.'

It's too late and I feel too emotionally fragile to interrogate what she's suggesting. Dami must see it in my face because she says, 'Look, it's late. I don't really know Max. But from what I've seen, he doesn't seem to offer you much except helping you stand still.'

I nod. I really, *really* don't want to stand still anymore. Dami kisses me on the head and goes to bed. I sit on the sofa for a bit. I'm not sure what I'm going to do about Max yet, but I know something that I *can* do. Using a sizeable chunk of my remaining funds, I book an open return train to Manchester first thing in the morning.

Chapter Twenty-Six

I'm starting to feel like I live at King's Cross station. I've probably been here more times in the last two weeks than I have in the last decade. At least today I can eat. I feel strangely cool and calm.

I'm going to see my dad today. For the first time in twenty years.

I find I don't have the compulsion to go over every possible scenario of what might happen. How many times in the past few weeks have I fantasised about how something is going to go, only to meet with disappointing reality? If I don't have illusions then I can't be disillusioned. I'm basically cheating sadness.

Plus . . . I really don't remember my dad all that well. A shadowy figure at a couple of early birthdays. A trip to Nando's. A few gifts and cards that tailed off in my pre-teens. It's not much to build a picture out of.

When I get to the address, it's smaller than I imagined. It's a pretty, red-brick house on the corner of a suburban street, split into flats. From the outside I can already tell there's no garden. For some reason, whenever I daydreamed about my dad, he'd always be in a garden. Kicking a football around with Leila or sipping a beer with Leila's mum. Although now that I've met Leila, I can't imagine her involved in any form of sport.

I ring the doorbell for the ground-floor flat. Nothing stirs.

Well . . . this is going to be anticlimactic if no one's home.

I ring the doorbell again. *Shit*. It's not like I could call ahead, but maybe I should have come on a weekend. Urgh. I can almost hear my mother's voice in my mind. 'Why did you think anyone would be home on a Monday afternoon? Other people have these things called jobs, Becky.'

I stand on the doorstep, thinking about all the things I could have bought with that eighty quid on the train ticket.

Then there's movement inside. Someone is shuffling along the hallway. The door opens and . . . Leila emerges. It takes her a millisecond to place me out of context.

'Oh, it's you,' she states. I can't read any emotion behind it, if there is any.

'And it's you,' I say. I haven't been letting myself think about Leila – I felt too heinous about the last thing I said to her – but unexpected warmth spreads through me at the sight of her. I realise that I'm thrilled to see her. 'You went home, then?'

'Didn't have a choice.' She shrugs.

We stand staring at each other for a moment. She's wearing bright turquoise pyjamas with sparkly rhinestones. Her giant slippers are white and fluffy, like she's wearing two dead poodles on her feet.

'Come in.' She stands to one side.

I follow her through the communal hallway and into their flat, noticing her pyjamas also say say 'Sleeping Booty' on the bum. We enter straight into the living room. There's a beige carpet, a cream sofa, a giant flat-screen TV that's a little too big for the room. There's a coffee table with Scrabble tile coasters. A close-up photo of a flower hangs on the wall. It's so . . . normal.

I don't know what I was expecting. Of course it's normal. Where did I think they lived? The inside of an alien spaceship?

'Do you want a drink?' she asks.

'Er, yeah.' I'm still looking around, trying to absorb every little detail. 'Please.'

'What do you want?'

'Er, tea?'

'Okay.' She pads into the kitchen. I take the opportunity to move closer to the bookcase, which has a few photos on it. There's one of small Leila in a ball pit. There's one of a slightly bigger Leila eating some candy floss. There's one of her in a uniform, standing between her two parents, presumably on her first day of school. I look at Dad and think, *if I passed him on the street, I wouldn't recognise him*. I'm not proud of it, but the next thing I think is, *I'll never have a photo like that*.

There isn't one here of me. Nothing that would hint that the man in the pictures has another child. Suddenly I feel like I want to cry. All my calm on the way over here has evaporated.

'Why do you look like you're about to cry?' Leila reenters the room and hands me a mug of tea.

'I . . .' I don't try to lie to her, because it's impossible. 'I'm not in any of the pictures.'

'Why would you be? We met the other day,' she comments with her usual grace and sensitivity.

I don't say anything and pull myself together. I decide not to keep looking around their flat, in case it upsets me further. I'll just stare at a bit of carpet as I wait for Dad.

'So when is . . . When are your parents back?' I ask. I try to sound casual but my heart starts racing.

Leila's eyebrows raise. 'After work,' she says. 'About six.'

I look at the clock. It's one.

'Is it okay if I wait here for . . .' I trail off.

'For Dad?' she finishes.

'Yeah,' I answer. I can't quite bring myself to call him that out loud or admit that I'm here to see him. Even though I blatantly am.

'You'll be waiting a while,' she says. 'He doesn't live here anymore.'

My head spins to look at her. 'Huh?'

'It's just me and Mum.' She gestures around the place.

'I . . . What?! Since when?'

'About eight years ago.' She shrugs as if she's telling me where the nearest Tesco is.

'I . . . *What?*' I nearly spill my tea. 'What happened?'

'They fought a lot. Eventually he had enough, I guess. I came home from school one day and he was gone. Mum was down for a while. Like, really down. But she's better now. I don't see Dad much.'

We stand in silence for a moment. Leila plays with her nails while a mixture of feelings flood through me. Disappointment that today is not going to be the day that I see my father again. Confusion as I scramble to piece together a very different picture than the one I've been living with. Sympathy for Leila going through that. Relief that it wasn't just *me* he left because I'm defective in some way. Which I know is irrational . . . Of course I'm not. But I can't help feeling that way.

'Why didn't you tell me?' I wonder aloud. I can't believe,

in the whole evening we spent together at Max's flat, she didn't say anything about any of this.

'You didn't ask.' Leila goes to sit down on the sofa. 'You didn't ask anything about Dad, or my home life, at all.'

Shame courses through me. She's right. I didn't. It was too painful for me, but I realise that I've inadvertently been selfish.

'Seeing as you didn't want to ask and it's not the most fun topic of conversation for me either,' Leila continues, 'I didn't see the need to bring it up.'

Leila hugs her knees to her chest, scrunching herself into a ball. The image in my mind of her life rearranges itself. She's not living a charmed life within the bubble of infinite, protective love of two steady parents who never do anything wrong; she's just like me. She's just like most people, really. Her parents are just human beings with their own special flaws and shortcomings, ready to pass onto the next generation.

I watch her playing with the fluff on her slippers. When I first met her I thought we were complete opposites. But I see now that we're not so different. Our defences just manifest in ways that look different. She keeps all her mess on the inside and I keep it on the outside . . . Both fine methods of avoiding dealing with anything.

'When did you last see him?' I ask. I timidly move across the room to join her on the sofa.

'For years I didn't. But now I do, sometimes,' said Leila. 'Saw him at Christmas. Months will pass and you don't hear anything. You have to be the one to make the effort.'

'So you have his new address?' Something inside me lights up.

'Yep,' Leila says. 'I'll give it to you. I never gave him your first letter, if you were wondering.'

'Why not?' I ask, although I'm glad that she didn't. Relief washes over me that he's never going to read it.

Leila eyeballs me. 'Wasn't sure you really meant it. Unless, of course, you're here now just to reinforce you never want to see him? In case he didn't get it the first time?' She smirks.

I smirk back. She's right, obviously. 'Yeah. Okay. I didn't really mean it.'

I think back to what Angie said, about not being honest with myself about why I sent the letters, about sending them in anger. I thought I was trying to find closure in my relationship with my dad, but I think really I was just trying to get his attention. Given that I felt compelled to come all the way here, it's become obvious that maybe what I wanted *is* to see him again. Whatever form that takes, however it goes. It might not be what I dreamed of as a kid but it could be . . . *something*. Maybe Leila could even come with me.

I realise Leila and I have lapsed into silence again. I remember that I'm still holding a cup of tea and take a sip.

'Sorry you're not going to see him today,' Leila says.

'That's okay.' I smile. 'I get to see you.'

'Thought you didn't want to see me.' Leila tries to sound impassive but she can't keep a hint of hurt out of her tone.

I wince. I feel so bad about what I said to her. Doubly bad because now I know I'd made all these wrong assumptions about her.

I take another sip of tea and ready myself for the most recent in a queue of apologies I have to make. 'I'm sorry,

Leila,' I say. 'I was being childish. I was in a bad place and, well . . . I was just jealous of you because I thought you had a dad and I didn't.' It sounds *so* incredibly lame when I say it out loud, but that's the truth.

'So now you know that I don't, we can be friends?' Leila remarks. 'What if I *did* have a good relationship with Dad? What if he *was* a shit father to you and the perfect one to me? That still wouldn't be my fault. It wouldn't make the way you treated me okay.'

'You're right.' I nod, my cheeks flushing. 'It wouldn't have. I guess I'm not excusing myself, I'm just explaining.'

Leila stops fiddling with her slippers and looks at me. 'Okay,' she says brightly. 'I accept your apology.'

I feel a rush of gratitude that she didn't leave me grovelling for longer. If it were me I probably would have milked that. I consider hugging her, but can't quite find the confidence yet. Maybe one day we'll feel comfortable enough. It's early days. I reach over and give her a feeble pat on the arm instead. She watches my hand on her forearm in amusement.

'So, are you heading back to London?' she asks, when I'm done patting her.

'I guess,' I say, realising I don't want to. I want to stick around. I want to know everything about her life, not the version I'd made up in my head. I have so many questions. But I don't want to impose. She's probably had enough of me, given everything that's happened.

'I mean, you don't have to go,' she says.

'Oh, cool.' My heart flutters. 'You're not busy?'

'No.' She smiles. 'Not busy. Want to watch something shit on TV?'

'Yeah.' I grin. 'I do.'

I have a lifetime to get my questions answered. For now it's enough that I have a real-life sister and we're about to hang out watching TV together, like real-life sisters do.

'Leila,' I ask. 'Do you have a pad of paper?'

Dear Dad,

I've been sad about the way things are (or aren't) between us for a long time and I know things may never be perfect, but it would be good to say hi over a coffee or something if you're up for it.

Your daughter,
Becky

Chapter Twenty-Seven

I smile all the way back to London. Okay, so the first letter I sent was all wrong. I wanted change, but I was going about it in the wrong way. But it worked out in the end . . . Really, it was just a cry for family and that's what I found.

My phone buzzes. It's Max again. I notice the shape of his name seems different. *Max Madigan*. I'm used to those letters spelling out excitement. Today I find myself tired at the sight of them lighting up my notification centre.

Once again, it's a message about something random and meaningless. My heart sinks. If he wants to talk to me, why doesn't he just talk to me?! I finally bite the bullet and reply, 'If you want to talk about our situation, I'm available, but I don't particularly want to chat about how creepy you found Paul from *The Traitors* right now.'

He reads it and goes offline.

When I get back to Dami's, Phil's booming rendition of Marvin Gaye is vibrating the floorboards and the sizzling smell of chicken and spices fills the flat. Phil and Dami are making fajitas together, which is a lovely sight. I take off my shoes and stand in the hallway for a moment, breathing in the sounds and scents of warmth and safety. I know I can't stay here forever, but it's so nice to feel at home somewhere I can also breathe, unlike Mum's house.

'Becky, how was your old man?' Phil yells as soon as I enter the kitchen.

I grab a knife and start helping them chop peppers.

Dami shoots him a withering look and turns down Marvin Gaye. 'Phil,' she urges in hushed tones. 'I told you she might not want to talk about it.'

'Oh, sorry, sorry.' Phil puts a finger over his lips. 'Sorry, Becky.' He turns around and slaps me on the back, then returns to cooking.

'No, it's fine,' I reassure Dami, who is still glowering at the back of Phil's head. Her face softens as she turns to me. 'I didn't meet my dad, though.'

'Oh!' Dami rushes over to rub my arm as I chop. 'What happened? Are you okay?!'

'I'm good. I saw my sister.'

'The one you . . .' She trails off.

'The one I told to get lost, yes.' I finish her sentence.

'Was it okay?' She blinks several times.

'Yeah, we made up. She's going to come and stay whenever I get my own place. And we might go and see our dad together.' It feels weird saying the word 'our', but I think I like it. 'He doesn't live there anymore,' I explain.

'Oh, that's lovely!' Dami beams. 'I'm so pleased.'

'It is, isn't it,' I say. 'I have a sister.'

'You have a sister.' Dami squeezes my shoulder.

'I always wanted a sister,' Phil adds as he throws more spices onto the chicken. 'Brothers smell bad. And smear hummus on your best shoes.' He sounds as though he's reliving a painful memory. When I leave, I'm going to miss Phil's well-meaning but irrelevant commentary on my life.

Dami and I set the table and we lay out all the food. We've just sat down to eat when the doorbell rings. Dami and Phil shoot each other a puzzled glance.

'You expecting anyone, babe?' Phil asks as he starts loading up a fajita.

'No.' Dami gets up. 'I swear, if it's downstairs complaining about the noise again. We've been taking our shoes off by the door *religiously* . . .'

She returns a minute later with a strange look on her face. 'It's, er, Max,' she announces.

I almost choke on a piece of chicken. 'Max?'

'He's just taking off his shoes,' she says. She's trying to communicate something with her eyes. I think it's, *what's he doing here? Is this a good thing or a bad thing? Should I have told him to go?*

Max's face appears behind her in the doorway. He's about a head taller than her. 'All right, Becky,' he says.

'I . . . Hi,' I say lamely, pieces of chicken and pepper dropping out of my fajita. My heart rate picks up speed. Why is he here?

Damilola moves to make space for him in the room. 'Max, we've just sat down to eat. Would you like to join us?'

'That would be great, thanks,' Max accepts without an ounce of awkwardness. He sits down in the last empty seat around the table. 'Fajitas, nice.'

Dami shoots me another questioning look. I think this one is, *are you guys together now and you forgot to mention it? How am I supposed to act around him?* I return a look that says, *I have no idea*. I barely know how to act around him myself.

'I thought you were in Paris,' I state.

'I was. Then I got on this thing called a train that brought me back to England,' he answers with a grin.

'*Haha*,' I say. 'I meant, I thought you were there until next week?'

'Ngeghhh.' He shrugs. 'Something else came up.' He locks eyes with me across the table. I can't help heat rising through my body. Did he leave Paris for me? So he could speak to Fran? He must have broken up with her now, otherwise he wouldn't be here.

'So how was Paris, Max?' Dami asks politely.

'Did you eat any good *les bugs*?' Phil asks in a French accent and roars with laughter. 'Never fancied *la cuisine* myself.'

The disdain on Max's face is clear. He's kind of a food snob. 'No, no escargot on this trip,' he answers. 'But a lot of wine.'

'What about galleries?' Dami asks.

'Did you go to that . . . Oh, what's it called, Dami?' Phil jumps in.

'The Louvre?' Dami fills in.

I can see the question causing Max physical pain. That anyone would forget the name of the Louvre, or think he was such a basic tourist as to go to there. 'Yes,' he says. 'I went there after the Eiffel Tower and before the Champs-Elysées, wearing my *I Heart Paris* T-shirt and my beret.'

'Sounds great, mate,' Phil says, not aware of Max's sarcasm. Damilola gives a half-hearted smile, not quite sure of Max's tone either. Max has this way of making fun of you as if he's having a joke *with* you, and you're never quite sure which it is.

We continue to make small talk through the rest of dinner. I've lost my appetite and nibble at my first fajita, eager to get Max alone. The only bit of conversation that captivates my attention is when Dami mentions that Angie is selling her house.

'She is?!' I repeat in shock.

'Mmhmm.' Dami makes an awkward noise in her throat. I can tell she regrets letting it slip. We've skilfully avoided mentioning Angie since I've been here.

'But she loves that place! She spent so long on it!' Angie has lived in that house for four years. She's always making new additions to it. I can't imagine her being apart from it.

'I guess she doesn't want to stay there anymore. What with all the memories. And she probably can't afford to keep paying the mortgage on it without Jacob.'

I can't think of anything else to say. I suppose it makes sense, but it seems so sad. I never even associated Jacob with that house. I know it was his house as well, technically, but it's all Angie. The brickwork, the garden, the modern chic glamour . . . Even the plugs feel like Angie.

These past few weeks have been so surreal that there have only been moments where it hits home that this is all happening. That I set all this in motion, with a crisis caused by a tarot reading. That I am a real person, with real impact on other people and their lives. And now Angie is leaving her beloved house.

'She'll make a killing,' Phil comments, oblivious to the spiralling happening in the seat beside him. 'What with everything she's done to it. It was a crap pile when they got it.'

Dami clears her throat.

'I mean, er, it was a real fixer-upper. It must have gone up tons in value.'

'True,' Dami agrees. She flicks me one last loaded look and we say no more about it. I know Angie and I aren't in a great place right now, but after hearing this I have to contact her. I text her under the table.

> Hey. I heard you're leaving the house. I'm sorry. I know you love that place. It must feel strange. Here for you if you want me. Love you. x

After what feels like a thousand years of watching Phil chomp his way through a mountain of chicken meat, we're done. Normally I would offer to do the washing-up but I'm so desperate to talk to Max I excuse us as soon as Phil takes his last bite and drag Max into the other room.

'What are you doing here?' I demand.

'What do you think?' He gives me that knowing look that feels as if his eyes are communicating directly with my innermost thoughts.

'You missed Yorkshire puddings?'

'Exactly right.' His eyes roam all over my face, which is blushing furiously. I try meeting his eye but it's like looking at the sun.

'So you spoke to Fran?' I say.

'I spoke to Fran,' he confirms. 'It was always you, Becky.'

It was always me.

The memory of wandering around Paris all alone without so much as a text message, and then being plagued for more than a week with random chit-chat as if nothing had happened between us, niggles in the pit of my stomach. But his presence washes all of that away. He's here now. He's here, telling me it was always me. He's here leaning in . . . to kiss me?

Our faces move closer together, when Dami coughs at the door. 'Ahem . . . Are you staying, Max? Do you want dessert?'

'That would be great, thanks.' Max pulls back and puts his arm around me.

Dami smiles. I want her to look at me, so that I get some hint of what she's thinking – I know she's had her doubts about Max – but she keeps her eyes on Max. 'Okay, great,' she says brightly and disappears back to the kitchen. Surely, her doubts will dissipate now Max and I are official. Things won't be like they were before.

'Shall we?' Max points to the kitchen. All I can think about is the fact that his arm is still around me.

'Yes, uh huh,' I answer.

We go back into the kitchen. I feel a lot more relaxed now, and stuff my face full of chocolate sponge pudding. I even find myself having fun. I am having *dessert*. With my *adult* friends in their *adult* flat. Max puts his arm around me as my *adult* boyfriend. For the first time in forever, I feel like I have a real seat at the grown-up table.

Phil is halfway through treating us to his rendition of 'Respect' when my phone lights up with an email that is the cherry on top of a near-perfect evening.

Becky,

I just wanted to let you know I gave you a good reference for the job at Shout Box. You'd be perfect for it. Why, every time I walked past your desk you'd be engrossed in some film or another. And your impression of Michael Myers that one office Halloween party has certainly stayed with me.

Good luck. Once you find the thing you want to do, I know you'll be as brilliant as you were when you first joined WWYW.

Margaret.

I squeal and nearly knock my plate off the table. 'Oh my God!'

Everyone stares at me quizzically.

'Margaret gave me a good reference! She didn't screw me over!' I put my hands together as if in prayer. 'I *knew* she had a soft spot for me, after all! Oh, thank you, Margaret, you beautiful, *beautiful* camel-covered angel.'

'Becky, that's amazing!' Damilola exclaims.

'Well done, mate.' Phil pats me on the back.

'Ah Margaret, I'm going to miss hearing about that old sour-faced lemon,' Max jokes.

I can't believe it. I can't *believe* I have a slim shot in hell of actually getting this job. I eat another bite of pudding and grin to myself for the rest of the night.

Dear Margaret,

Thank you for putting in a good word. I owe you one.

Let's call it even for the sandwiches ;)

Becky

Chapter Twenty-Eight

As it gets later, the question of whether Max is going to stay over starts hovering in the air.

'God, is that the time?' Dami looks at her phone. 'I've got to go to sleep.'

'Mmargh.' Phil makes an indistinguishable noise of agreement. He looks like he's about ready to pass out.

'Yup, suppose I'd better be getting back to ole Brixton,' Max adds. He stretches and yawns.

'Uh, I mean, you can crash here if you like, obviously, Max,' Dami offers politely.

Dami and Phil nod. 'That's cool, mate,' says Phil.

Dami jiggles Phil's leg to rouse him from the sofa. 'Night then, folks,' Dami says as they head upstairs. A few seconds later the sound of Phil's electric toothbrush buzzes through the house.

'So, bedtime.' Max reaches for my hand and squeezes it.

I flush. This evening has been ridiculously wonderful. How long have I imagined spending an evening like this? Actually being with Max like proper boyfriend and girlfriend again? Having job prospects? Not feeling left out, left behind. I'm living under a beautiful spell.

There's a part of me that wants to ask him what's been going on. It's on the tip of my tongue to have a go at him for being cryptic before he definitively ended his relationship with Fran. But he did do it, and that's what counts, right?

'Let's go upstairs,' I say.

It feels *totally* bizarre going to bed with him. It's not like it was in Paris. Paris was a wine-fuelled dream a world away from our actual lives. Having him here in Damilola's bedroom – in what I have come to think of as my bedroom – brushing his teeth, washing his face and walking around in his pants when I am stone-cold sober, feels utterly absurd.

He sits down on the bed next to me and I burst out laughing.

'What? What's funny?' He climbs under the covers.

'Just . . . this is *weird*.' I climb under the covers too. 'Don't you think it's weird?'

'I guess.' He sounds a little defensive. Max has a brilliant sense of humour until he thinks someone is laughing at him. Even though he laughs at basically everybody on the planet.

'I don't . . .' I correct myself. 'I don't mean it's bad weird. It's good weird.'

Max doesn't say anything. He *must* be finding this odd. He's had another girlfriend for the last two years and we've not dated since we worked at Scintilla. I know Max likes to be entirely in control, and never let anything unsettle him, but there's no way even the most cool and collected person wouldn't need to adjust to this.

I don't say any of that, though. I just turn out my bedside lamp and lie down facing him. Max mirrors my body language and we stare at each other across the bed.

'Night, Becky,' Max says softly.

'Night, Max,' I reply.

There's a moment's hesitation where I wonder if he's going to move any closer. But then he turns out his light and we're plunged into darkness. Briefly, I wonder if it's okay that we're not having sex. Or touching one another. Should we be? I attribute our lack of contact to this being so new and strange, despite Max's claims that it isn't.

We've been friends for so long now, that navigating being in a relationship with one another won't come back *instantly*, will it? Even though we're obviously right for each other and meant to be together. There's bound to be some sort of slightly awkward transition period.

I lie listening to the sound of his breathing as it goes from conscious and jagged to slow and rhythmic. I wonder how he can fall asleep so quickly. Maybe he really doesn't find this peculiar. Maybe this *is* totally normal for him. Maybe because deep down we both always knew this would happen . . . If you look at it that way, I suppose he's right, it shouldn't be weird at all. Still, I already know I'm too buzzed to get any sleep tonight.

I spend the whole night lying awake, thinking about how wild it is to be in Dami's house, in bed next to Max. The next morning, I'm scrolling mindlessly on my phone with the frenzied zombie stare of someone who has barely closed their eyes, when I see an email from ShoutBox inviting me for an interview.

'Oh my God!' I squeal, forgetting how early it is. Suddenly I'm wide awake despite not getting a wink of sleep. My body is flooded with adrenaline. I gently shake Max. 'Max! *Max!*'

'Mmm.' He rolls over, rubbing his eyes.

'I got an interview! On THURSDAY!'

'Mmm?'

I give him a second to wake up. 'A real-life interview for a real-life job I actually like the sound of and could actually be good at!'

'Oh yeah?'

'Yeah, it's at the entertainment agency I was talking about last night. The one Margaret gave me the reference for. I'd be marketing and doing lots of stuff I already know how to do but . . . for films and stuff. Actual proper films and TV shows. Look at this list.' I sound breathless as I'm talking. I scroll through the long list of productions they've worked on, some of which I know Max has seen and liked.

'That's cool,' he says. It's not disingenuous, but there's a noticeable lack of animation in his voice. Then he gets out of bed and goes to the bathroom.

His reaction is a bit disappointing. All the enthusiasm I've shown for Max's career over the years flashes through my mind. All the freezing-cold galleries I stood around in until my feet hurt, pretending I liked the bizarre photography I didn't really get. The countless celebratory drinks we've had after he landed a job. The hours spent looking through film after film and helping him decide which shot he liked best. The cheerleading, the interest, the support. And all I get is 'that's cool'? I know I'm not exactly a globe-trotting photographer like he is – it's just an interview, I haven't even got the job – but this is a big deal for me.

Then I shake myself. I'm being stupid. Of course Max is supportive of me. He's listened to me complain about We Work, You Win more than I've listened to stories of his work successes. He's always there to hear me moan about my awful dates and laugh about them with me. He's always there to cheer me up when I accidentally eat my mum's fancy yoghurt and she goes batshit crazy. Max is there for me more than anybody.

But I can't help but think of what Dami said the other night, about partners taking the bad with the good, rather than just wanting the bad . . . Max is very sympathetic when things are going badly for me. But can I think of a single example of when he's encouraged me or been pleased about something going well?

Is it possible that Max is more interested in messy Becky, drunk Becky, sad Becky, desperate Becky, than he is in any other kind of Becky?

He comes back into the room, fully dressed. He smiles at me and my paranoia dissipates. Of course Max doesn't want me to be miserable. This is *Max*. I can't think of any examples of him being pleased about things going well for me because . . . well, hardly anything has in a long time. He was probably just sleepy because he'd only just woken up. What kind of reaction do I expect when someone is barely conscious?

'Are you leaving?' I ask.

'Yeah, I've got to get back to the flat to sort a few things.'

'Fran?' I ask.

He nods.

'Yeah, she's just collecting her stuff. There's not that much as she'd only brought some of it. But it just felt like a dick move to not be there, you know?'

I nod.

'Then, the magazine guys are pretty pissed with me for

leaving early,' he says. 'So I need to go and cobble together what I've got and convince them I really did get enough material.'

'Oh,' I say, feeling instantly guilty. He left Paris for me and now he's in trouble. I don't ask any more questions. 'Well, good luck. Hope it all goes okay.'

'Bye, Becky.' He picks up his camera bag and heads towards the door. 'Call you later?'

'Yeah.' I wonder again if it's weird that we didn't kiss, last night *or* this morning. And again, I tell myself it's fine, that it will just take time to adjust.

He leaves. I sit on the bed, soaking up the silence. Last night I felt so happy and this morning I feel oddly unsettled. I'm not sure if it's the lack of sleep, or that Max is gone, or what. But eventually I make myself get up and start preparing for my interview. My Interview. I try to remind myself to be excited, to bring back the energy I felt only fifteen minutes ago seeing the email pop up.

I was twenty-four the last time I had a successful interview. *Twenty-four.* I can barely remember it. I can't for the life of me recall what I was asked or how I responded. I just remember staring intently at Margaret's furry gloves.

I google some bullshit interview questions. *How would your co-workers describe you?* . . . Inconspicuous? *What is your greatest professional achievement?* Avoiding my turn on the kitchen rota three times in a row? *Tell me about a time you demonstrated leadership skills?* One time someone did a really foul-smelling shit on the sixth-floor loos and I sent an all-staff email warning everyone to give it an hour?

I cannot think of a recent good answer off the top of my head. I spend all of Tuesday and Wednesday scraping together passable achievements from when I first started at the company, and thinking about how best to phrase them. Phil helps me do mock interviews in the evenings. By the end of Wednesday night I'm as prepared as I'm ever going to be.

The night before the interview, I'm watching more *Sopranos* with Dami and Phil, trying to take my mind off how nervous I feel, when my phone buzzes. I assume it's Max, but I look down to see Angie's name. She replied to me. The sight of her name on my screen again is wonderful.

Hey, thanks <3 Heard you have a big interview tomorrow. Good luck. Ax

ps love you too x

My face breaks into a huge grin. With everything she's got going on – that's partially because of me – she still cares about how my interview goes.

Dami peers coyly at my phone and smiles. I assume she knows it's Angie. She must have told her about the interview and they probably discussed at length whether Angie was feeling ready to reply to me.

'I think I'm going to go to bed,' I announce, even though it's only ten o'clock. 'I'm shattered. And I want to get a good night's rest.'

'Yeah, you wanna be fresh,' agrees Phil, without looking away from the TV.

'Night, babe.' Dami reaches for my hand and squeezes it as I pass her. 'If I don't see you in the morning, good luck!'

'Thanks. Night.'

But when I get upstairs, I don't go to bed until I've worked out exactly what I want to say to my friend.

Dearest Angie,

I love you so much. You and Dami are my best friends in the universe and I miss you more than anything. I'm so sorry for the letter I sent you and where it ultimately led you.

You were right about most things. I wasn't being honest with myself about the letters, and I did write to you partly out of bitterness.

But you were wrong about why I was angry. I want you to have all the happiness that you deserve . . . I just want to be a part of it.

I don't know when we stopped being as close as we were. But I know now that it is partly my fault, and I would really like that to change.

I think we can find our way back, if you can forgive me.

Love you lots,
Becky

P.S. just a thought . . . Now you're selling the house, do you need a new flatmate? One who has a lifetime of making things up to you to do? E.g. in cleaning and home baking?

Chapter Twenty-Nine

It's the day of The Interview. I can't stop shaking and I feel glacial even though it's like a sauna in Phil and Damilola's flat. As soon as I'm dressed I message Max:

> I'm so nervous I'm as cold as ice. I might freeze to death on my way there. I won't make it

He replies:

> Ah, classic hyperventilation reducing efficiency of blood flow

We've not been messaging much more than usual since the night he came over, but I wanted to give him space, after everything with Fran. He said things went okay when she came to get her things, although he didn't give loads of details. I hope she wasn't too upset.

I go downstairs to eat but I barely touch my breakfast. Phil is babbling about something and I've not been listening.

'She's not listening to you,' Dami points out.

I tune in three seconds later. 'Oh, er, I am . . .' I try to recover.

'She's nervous,' Dami explains. 'Stop talking about lollipop men. Say something encouraging.'

'Sure.' Phil thinks for a second, then says, 'See, the thing is, Becky, you probably won't get it.'

'Phil!' Dami hisses. 'That is *not* encouraging! Of course you'll get it, Becky.' She pats me on the arm.

'How is *that* encouraging?!' Phil booms. '*That's* applying unnecessary pressure. My way she'll be way less angsty and less likely to fuck it up.'

'*She's not going to fuck it up.*' Dami's voice is practically a whisper.

'Not if she thinks she's not going to get it. Reverse psychology, innit.' Phil taps the side of his head.

Jesus Christ.

'Er, thank you both for your heartening words of inspiration, but I'm fine, thanks,' I say.

'Of course you are,' says Dami. She means it sincerely but it sounds like she's talking to a four-year-old.

When Phil starts reeling off all his mates' worst interview horror stories, 'so mine won't feel so bad', I leave and walk around the block for half an hour.

God, I really am nervous. What if they find out I accidentally wore my pyjamas into the office once? And had to keep my coat on all day to try to hide it? What if they can sense I took Ted's lip balm from his top drawer because it was funny to watch him anxiously licking his unmoistened lips during meetings?

I realise I haven't taken a breath in thirty seconds and remember to inhale. They probably won't be able to tell any of these things just from looking at me. Probably.

I finally get on the train. The journey to Barbican has never felt so short. I'm clinging to every tube stop like a baby roo to its mama. I'm safe on the tube. I can't say anything stupid on the tube. The interview hasn't happened yet and therefore I could, theoretically, still get the job. Once I go in there and screw it up there will be no other outcome except failure.

I arrive and dither around outside because I'm early. My jerky movements scare some woman so much she nearly spills coffee all over herself. I'm definitively *lurking*. This is what a lurker looks like. Lurkers don't get cool jobs in film and TV. *Come on, Becky.*

I go inside and register at reception. I get a little 'visitor' tag and sit on one of the sofas in the reception area. Oh God. Sitting is worse than lurking. I have so much nervous energy that's not burning off, it's just coursing through me . . . Oh God. I can't tell if I need to do a shit or not. And now my face is twitching. Great. Just great.

'Becky?' A woman in a shirt and black jumper with plaid trousers and chunky black boots comes out to greet me. I suddenly feel very drab in my suit. Of course they wear proper human clothes here . . . What was I thinking?! I may as well have worn one of Margaret's ensembles. Even that would have been more interesting.

I quickly take my hair out of its bun so she can see my pink tips.

'Monique?' I ask. Twitch, twitch.

'Yes, hi.' She beams. Her hair is so sleek. Angie would approve. 'Come on through.'

I follow her through the ground floor, which must be some sort of publisher. There are a lot of bookshelves and books piled up high around people's chairs, on desks . . . Some just in the middle of the floor. We weave our way through to the stairs. Towering heaps nearly fall on top of me several times.

Upstairs it's a little less cluttered, but still casual and vibrant. Framed movie posters decorate the walls and there's the odd plant dotted around.

'Welcome.' Monique holds her arm out. She sits down on a bright orange sofa in the middle of the room and gestures for me to sit.

It's stupid but . . . I already feel at home here.

My face is still twitching, though.

'So Becky, long journey?' Monique smiles. She seems very at ease in herself. But not in an arrogant way. Just in a down-to-earth way, like she's not plagued with embarrassing flashbacks of things that happened to her ten years ago when she's on the loo.

'Er, no,' I say. 'Not really. I'm based in London.'

I tell her where I'm living and successfully manage to skirt around the fact I'm staying in my friend's spare room. After a few minutes of small talk, another guy joins us, whose name is Will. He's wearing human clothes too. FFS.

He's very pale and super tall and skinny with clear-frame glasses. He looks kind of geeky, but in a cool way. They talk for a bit and make some film-related in-jokes I pretend to understand.

WHY ARE BOTH OF THESE PEOPLE SO EDGY?! I don't belong here . . . I belong with creepy Ted! And basic Jess! All this time I thought I deserved to fit in somewhere cooler I was mistaken. I'm a dolt, a Mary, a dullard! I can never be fashionable or confident or have *proper, well-*

formulated opinions . . . I live to mock others and slither under the rocks of functional society like a little malignant worm, peering up at people like Monique and Will from the shadows of self-loathing.

We chat casually for a bit longer. I'm on edge, waiting for the torrent of painful, banal interview questions to hit me. But they never do. It seems like they just want to get to know me. They do ask about my last job and why I wanted to leave We Work, You Win, and why I want to move into this area. They ask why this company specifically. But they're all fairly easy questions to answer . . . It doesn't feel like they're trying to test me or catch me out. It's going well, and I feel myself starting to relax, until Will asks, 'What's your favourite film?'

Oh God.

Mind . . . Stopped.

Blank. Gaping. Void.

Think of a film. ANY film.

Have I ever seen a film?

What is film?

Eventually, after fumbling madly in the dark recesses of my mind, I come out with *The Hobbit*.

The Hobbit?

THE HOBBIT?

I think I see Monique crack a smile. Will shuffles in his seat and his eyes slide to one side as if he's thinking my choice over.

'Interesting,' he says.

Immediately I think of a million other films I could have said. Recent, old, classic, funny, scary, arty, Hollywood, independent, just plain brilliant. *Taxi Driver. Moonlight. The*

Terminator. Get Out. The Graduate. Silence of the Lambs. Jennifer's Body. Boyhood. American Fiction. When Harry Met Sally. Fish Tank. Clueless. Parasite. Psycho. The Substance. Spirited Away.

Urgh. I can't take it back now. Will has already moved on.

We chat about other things and thankfully I seem to rediscover my brain. Before I know it an hour has passed and Will and Monique are briefly parading me around the office to wave at the rest of the team, before seeing me out.

'Thanks so much for coming in,' Will says.

'Yeah, thanks, Becky, it was great to meet you,' Monique adds.

I shake hands with each of them in turn. They both smile warmly. I've slipped in at least ten other great films by this point, just to demonstrate I do have a knowledge of cinema, and it feels like *The Hobbit* moment is safely behind us.

The journey home feels *long* as I analyse every second of the interview. At times I feel elated . . . I think, maybe, I didn't totally fuck that up? I mean, I was a bit nervous and I stumbled over my words a couple of times, but who doesn't do that in an interview, right? I feel like we got on. There was a vibe. I keep running through every single thing I said, trying to work out if it was stupid or not. Apart from *The Hobbit*, I can't come up with anything.

But then I get the flattening doubt. Did I take too long to get one of Will's puns? Was Monique offended when I took the last bourbon biscuit? Was it okay to eat the biscuits at all, or were they just offering to be polite but really you're not supposed to eat crumbly chocolatey snacks in an interview setting? Did I have a crumb in my teeth? Did they see how many times I was running my tongue across my teeth to check for said potentially rogue crumb?

When I get back, I take off my shoes and breathe in the comforting scent of whatever it is Phil is cooking tonight. It smells like some kind of curry. I hear Dami speaking. She's back earlier than usual today. Then I hear an unexpected bark of controlled yet manic laughter.

Angie. She's here.

My heart starts thudding wildly. I thought the interview had rinsed all of my adrenaline but apparently I have some left.

I take a breath and walk through to the living room. Angie is curled up on the sofa, gracefully clasping a glass of wine. She looks flawless as usual. She's wearing her standard green silk blouse and black leather skirt and her make-up is perfect. You wouldn't think she'd just broken up with her long-term partner.

When I come in she gives me a tight smile. It's not fake, just uncertain.

'Hi, Angie.' I clear my throat.

'Hi.' She swirls her wine and holds eye contact. I never knew the word 'hi' could say so much but her greeting is loaded.

'How was it?!' Dami asks. Angie's gaze is still fixed on me.

'Yeah . . . I'm not sure,' I answer. 'I don't think I *totally* fucked it up. But I did say my favourite film was *The Hobbit*.'

Angie snorts. I smile. It feels good to have her making fun of me again.

'Is that bad?' Dami asks. 'I've never seen it.'

'It's not exactly a *cultured* choice,' Angie explains.

'Right.' Dami nods. 'But . . . apart from that? It was okay?'

'I think so,' I say. 'I mean, I analysed every other moment on the train home and even the most paranoid and irrational parts of my brain couldn't find *too* much else to stress over, so . . .'

'That's good!' Dami claps.

'Yeah, well done, Becky Baggins,' Angie adds.

There's a moment of silence.

'Well.' Dami pats her lap. 'I think I'll just go and check if Phil needs a hand . . .' She smiles awkwardly at both of us in turn and leaves the room.

Without Dami's buffering presence it's harder to look Angie in the eye. I sit down in Dami's vacated seat.

Angie breaks the silence. 'I read your letter. D gave it to me.'

'Oh,' I say.

'It was much better than the first.'

I look up to check Angie's expression; she seems to be smiling. Faintly, but it's a smile nonetheless.

'You were right,' I say. 'I wanted my life to change, but . . . my delivery left a lot to be desired.'

'Yes.' Angie picks her nail. 'And *my* life.'

'I'm sorry, Angie.' My voice is heavy with guilt.

'Yeah, I think I read that somewhere.' Angie presses her lips together and takes a deep breath. 'Look, I should say sorry, too.'

My eyebrows raise. 'You're sorry? For what?'

'I think I came down on you a bit hard about the letter. I don't know, I think I've been walking around pretending everything was *hunky-dory* until you sent it. And, if I'm completely truthful . . . it wasn't.'

I'm confused. 'What do you mean?' I ask.

She takes a sip of wine. 'I already knew.'

'You *knew?* Knew what? That he was hiding stuff from you?'

Angie looks like she's gathering strength. She sighs. 'So one time, he said he had to work late and my messages weren't delivering, so I rang up the office, and the receptionist said the entire floor had gone out to the pub.'

'Why would he lie about going to the pub?'

Angie shrugs. 'Not a clue. I don't care if he goes to the pub. But I couldn't ask because then he'd be like, why did you ring the office, were you checking up on me? Anyway, yeah, then a few months ago I noticed he'd left his Slack open,' she says. 'And I saw his friend Mark making jokes on a group thread about where he and *Delith* had disappeared to the other night.'

'Hilarious,' I say. 'This Mark sounds like comedic genius.'

Angie smirks. 'Anyway, I wasn't looking, he left it open,' she adds, like I might judge. As if I wouldn't have shown up at his building in a trench coat and sunglasses by this point, if I were her. 'But I couldn't ask him about it, obviously, because then it would look like I was snooping.'

This conversation is baffling to me. Angie is the *last* person I ever would have thought cared about looking like she was 'snooping'. I always thought if she suspected her boyfriend was actually cheating on her she'd be straight in there, shining a light in his eye.

'He's always flirted, but it wasn't just that. There have been lots of little hints. Things that didn't quite add up. Things I've been willing to overlook. And when I got your letter, I just couldn't pretend I didn't see them anymore. I guess because then I knew other people saw them, too. I've been lying to myself for a long time.' She looks down into her glass, avoiding eye contact.

None of this tallies with the Angie that I thought I knew so well. I knew that Angie must see Jacob's flirting, but I always assumed she was so secure she was genuinely okay with it. I'm not sure what to do with the information that confident, outspoken Angie has things that secretly bother her, too.

'I guess that makes two of us.' I laugh.

Angie draws breath. 'So . . . Yeah. I'm sorry for making you feel like it was all your fault. It wasn't.'

'I still shouldn't have sent it, in the way that I did,' I apologise. 'And I am sorry.'

'Yeah, well, next time maybe just gently point to the red flags. Just don't sit in silence, stewing for years, then lob them at me.'

I laugh. 'Okay, so honesty is our new policy?'

'Well, if we're being really honest . . .' Angie pauses, like she's about to say something important. 'I *hate* your hair. Lose the pink tips.'

I burst out laughing. A warm, tingling sensation rushes down my back, like when someone you barely know remembers your birthday or the way you take your tea. *Angie is insulting me like normal.* 'You're wrong,' I assert. 'The pink tips stay.'

Angie grins. 'Becky, look, in all seriousness. In the spirit of helping each other see things we might rather not see, there is something I've been wanting to bring up with you. Don't hate me, okay?'

I sit up, intrigued. I genuinely have no idea what she's about to say.

'It's just... I know you have this *version* of what happened with you and Max. That he was *perfect* and you ended it because of *circumstances*...' She waves her hands back and forth, her wine swishing against the sides of the glass. 'And he was like... the one that got away. But, that's not how *I* remember it.'

'Oh,' I say.

There's a silence. Angie puts her glass down on the table.

'How do you remember it?' I ask eventually. I can't not want to hear about this, now she's brought it up.

'Well.' Angie grimaces. 'You have this version that you broke his heart. I mean yes, *you* broke up with *him* technically, but he decided to leave, so... I think the break-up is on him just as much as you. I mean, did Max ever suggest long-distance?'

No. Max didn't abandon *me*. I abandoned *him*. Didn't I? But I can't deny there's some sense in what she's saying.

'I remember him being a bit of a shit boyfriend, to be honest,' she goes on. 'Unreliable. Uncommunicative. I kind of thought the only reason you made it work was because you practically lived together and worked together. But, even then, I remember it being... *difficult.*'

Difficult? Was Max difficult? We were so young. I do remember wanting to be told how he felt about me more, but it didn't matter because I always *knew*. He's never been great at sticking to plans... but I don't remember it bothering me too much. Did it?

'And I know you think that you got over it at the time because you were too distracted by life in the big city, you were a naive fool with the world at her feet, yada yada. But . . . I kind of always thought you got over it because it ended at the right time. Then when he came back and things weren't going so great for you, I think you kind of rewrote history, to be honest.'

When she stops talking, I don't know what to say. I'm aware of my brain working overtime to contradict her words. *Max might be shit at expressing his feelings directly but he's not 'uncommunicative'. He communicates in lots of ways that aren't verbal. And he's not 'unreliable'. He might be difficult to pin down sometimes but he always shows up when I need him.* But a little voice in my head reminds me of him ditching me in Paris, and the fact we still haven't spoken about anything properly since.

But he did break up with Fran, and he did say it was always me. What more needs to be said, really . . . ? I rationalise.

'Look,' Angie says, as I go over the past from a new perspective. 'We don't need to discuss it. Maybe I'm wrong. But if you or Dami had suggested Jacob was untrustworthy earlier on in our relationship, I might have done something sooner. So there. Now I've said it. Let's say no more about it, okay?'

I nod. I'm sceptical. Her version of the past doesn't match up with mine at all. I mentally shelve it; I'll think more about it later, but for the moment I'm just pleased that Angie and I are friends again.

'Anyway, Becks,' Angie carries on, 'I understand why things got blown out of proportion. I know I've been a hag, too. I've been so focused on the things I want, I forgot to be considerate of your feelings.'

I don't say anything. Now feels like the wrong moment to agree too emphatically with that statement.

'I also know that we love each other. And I just lost a boyfriend . . . I can't lose anyone else that I love.'

Hot tears start prickling the back of my eyes. *She still loves me.* 'So . . . ?'

'So. I guess . . . What I'm saying is . . . Yes. I am in the market for a flatmate.' She looks up, smiling, and puts down her wine.

'Really?!' I feel like storm clouds I didn't even know were hovering over me start clearing. Sunshine starts peeking through.

'Yes.' Angie nods.

I launch myself across the room and throw my arms around her. Angie's thin frame seems so fragile in my arms and I feel an overwhelming sense of protectiveness.

Angie hugs me back. 'But only because you promised me baked goods,' she says. 'Renege on this and I'm out.'

'That's fair,' I mumble into her blouse.

We hug for a minute longer. I breathe in her familiar perfume and think of how perfectly everything seems to be working out. Angie forgives me. We're going to live together. I had a job interview today that actually went well. I am with Max. It feels almost too good to be true.

Dear Mum,

I'm really sorry if I hurt your feelings by leaving so abruptly; I think I just wanted things to change and I didn't know how to go about it.

I still don't think we should live together anymore – I'm actually going to be moving in with Angie – but I'm not planning on flying off to Bali anytime soon. I would love to live close enough that I can come round and watch Grey's Anatomy whenever we feel like it.

All my love,
Becky

Chapter Thirty

We spend the rest of the evening giggling and catching up. Phil tactfully stays upstairs so that Angie, Damilola and I can be alone. There's no wedding talk, job talk or kitchenware talk . . . Although I do find myself more interested in fridges now I'm actually faced with the concept of choosing one.

Who *am* I?

I feel giddy with how lovely the evening has been. Eventually, Angie decides to head home. As I'm seeing her out, a shadowy figure appears at the end of Dami's path. It's Max.

'Oh . . . Hi, Max.' Angie walks past him. 'Looks like I just missed you, sorry. Next time.' She doesn't sound in the least bit sorry.

'Good to see you, Angie.' Max smirks as she gets into her car. 'She still hates me, then,' he says as we both watch her drive off.

'I guess so.'

'Ngegh. Oh well.'

In the past Max and I have always joked about Angie disliking him, but tonight it doesn't seem so funny. Maybe because what Angie said is still playing on my mind, or because Angie and I are moving in together and Max and I are beginning an actual relationship. I suddenly wonder how on Earth that's going to work, if my boyfriend and my flatmate can't stand each other.

'Better try harder,' I reply. 'Angie and I are going to be roommates.' I wait eagerly for his response to this news.

Max keeps staring down the road. 'Well, I guess I can let her win an argument every now and then,' he jokes. He doesn't show any sign of reaction.

'Did you hear me say Angie and I are going to move in together?' I repeat.

'Yeah. That's cool. Will you be living in her massive house?' He finally turns to face me.

'She's selling it,' I reply. I don't say anything else about how Jacob's letting her keep half from the sale of their house, even though the deposit was his – he must feel guilty, now he's stopped gaslighting her – or how she'll buy somewhere and I'll give her rent to help pay off the mortgage, or the flats we've been looking at on the internet. He doesn't seem to be that interested. Am I making a big deal out of it? Maybe moving out of my mum's isn't such a huge thing . . . I guess we all did this years ago. Maybe I can't expect him to jump up and down in excitement for reaching a milestone a second time. 'I didn't know you were coming,' I say instead.

'Yeah, I was working near here.'

'Oh, you got another job? That was quick.' Being freelance, Max usually has a bigger gap between projects.

'Nah, they lined me up for this ages ago. Beating them off with a stick these days,' he jokes.

I frown. That doesn't add up. Max made it sound like he left Paris suddenly – like he had to race back to break up with Fran and come to be with me – but if that was the case, how could he have had another job booked? Max notices my confusion and realises he's said something amiss. A flash of something crosses his face as he recognises I've caught him in a lie. He was always supposed to leave Paris on that date, and he was lying to make it sound like he left just to see me.

'You gonna ask me in, or . . . ?' There's an edge to his voice now.

'Er, yeah.' I wave him past me. I feel a little unsteady on my feet. Max lied to me. He outright lied. And for the life of me, I can't understand why. Why would he pretend he rushed back just for me, if he didn't?

Max has disappeared inside and I stand on the pavement for a moment, my head spinning. I think of all the times Max has implied he made some sort of special effort to see me. Even my birthday. He said he couldn't come and then turned up at the last minute like he blew off work because he couldn't *bear* not to be there.

Was any of that true? Is he sometimes pretending like he made more effort to see me than he did? I shake my head. I'm being paranoid. He *did* lie, there's no way around it, but he probably just wanted to impress me and make things right because we left on weird terms. Stupid, but not earth-shattering. There's no reason to assume every time he went the extra mile for me was made up. This is Max. My Max. Best friend Max. Love of my life Max. Always there for me Max.

Unreliable Max? Uncommunicative Max? I can't help but think about what Angie said.

I go inside. Max is waiting for me in the hallway. Any blossoming doubt shrivels up and recedes as he takes my hand.

We go to bed and I am so, so tired that I don't interrogate any of this further. I don't think too hard about whether Angie's words have any weight, or analyse that once again we don't kiss before we fall asleep.

I get a blissful night's rest as a girl who is madly in love and has exciting job prospects. But when I wake up the next morning, I see two things that blow that dream to pieces.

My phone is lying on my bedside table charging, and a message from Sara pops up on my screen.

> Hey babe, glad you didn't die lol. Are you coming to my show tonight? Max and Fran were coming but he told us you're together now? I was always backing you guys to get back together tbh. Ed has food poisoning because the man never reheats his risotto properly, but Aurelia will be there x

I blink at the message and shake my head. At first I think Sara must have it wrong. Max would never go out with these guys without me? Would he? This is *our* group of friends. He always made out like he hardly sees them that much anymore. It's a smack of reality that, in light of my recent chats with both Dami and Angie about him, I can't quite manage to feed to the denial monster. He had plans with our friends from Scintilla . . . without me. And with Fran.

What the hell? Is that a regular thing? Does Max take Fran out and purposely not invite me? I think back through a million little niggling memories . . . Fran knowing what Sara's next theme party was going to be before I did . . . Sara knowing about Max and Fran moving in together . . . Max said Fran bumped into Sara, but what if that wasn't true?

I'm still reeling from this bewildering theory when I pick up my phone, and see I have an email from Monique at ShoutBox.

Dear Becky,

Thank you very much for coming in yesterday – everyone enjoyed meeting you. However, I'm not going to be offering you the job and I wanted to let you know quickly so you could pursue other avenues as soon as possible.

I hope you are not too disappointed. You got down to the last five out of 250 applicants which is an accomplishment in itself.

Wishing you all the best,
Monique

It is a brutal double digital attack.

I stare at the email, reading it over and over to check the words still say the same thing. *I hope you are not too disappointed.* The sentence taunts me. Disappointed doesn't even begin to cover it. I am crushed. Monique has broken my heart.

If nothing else, it at least makes me forget Max for a second. I don't have space in my brain to work out what's going on with him in the face of this rejection. It's immature – I realise people don't get jobs all the time – but I can't help it . . . I start sobbing. I wanted that job *so* badly. I really thought I'd be good at it. Stupidly, on some level, I had faith that I'd get it.

My shuddering and sniffing wakes Max. He rolls over and sits up. 'Hey, what's up?'

I pass him my phone. He reads the email and squeezes my arm. 'Ah, Becks. I'm really sorry. Look, there will be other jobs.'

'Not as good as this one.' I wipe my nose with the back of my hand and look away from him so he can't see how red and blotchy my face is. 'Ugh, I can't believe I actually thought I had a shot. I'm never going to be good enough.'

'It was your first proper interview in years,' he reassures. 'Don't beat yourself up.'

'Maybe it's stupid,' I say. 'Trying to make the leap into something I actually care about. I should have never left We Work, You Win.'

'Well, it's true you may never find another boss with such a fine collection of hats,' Max jokes.

I laugh through my tears.

'Come on.' Max turns my face to his. 'It's okay. Everything's going to be fine.'

'What if I can't find a job and I can't move in with Angie? What if I have to work at another recruitment company?' I wail.

'It wouldn't be so bad. Maybe you will, that's okay.' Max cups his hands around my cheeks. 'Think how many more Tequila Trollops you'll be able to afford. Hey, I know what would cheer you up . . . shall I bring you a mimosa in bed?'

When he says this, my heart sinks. Working at another

recruitment company 'wouldn't be so bad'? 'Maybe I will'? He knows how unhappy it's been making me for years. How hard it's been to pull myself out of the rut. His tone is so . . . *light*. Ostensibly it's supposed to be comforting, but it feels like he's kind of enjoying it. He doesn't sound disappointed about this for me at all.

I tilt my face up, daring to look into his eyes and be honest with myself about what I find there. With earth-shattering sadness I realise it's glee. I don't want to see it, but I can't not. He's *pleased* that things have gone wrong for me. On some level, he's delighted that my plans are crashing and burning and at the prospect of me staying exactly where I've always been.

I am split in two. One side wants to laugh at his joke, to curl up in the cosy, protective warmth of familiarity, to regress. To drink a mimosa and pretend everything is fine. Perhaps it's not so bad here, having nothing of my own and not being able to respect myself. I know it well. Maybe it's just who I am. The other side pushes against it. I've come so far. I can't go back to the way things were. I don't like my life, I don't like who I've been and I'm ready to move on and become someone new.

'Max . . .' I look straight at him. 'Can I ask . . . When you said it's always been me . . .'

'Yeah?'

'What did you mean by that?'

'I mean, it feels pretty self-explanatory.' He laughs.

'Sure. It's just, after Paris I had no idea what you were thinking . . . I *never* have any idea what you're thinking. And I want to know. Did you know that you still had feelings for me when you were with Fran but didn't think I felt the same? Did you not know it and then realise it suddenly when you read the letter? I just . . . I want to know more.'

He knits his eyebrows together. 'What letter?' Max asks.

I blink slowly. 'What do you mean . . . What letter?! THE letter.'

Heat rapidly travels up my neck. I essentially did the emotional equivalent of jumping up and down naked on a trampoline and he is *having trouble remembering it*? How can that be?

Max shakes his head. 'Still don't know what you're talking about.'

'The letter where I . . . Well. The letter where I tell you . . . You know. About my feelings for you.'

Max continues to look blank.

Oh my God.

He didn't get the letter. I can see it in his face. He really has no idea what I'm talking about. Somehow, my words never reached him.

This entire time I've been working on the assumption that I confessed my feelings, which brought him to realise his own, that my letter was what instigated change . . . and he *never even received it*?

My mind starts turning things over at a million miles an hour. I was working so hard trying to read between the lines, spot the clues, figure out the hints, that I found something that wasn't even there. HE NEVER EVEN READ THE STUPID LETTER.

So what happened to it?! Did it get lost in the mail? Max's building has a lot of people in it . . . I suddenly remember the number of pigeon holes there are in the mail room. I faintly recall him complaining once about post going to a Max Martin on the second floor. Oh my God . . . Was my hideously embarrassing soul-bearing opened by some random dude? I bet he had a great laugh!

But then why this massive shift in Max's behaviour? Why did he suddenly start acting differently? Why did he do the hug?! And the invite to Paris? If he didn't get my letter then how did he know how I felt . . . ?

Oh.

OH.

The truth starts falling into place. I'm an idiot. A colossal idiot. Suddenly all the pieces start coming together and I feel a million times more humiliated than when I thought Max read it.

Max didn't *need* to read it. He didn't need me to tell him how I felt. He already knew.

'Max, how long have you known that I'm in love with you?' I ask. I'm past feeling embarrassed about it, now.

He looks uncomfortable. 'Well . . .' he says.

The look on his face tells me everything. He's always known. And if he's always known, that means he can't *really* want to be with me now, because otherwise he could have been with me at any moment over the past three years, since he came back to London.

I think of his hurt about me flying to the other side of the world. What if it wasn't really that he realised he loves me and was going to miss me? What if he just didn't want me to be the one doing something exciting for once? The invite to Paris . . . What if it wasn't that he was desperate to see me? What if it was to put himself back in the driver's seat? Taking pity on me, splashing the cash on expensive tickets to *his* exciting trip? What if he didn't bail the next day and stop speaking to me because he was feeling guilty about Fran, what if he just felt he'd got me back where he wanted me? And then, once he felt me slipping away again, he knew in order to keep me where I was he had to break up with her, and show up here in some big romantic gesture?

Except . . . it's not romantic. Not even slightly. It's control, it's ego, it's clinging onto something that makes him feel good about himself. I race frantically through all my memories. Even Max saying it's always been me felt slightly half-hearted, if I'm really, painfully honest with myself. If it had always been me, and he knew how I felt about him, then it would have been me a long time ago.

We haven't even kissed since. Again, I assumed it was because he felt guilty about Fran, but is that really why? Maybe we just don't belong together in the present. Maybe, together, all we have is the past.

'Max,' I ask. 'Why are you here? Is it because you want to be with me? Genuinely?' It physically hurts me to say this. To finally put this niggling feeling into words and then actually say them out loud.

'Why else would I be here?' He's in full defensive mode now. His jaw is clenched. He's pulling at his hair, massaging his temples, avoiding eye contact.

'Well . . .' I've never challenged Max on anything and it's not easy. I can't remember us ever having a confrontation, but then, why would I have done? Our entire relationship is exchanging memes and bizarre facts and bitching about other people over drinks. Joking. Laughing. Not talking about anything real. And when we went out in our early twenties we were so . . . *young*. We had no life, we just rolled around in bed and in bars. But if we have any hope of dating each other as adults we need to be able to say hard things to each other, surely?

'I suppose, I'm wondering if you could be here . . . because you felt me moving on, and you don't want that to happen. You don't really love me, but you love that I love you. You love having me waiting there, hanging on for you, like some kind of sad, adoring . . . *back-up option*.' There. I've said it. There's no taking it back. It's out there in the world.

Max makes a spluttering sound.

'If you were just a back-up, why would I have broken up with Fran for you?' he asks.

I bite my lip. 'Because you don't want to lose me. But . . . you don't really want me either.'

I wait for a denial, but it's not forthcoming.

'How often do you go out with Fran and our friends from Scintilla without me?' I hold up my phone and point at the message. 'I guess my invite got lost in the mail.'

Max makes another indistinguishable sound. 'I mean, Fran was my girlfriend. Obviously, I'd bring her out with my friends.'

'But why lie to me about it?' I ask. 'You always made out like you barely saw her, quite frankly. Like you weren't that involved. That's partly why you moving in together came as such a shock to me.'

I'm going over everything and rewriting it. I always thought that *I* was the one making sure Fran and I were never in the same room . . . which I was, but now that I think about it, he must have been too. He never suggested she come along to any of our drinks. And he's clearly been involving her in group situations and conveniently forgetting to invite me. The only times we've met is when he absolutely couldn't avoid it.

'I didn't *lie* about it. I don't tell you, or Fran, everything. Look, I'm sorry you haven't been in any real relationships, so you wouldn't understand, but people don't need to track each other's every move,' he retorts.

Ouch. That stings. 'I haven't had any real relationships because I was pining after *you*.' I'm incredulous. 'And you knew that, didn't you?'

'Don't blame *me* for your complete inability to function, Becky,' Max retaliates.

Wow.

WOW.

I can't believe how quickly this has degenerated. Five minutes ago he was talking about mimosas in bed. This doesn't feel real. Part of me wants to stop fighting and just go get the champagne. That would be *so much* easier.

But part of me knows this moment was coming for me. If not today, if not tomorrow, it was on its way. Our relationship is flimsy. Under any sort of real pressure it was always going to fold. I think I've been becoming aware of it for a while now.

It suited me to think I was in love with Max, because dating was so difficult and scary that I wouldn't have to try and fall in love with anyone else. It suited him to have me waiting in the wings like some second, supplementary pseudo-girlfriend.

Clearly he's known how I felt, or *thought* I felt, for a long time.

This isn't some great, novel-worthy romance that never got its chance to shine. We were both just overly invested in keeping a foot in the past – him for the ego boost and me for the shield from reality.

At that moment, I think of the Death card and its real meaning. *An impactful ending of sorts; the death of a relationship, a friendship, an identity, an era in order that new life can take root.*

It really does feel like everything is ending now, hopefully in order that everything can begin again.

'Becky, I'm sorry.' Max softens and moves towards me. 'I didn't mean that. Fuck this. Can we stop arguing? Let's just rewind, yeah?'

I desperately want to, but I can't. I can't unknow what I know now.

'Max, I think you should leave,' I say.

My heart is broken. But it's not really broken for Max. It's broken for the idea of Max and knowing that I can never hide behind him again.

Dear Fran,

This is a bit awkward but, um, I was sort of always in love with your boyfriend. (Or at least, I thought I was, but it turns out, I need a reality check about what real love looks like.)

    Either way, I'm really sorry about any part I played in causing you any hurt. I'm not writing to you to absolve my guilt or ask for your forgiveness; I don't deserve either. I'm only writing because I wanted to say you deserve better.

    Sorry that I didn't get to know you, you seem cool.

Yours,
Becky

Chapter Thirty-One

After Max leaves, I sit for ages on the bed, staring into space. Did that really just happen? Did I really just end it with Max? The person I've been wishing I was in a relationship with for the last three years? And now, within a week, it's over?

It can't be over. *Surely*. I've been hoping for this for so long and now it's just . . . gone? Am I wrong? Am I overreacting or misreading the situation? But no. I think this is the first time I'm seeing clearly. Every time I run through the events in my head I can't come up with a different interpretation. I was kidding myself. The whole thing was a fantasy that collapsed like a house of cards.

I still don't have a romantic relationship. Or a place of my own to live. I didn't get the dream job. Ostensibly, all my efforts have failed spectacularly. But maybe a couple of – albeit pretty massive – setbacks don't have to mean I'm a total failure. Maybe the real failure is giving up. Repeating my patterns. Continuing on in an unhealthy but familiar and easy dynamic with Max. Begging my mum to take me back. Finding another job I don't want and remaining there, complaining but never doing anything about it.

I start getting dressed on autopilot. I barely realise what

I'm doing until I'm pulling on my jeans and I'm halfway down the stairs before I register I've forgotten to put on a bra.

'Becky?' Dami calls from the kitchen. It's still super early and she hasn't left for work yet. 'Are you okay?'

She steps into the hallway, takes one look at my face and rushes towards me.

'Oh Becky.' She puts her arms around me. 'I heard Max leave.'

I hug her back for a moment, but there's only one place I want to be. I clear my throat. My voice feels shaky. 'I'm just popping out.' I just about manage to make it through the sentence without crying.

'Okay.' Dami stands back and rubs my arm. 'I'm in the office today, but call me if you want me.'

'Yeah.' I make a half-hearted attempt at a smile. 'Thanks.'

I leave the house and start walking. I don't feel like getting on public transport. My mind feels too crowded to be packed inside a narrow tube with hundreds of other minds, all sifting through their own problems.

I walk for nearly an hour, but I hardly notice it. My feet take me in the right direction and my brain gets some time to breathe.

Finally, I get there, and every single part of me starts relaxing into solace. I knock on the door. The familiar beeps and buzzes of the alarm system unlocking are sweet music to my ears.

Mum opens the door.

'*Mum*,' I start to say, but I barely make it through because I am blubbering. I am just a big incoherent mess of feelings disintegrating into a pool of tears on the doorstep.

I lunge at her. I cling to her in a giant hug, breathing in the comforting smell of my childhood home, and think how I will always want my mum when things fall apart, just a little bit, and that's okay. She hugs me back and we stand there for a bit.

'Mum . . . how long would it take us to drive to B&Q?'

Two hours later, after traipsing through floor after floor of various showrooms, and sorting through so many imperceptibly different shades of paint I wanted to eat my own fingers in frustration, we're back at the house with rollers, brushes and two tins of 'daffodil spring matte finish.'

'Becky, what is all of this for?' Mum asks again as we lay the tins against the wall in the corridor, but I think she already knows.

I march upstairs and head for the back of the house, towards my bedroom. I pause in the doorway and take one last look around, capturing a mental snapshot of my bedroom as it's been preserved for over a decade now. It's time that time caught up with this room. It's time that time caught up with *me*.

I lie down on my bed, next to a pair of my pyjamas that Mum's washed, dried and folded neatly in a pile. I stare up at Bowie one last time. 'Things are going to be different, friend,' I whisper. Then I hear myself and laugh. Possibly I've gone insane but that's okay.

I stand on the bed and carefully take him down, then roll the poster up and put an elastic band around it. I stare at the blank square on the ceiling, a slightly brighter shade of white than the faded paint around it. I breathe. That wasn't so bad.

I start taking down more posters. Mum appears in the doorway behind me and watches for a moment. She swallows hard, like there's a lump in her throat. Then, wordlessly, she begins helping me. Soon the garish yellow walls are completely bare, apart from leftover smudges and Blu Tack marks.

We strip the bed and dump the sheets in a corner. After moving the mattress into the hallway, we begin dismantling the bed frame. We push the wardrobe, the bookcase and the bedside table into the centre of the room and cover them in my old bedding. I grab a newspaper and lay out the individual sheets across the floor.

Then, before I can think too much, I open the first tin of paint and dunk the roller in. I start spreading it up the walls. The splodge of creamy 'daffodil spring' looks classy and sophisticated next to my childish buttercup yellow. There's no going back now. Mum goes to put on an old shirt, and then comes back and grabs the other roller. We put on Magic Radio and keep rolling until there's no buttery yellow left in sight.

When the room is completely transformed, I sit down on the floor and cross my legs. To my surprise, Mum places herself opposite me. I don't think I've ever seen her sit on a floor in my life.

'Did you get my letter?' I ask. 'The second one.'

'Yes.'

'Well, I, er . . .' God, I love her, but the woman still makes me nervous as hell. 'I think Gavin should move in. I thought this could be his study.' Gavin's a solicitor and works from home a lot. He's always moaning about how he gets neck cramp from having his laptop at his kitchen table. 'Or, if you really don't want Gavin to move in, maybe this could be a library.' She's always complaining about not having enough shelf space. 'Or a really gorgeous spare room or . . . whatever you want it to be. But it can't be *my* room anymore.'

She doesn't say anything and I carry on. 'I think keeping my room like this is too much of a safety net. It's too easy to fall back on it, it's too easy for me to stay stuck where I am. And, well . . . for you as well. How long have you been with Gavin now? Since I was at uni, right?'

God, has it really been that long? Gavin has become a steady background presence in my life over the years without me even noticing it. The operative words being 'background presence'. He's there on birthdays, Christmas, Easter. Occasionally we all go out for Sunday lunch together. But mainly, he and Mum see each other alone outside of the house for a few hours – to go to the cinema, for a coffee, the garden centre. They never evolved past 'dating'. To some degree, that's how Mum likes it – she's very independent – but guiltily, I now wonder if it's partly because she was keeping everything the same for me. And then I moved back in.

'Nearly ten years,' Mum answers. 'It must be, yes.'

'So,' I say. 'Maybe it's time to move forward. You don't have to. Maybe you'd like to keep the set-up as it is. But, I don't know, maybe without me here you'll have the freedom and the space to consider it.'

She takes a deep breath and looks around. 'Well, if this was his study, he might stop complaining about his neck,' she remarks.

I laugh.

'I just . . . I never wanted you to feel like you don't have a solid base here,' she goes on. 'You were so young when your father left, so with anyone I dated . . . I never wanted you to feel like *I* was abandoning you. I never wanted you to feel like your home was being intruded on. I wanted everything to be stable for you.'

I think back to my childhood – how Mum's other relationships usually stopped at the doorstep – and realised I'd never thought about it like that before. About what a conscious decision that must have been. Gavin is definitely the boyfriend I've had the most contact with, and it's still fairly restrained even now I'm an adult. My heart swells thinking of my mum making sacrifices so that I wouldn't feel sidelined.

'Mum, I love you for that,' I say. 'But I'm nearly thirty. I don't need everything to be exactly the same anymore. You're allowed to have a life and . . . well . . . I'm sorry I've made that difficult for you by continuing to be such a massive baby. I'm sorry I've been such a let-down.'

Mum reaches over and holds my hand. 'You're not a let-down, my love. I think I've let *you* down.'

'Of course you haven't,' I protest. 'That's preposterous. You do so much for me. You've given me *everything*. And I took it all for granted and . . .'

'Yes, I've done so much for you,' Mum interrupts. 'Too much.'

'What do you mean?! I'm sorry I made you feel that way, Mum. I'm sorry I've been ungrateful.' I squeeze her hand. I'm flooded with so much love for the woman sitting in front of me that I can barely breathe with the guilt of knowing I made her feel like she's been a bad parent.

'Becky,' Mum goes on. 'I've always wanted the best for you and to help you. This began with the best of intentions. But, well, as time went on I could see it wasn't helping, or making you happy. I think for a long time I've been convincing myself that it was still the best thing for you, when it wasn't, because . . . *I* wanted you here.'

I blink. 'You wanted me here?'

In all my time living here, I've never thought of my mum as having taken any pleasure in my presence. I'm a nuisance. A parasite. A money-sucking, hot-water-draining, grocery-consuming leech.

'But . . .' I start. 'But I make rings on the table and leave my pants on the bathroom floor and eat your yoghurt.'

Mum smirks. 'Yes, you do. But when you do those things, when you're still here, you're still my baby. I think it was easy for me to criticise you for being irresponsible, without really wanting you to move on and be responsible. I've let it all slide, instead of pushing you like I should have. You'll understand this one day, if you ever have children, but . . . it's hard to find your kids don't need you anymore.'

I let her words settle for a moment. I've never thought of it like that before. I always knew Mum was controlling, but . . . I always blamed myself entirely for still being here. The fact that she's admitting some mutual responsibility in our dynamic makes me feel ever so slightly less pathetic.

'I still need you, Mum,' I say. 'I'll always need you. I just . . . maybe don't need you to buy my underwear.'

Mum laughs.

'I think, maybe I will ask Gavin to move in,' she says. 'Christ knows he's been hinting at it enough.' She smiles, and I can tell that's what she really wants.

I look around at the freshly painted room. I picture Gavin sitting in here, taking calls and drinking cups of coffee and drawing his neck pillow tight, right in the spot where I've slept, not slept, cried, snuck boys – and then, later on, girls – in when Mum was out, laughed, hated all my friends, loved all my friends, where basically every passing thought has swept through my mind for the last twenty-nine years. This will be his space now. There is no going back.

I barely realised how much I took for granted having such a solid base here. Now that someone else is *actually* taking my room. *My* room. In some ways, I feel like someone just pulled the floor from under me. And then the ground beneath the floor. I'm falling, falling, falling into a terrifying abyss of unknown.

But in another way, I know it's completely right and way, way overdue. It hurts, but I can already tell it's the kind of pain you need to feel in order to grieve, heal and renew. Kind of like the real meaning of the Death card.

We sit on the floor for a while longer. Eventually Mum says, 'Shall I make us some tea?'

I nod gratefully and we move downstairs, through to the living room. I take my seat on the usual side of the sofa while Mum goes to put the kettle on. The cushions still have my imprint in them and I nestle into it.

Then I see something in the corner of the room. A pack of

familiar cards with little figures on them and a book that says *Understanding Tarot*.

'Mum,' I say, hardly believing my eyes. 'Are those . . . *tarot* cards?'

'Hmm?' she says over the noise of the kettle boiling. 'Oh, those! Yes. Anne from Poker Club brought them over for a laugh and forgot to take them with her.'

I stare at them in disbelief. 'Can I . . . ?'

'Oh, yes, go ahead. I'm sure Anne wouldn't mind.'

I move over to the pack of cards and the book and pick them both up. I sit back down on the sofa, holding the cards reverently. On the front of the pack, a man in a frilly tunic is holding a pole and a rose and tilting his head back under the sun in a carefree manner. I open the pack and begin to shuffle the cards.

I hear Spellbound Sue, telling me to stop when I 'feel' it. I break midway through the deck and lay three cards face up. Past. Present. Future.

First I lay The Fool. The same carefree man on the front of the pack stares back at me. Then I lay Strength. A woman in a white dress bends over a lion, holding its jaws in her hands. Finally, I reveal The World. A woman stands dancing on some clouds, waving some wands around in the centre of some kind of wreath.

I read about my past: The Fool.

The fool is a naive adventurer, about to begin a significant journey. Idealistic, but not grounded in reality, he sets off into the world blissfully ignorant of the dangers and hardships that lie in wait . . .

I cringe. Yep. That definitely sounds like the me of a few weeks ago. Innocently believing that I knew my own mind, that my unhinged letters were dishing out necessary truths to those who needed it, that I knew exactly what needed to change, and it wasn't me.

I flip to my present: Strength.

The woman is strong in the face of the lion, representing her base instincts. Although her position is dangerous and she may have reason to be afraid, she does not cow to her fear. This card is about having the courage to listen to our own, most difficult inner conflicts, and tame them in order to live boldly and confidently as our true selves. This card is about resilience of character.

I sit with this for a moment. It resonates profoundly. I do feel, right now, that is what I'm doing . . . or at least trying to do. I don't want to give in to fear anymore. I turn to the page about my future: The World.

One of the most positive cards of the Major Arcana. The dancer in the centre is the Fool, but he has travelled the world on a spiritual quest and is reborn, with a new understanding of himself. This is a card of success, harmony and renewal. It is a card of deep joy as dedication to transformation pays off.

You know . . . I'm starting to believe that maybe Spellbound Sue was actually onto something all along?

I feel ten times lighter than I did when I walked into the house.

I'm still not sure I *really* believe in spiritual divination, as such, but . . . isn't it strange that these cards and this book were lying here in wait for me? And that I would pick these three cards, in this order? It feels like the universe is trying to tell me something. Or, maybe, the cards being here is just a massive coincidence and my own subconscious is trying to tell me something . . . But in any case, I sense that 'something' is very important and should be listened to.

Mum pours two mugs of tea and comes to sit beside me. She puts them on the table.

'Good reading?' she asks.

'Very good.' I smile, looking at the cards on the table, thinking how they're a world away from the last reading I had.

'I was thinking.' Mum folds her hands in her lap. 'I think a sofa bed might look nice in the corner of Gavin's study, don't you? You know, just in case you ever do want to visit.'

I hug her. We sit there clutching each other for a few minutes.

'Why don't you go and run a bath and get into something comfy? I assume you're staying, tonight at least?' Mum suggests. 'I'll put my pyjamas on, too.'

We hang out for the rest of the evening, watching *Grey's Anatomy* and eating everything left in the fridge. I fall asleep on the sofa, listening to the comforting sounds of Meredith Grey having a major life crisis and my mum making her pre-bedtime decaffeinated tea.

The next morning, I head upstairs and push the door to

my old bedroom open gently. I hover in the doorway for a moment, taking it all in, saying goodbye one last time. The future is blank and daunting, but I'm happy and hopeful for Mum and Gavin. They've got their World card, and I need to go out and get mine.

Dear Becky,

Thank you for your letter. I have my own apology to make. Your letter to Max ended up in the wrong pigeon hole. A neighbour passed it to me the day after you and Leila left and I hid it. I know I shouldn't have; that was wrong of me.

I think I always suspected that Max still had some sort of romantic attachment to you and I chose to ignore it. So when he broke up with me because he still had feelings for you, I can't say I was entirely surprised.

He tried to get back together with me, so I assume things didn't work out between you. I said no. You're right that I deserve better and, frankly, so do you. I know in my next relationship I will find someone who is fully present, and I wish the same for you.

I'm not writing to 'absolve your guilt' as you put it, or forgive you, but I just wanted to let you know I'm glad you wrote to me.

Yours,
Fran

P.S. I hope things are going well with the London Fire Brigade

Epilogue

Three Months Later

'We looked so nice at Rob and Gia's anniversary.' Angie is flicking through pictures on her phone that are being projected onto the wall. I look up to see a photo of just her.

'I wasn't at Rob and Gia's anniversary,' I say, continuing to lay out paper plates.

'Right,' she says, tilting her head to one side to admire past-Angie's hair.

I smirk. I'm secretly thankful there will be way more pictures of Angie than me, because I never would have chosen to project giant images of ourselves onto a wall for all our friends and acquaintances to see, but it is quite iconic.

'What time is it?' she asks.

'Eight.'

'Oh my God, we're running out of time!' she shrieks.

Periodically for the past two hours she's asked me what time it is and had a freak out when I tell her. Yet each time she doesn't move to do anything except select more photos for the projector. I roll my eyes. Still, she found this great flat and is giving me rental mates' rates, so I can let it slide. It's not quite as fancy as her and Jacob's house, but they sold it and split the money fifty/fifty even though Jacob put in more initially, so she was able to afford this place. I am relieved to move out of the little dark hole we were renting together on a rolling contract, because I don't think I could take another second of Angie moaning about the dingy bathroom grouting.

'Oh, your mum replied by the way,' Angie informs me. She was in charge of invites.

'Oh yeah?'

'Yeah, she said thanks for including her, but she and Gavin are going to a movie. She's going to come over and see the place tomorrow instead.'

I smile. The mum of three months ago would *never* have left me to do my own thing. She would have been here early, commenting on optimum balloon placement and our choice of snacks. She seems so much happier now Gavin's living with her.

Three more stunning pictures of Angie flash past and then finally one of me pops up. I'm doing a tarot reading at Dami's birthday party last month. I'm really into it now, much to Sara's excitement. I'm still not sure if I fully believe it's magical or a higher power – I mean, maybe, every reading I've had has been pretty spooky – but I definitely believe that it helps me to get in touch with myself and work out how I'm feeling about things. The cards are very wise.

I hear Max laughing in my head, saying, 'Yes, and the tooth fairy is my grandmother.' I still think about Max. I have weak days where I want to message him like nothing happened. He messaged me, at first; more little snippets of nothingness, acting like everything was the same. I'd be lying if I said I wasn't tempted to reply, especially after a few drinks, but I gave myself an especially 'cathartic', as Sara would say, tarot reading where I pulled The Devil card – about not giving in to negative cycles and self-defeating patterns – and I blocked him instead.

I have no idea if he's dating someone else by now or even in the country. I don't actually want to know . . . It doesn't change anything. I almost can't believe that I haven't seen or spoken to him in three months. I'm having a housewarming party and he's *not invited*. Six months ago he would have been the only guest I cared about.

Part of me longs to call him and laugh it all off. Another part of me still expects him to show up unannounced. If I did call him, he probably *would* come. I could pretend for an evening that we really do belong together. That he's not only interested in a version of me from the past. That he wants me to grow and change and have good things, rather than staying forever in a role that serves his ego. I could return to pining after him. It would be bliss, living in memories, in dreamland, for another evening or however long I was able to live in denial. But we'd just end up back in the exact same place and I'd have to accept the truth all over again.

'Remember, four-drink limit,' Angie reminds me as I put the punch bowl on the table. 'And plenty of food.'

'Yeah, yeah, mum.'

'I'll be watching you.' Angie puts her fingers to her eyes, then points them at mine. She claims this is for my own good so I don't ruin my first day at my new job on Monday, but I suspect it's partly because she's frightened I'm going to throw up on the new beige carpet.

Anyway, she needn't worry, because I wouldn't do anything

to jeopardise getting off to the right start on Monday. Besides, I don't feel the urge to drink half as much as I used to. Realistically I don't think I'd ever go tee-total, or even as far as Dry January, but I don't feel the same self-destructive magnetic force towards getting obliterated anymore. All of my worst decisions were made when I was drunk. I can't totally blame the alcohol; I think, on some level I drank that much on purpose because I knew it would *allow* me to make terrible decisions. I'm not in that place anymore, so it's not like I'm forcing myself to keep away from it exactly, but I want it less.

My stomach flips over, thinking of Monday. When I will have a new desk and new colleagues and a new commute at a new place I actually want to work in. The ton of degrading interviews I've been doing over the past three months – in between selling popcorn at the local cinema for quick cash, which wasn't all bad because of the free movies – were actually worth it. Even the man who asked me what colour I'd be. In front of a room full of people. I said, 'Orange, because I'm always bright and sunny?' and loathed myself for an entire week.

I hope it was all worth it, anyway. Unless . . . What if I hate it straightaway?! What if the job's only pretending to sound really fun and cool and 'oooh we get to go to lots of free screenings and get paid to watch films' but when I get there I'm instantly sent to buy the office milk and denied tickets to anything? Or I get given a desk next to Ted 2.0 who breathes really loudly, and all the fun people are on the other side of the room? And because I'm in a corner, by the Ted lookalike, no one ever remembers to give me anything good? And then

I stay for years and years, doing all the worst tasks, and a girl called Amanda who joined five minutes ago gets sent to a premiere with Timothée Chalamet and they fall in love and get married?

Breathe. It will be fine. It will be good. You have been out with your colleagues already and you liked all of them. Mostly because you actually gave them a chance.

Either way, I tell myself, even if it is shit and even if I haven't found the thing I want to keep doing forever . . . at least I'm trying.

The doorbell rings. I realise, in my dread-filled daydream, I've just been standing staring into space, clutching a bag of Pom-Bears.

Dami and Phil appear in the doorway. 'Snazzy, guys, snazzy.' Phil whistles as he looks around the room. Dami's been over, but no one else has seen the place. Angie wouldn't let anyone in until it was perfectly decorated.

'Thanks,' I say, surveying the room with fresh eyes. I am genuinely pleased with the way it turned out. At first, I worried anywhere we lived was going to look exactly like Angie's old place, one hundred per cent Angie. After all, I'm supposed to be paying her rent and the flat is technically hers. But after a giant glass chandelier arrived for my bedroom and I expressed it wasn't *quite* to my taste, she apologised for 'dominating' (she 'didn't know if I'd noticed but she has a tendency to do that') and suggested that I could help pick things for my own room.

We found a sweet, unfurnished flat that suits both of our commutes, and she included me in decisions on what furniture she was buying. The place really does feel like ours.

'Oh, Becky, thank you *so* much for the playlist! It sounds great!' Dami claps.

Dami had complained that hers and Phil's music tastes were so different – Phil is a big fan of country – that their wedding playlist was going to be a confusing cacophony of sounds. I'm pretty good at mixing so I offered to help sort it out and somehow managed to fashion Dami's love of modern pop music and Phil's obsession with Dolly Parton into something vaguely flowing, using Beyoncé's rendition of 'Jolene' as a midpoint.

'No problem,' I say, thinking how I'm actually *excited* for their wedding, and how much more fun it's been since she agreed to stop talking about it 24/7 and I actively involved myself in helping to plan it.

Dami, Phil, Angie and I open the snacks. Halfway through the bag of Pom-Bears, Angie calls that my sister's here. I race through to the hallway. She and her new girlfriend Mia are staying in the spare room. They make quite an odd-looking pair, with Leila covered in sparkles and garish colours and talking non-stop, and Mia wearing all black and barely saying two words together, but since gaining a fresh perspective on Phil and Damilola, I'm trying this new thing where I don't condemn other people's relationships. (At least not until I have all the relevant knowledge. Obviously, I still live to judge once fully informed.)

'You made it!' I raise my glass.

'Yes.' Leila's forehead crinkles in confusion. 'Did you think I wouldn't?'

Ah, I have missed her. We talk on the phone every couple of weeks or so, but there's nothing like having her obliterate all my meaningless small talk to my face. We still haven't seen our dad, but Leila's been in touch saying we'd both like to see him and he's agreed. We just need to set a date, but I asked if it could wait until I was settled in at work. I'm trying this other new thing where I deal with one thing at a time, instead of throwing myself headlong into the shark-infested waters of all my problems and hoping I won't get eaten.

'What is this?' Leila points to a table covered in a red cloth, with a tarot deck, guide book and a candlestick laid out.

'It's my new party trick,' I say. I'm coming for Spellbound Sue's job. 'Would you both like a reading later on?'

'I love tarot,' says Mia, deadly seriously. That doesn't surprise me.

I show them to the spare room and leave her and Mia to unpack. An hour later, I haven't had another drink, but I am still somehow managing to have fun. Incredible. I guess parties *can* be fun if you try talking to other people, instead of spending them in a dark corner by yourself, tracking your ex-boyfriend's movements. I've also given several, dare I say it, very insightful readings. One of Phil's mates said his 'mind was blown' and keeps glancing at me in horror from across the room as if I'm an actual witch.

At that moment, I catch a glimpse of a familiar side profile. I recognise that slope of shoulder . . . that blonde, wavy hair . . . that laugh.

NO.

WAY.

It takes me a moment to adjust to what I'm seeing.

It's *Vera*.

Vera, the only person I actually fancied on a date in years.

The only person that, no matter how hard I tried, I couldn't turn into an amusing anecdote or convince myself was subpar in some way. Vera, the woman who inspired that first glint of recognition that I might be partly to blame for my own tragic love life.

Is this it? My big movie moment where I finally cross paths with That Person?

Has fate come knocking?

I move closer . . . and see she's holding hands with another woman.

Ah, okay . . . not fate.

Vera catches my eye and almost spits out her drink. 'Becky!' She turns towards me and reaches in for a hug.

'*Hey*.' I try not to sound as uncomfortable as I feel. The woman she's with carries on her conversation with one of Angie's work colleagues, thank the Lord.

'So how's Bali?' Vera grins. There's no animosity in her tone.

I laugh awkwardly. 'Ahem, yeah, that didn't exactly work out . . . Funny story . . .'

'It's okay, Becky, I'm only joking.' Vera playfully touches my shoulder.

'But . . . I really *was* moving there!' I protest. 'And it really *is* a funny story. I didn't lie. I mean, not that you *care*, but you know . . . Just so you know,' I tail off weakly.

'Thanks. You *did* break my heart, I can't lie. But it's cool. We're cool.' Vera smiles. Her eyes crinkle at the side and glint mischievously.

Urgh. Urghhhhh. There's a palpable vibe between us. And she's so nice and STUNNING. How did I not notice how beautiful she was the first time we met?! I mean . . . I noticed. But like, I didn't *notice* notice. Now I'm . . . NOTICING.

Did I really pass up sex with this woman because I was more interested in meaningless text exchanges and loaded glances with Max? I am so angry with past me.

'So how do you know Angie?' Vera asks.

'She's my best friend. I live here!' I explain.

'No way!' Vera shakes her head fervently, then brushes a stray hair out of her face. 'Such a small world. Angie works with Keira.' She nods to the woman she was standing with.

Ugh. Keira. Lucky hag. I pray she is making full use of all the sex I missed out on.

We chat for a bit longer before going our separate ways.

'Well, it was nice to see you, Becky,' Vera says.

'You too.' I smile.

'Will you give me a reading later on?' she asks.

'I can already tell you what it will say. *You will bump into some dickhead you once went on a date with, who is now kicking themselves a bit, but is glad you seem happy.*'

She laughs. And although I am obviously kicking myself, I feel all right. Okay, so it won't be Vera – unless she and Keira break up and then I'll be straight in her DMs – but there will be others. Now that I'm actually open to the possibility of meeting someone, the next time I come across a Vera I'll be ready.

As I walk away, I take note of how well I handled that situation and how it didn't send me into the depths of despair like it might once have done. I am collected and together and, dare I say it, *mature*. Obviously, I drag Dami and Angie into the bathroom like we're at school to tell them about every second of the encounter in between periodically groaning, so not entirely mature. But baby steps.

The rest of the night passes by without drama. I don't get so drunk I end up vomiting on the carpet. Or *even* in the toilet. I hang out with my friends and my sister and listen to Phil's long, loud anecdotes, gasping in all the right places. I pay attention when other people talk about their lives; more than that, I *want* to hear about other people's lives, because I don't hate my own. Every now and again, I can't help looking around, thinking about how lucky I am to live here.

When everyone is gone, I go upstairs and write one final letter.

TO BE OPENED AT MIDNIGHT ON 30TH BIRTHDAY (WITH CANDLES AND INCENSE AND CHARMED SOUNDTRACK PLAYING)

Dear Becky,

Ah, the big day has finally arrived; that's right, the one when all women on Earth magically crumble into dust and irrelevance. So, with death being nearly at your door (once again), it's time for some congratulations and a review of just how far you've come since twenty-nine:

1) After half a decade of the world's most boring job, you finally have one you don't despise!
2) You no longer live with your mother, although sometimes Angie acts like one.
3) Your friends do like you, and you like them, even when you are both being truly detestable.
4) You may never have the relationship you want with your dad, but you do with your sister.
5) Your ex-boyfriend has moved on . . . but, thank God, so have you.
6) You **will** find a decent relationship, now that you're prepared to put your heart back into the soul-crushing dating-app scene.

7) You may never get married, but that's okay, given your apathy towards event planning.
8) You may never have babies, but that's okay too, given your suspicions that their being worth the physical pain, money and fatigue is a bit of a con.
9) You have made peace with the fact you will never be on Strictly Come Dancing.
10) You have invested in a pack of tarot cards and will continue to spread the good word.

Happy 30th birthday! You are (sort of) growing up.

Best wishes from,
Yourself

Acknowledgements

I am indebted to Silé for always going to bat for me and for her incredible creative instincts (which are always right), to Lauren for being Becky's first champion, and to Ginger Clarke for being a complete bad ass.

Thank you to Clare Gordon, Kate Byrne and Tessa James for being brilliant editors and making the book so much better. Thank you to Eldes Tran, Stephanie Evans and Hope Breeman for a fantastic copyedit. Shout out to Grace Marshall for being a lifesaver, Felicia Hu and Sophie Rosewell for doing a wonderful job in MPR and to everyone else at HQ and William Morrow; I am so appreciative for what you do.

Forever grateful to my lovely authors and colleagues at Madeleine Milburn for being so supportive.

Love to my mum, who is the best always, and to Dad, Fiona, Ellie and Tom.

Nell Gooch, the best friend a girl could ask for; you will always get your own section in the acknowledgements of every last one of my books.

Thank you, Patrick, for all your support over the years and to Sarah C, Marcus, Sarah B, Ryan, Syd, Rachel, Catie, Hayley, Rosa, Barla, Sophie, David, Kate, Katherine, Gabriel and all my other kind, encouraging pals.

Thank you, Erin, for reading a draft and being nice, because your cutting opinions about books are quite terrifying.

Hooked by *P.S. You're The Worst*?
Discover *Open Minded* . . .

What if The One isn't the only one?

After nine years of dating, Holly is sure Will is going to propose. Instead, he shocks her by suggesting they open their relationship and date other people.

For the last three years, Fliss and Ash have been in a happily open relationship. But now they're turning thirty, he wants to close it, casting Fliss's whole approach to life into doubt.

When Fliss overhears Holly crying in the toilet during her first date in nine years, they agree to teach each other everything they know about open relationships and monogamy.

But perhaps they'll both learn that there's no one-size-fits-all when it comes to relationships . . .

ONE PLACE. MANY STORIES

Bold, innovative and
empowering publishing.

FOLLOW US ON:

@HQStories